POPULAR PUBLICATIONS · FACSIMILE EDITIONS

Dime Detective Magazine #1 (November 1931)

Dime Detective magazine was the flagship detective pulp in the Popular Publications stable, running for almost 300 issues over twenty years. This premiere issue contains stories by Frederick Nebel and Erle Stanley Gardner, and the first appearance of Nebel's long-running series character, Cardigan.

Authors:

J. Allan Dunn, Frederick Nebel, Erle Stanley Gardner, T. T. Flynn, Edward Parrish Ware

Illustrators:

William Reusswig, John Fleming Gould, Charles E. Dameron

"We can't get Married Until-"

"WE CAN'T get married until I can earn more money." Thousands of young men are saying that today. Thousands of girls are giving that as the reason the marriage date is being put off and off. Sometimes it gets a little embarrassing, too, to have to keep on giving that excuse. *For no girl likes to admit that the man she is going to marry is a failure!*

It takes money to support a home these days. And you're right in waiting. But don't wait too long. The years of youth are precious years. Once gone, they will never return.

Thousands of men have happy, prosperous homes because they had the foresight to prepare themselves for advancement through the home-study courses of the International Correspondence Schools. Hundreds of them report salary increases of $10, $15, and $25 a week. Many are earning $75, $100 and $150 a week. Some have doubled and even tripled their salaries. Some are earning $10,000 and $15,000 a year. Others have become owners of businesses of their own.

If the I. C. S. can help other men to raise their salaries, it can help you. At least find out how. It won't obligate you to ask for our Free Booklets, but that one simple act may change your entire life. Do it now. Do it for HER!

Mail the Coupon for Free Booklet

10¢ DIME DETECTIVE MAGAZINE

Every Story Complete   *Every Story New*

Vol. 1   CONTENTS *for* NOVEMBER, 1931   No. 1

FOUR COMPLETE MYSTERY-ACTION NOVELETTES

Watch for the December Issue   On the Newsstands Nov. 15th

Published every month by Popular Publications, Inc., North Broadway, Albany, New York. Editorial and executive offices 205 East 42nd Street, New York City. Harry Steeger, President and Secretary, Harold S. Goldsmith, Vice President and Treasurer. Application for second class entry pending at the Post Office at Albany, New York, under the Act of Congress, March 3, 1879. Title registration pending at U. S. Patent Office. Copyrighted 1931 by Popular Publications, Inc. Single copy price 10c. Yearly subscriptions in U. S. A. $1.00. For advertising rates address H. D. Cushing, 67 West 44th Street, New York, N. Y. When submitting manuscripts, kindly enclose sufficient postage for their return if found unavailable. The publishers cannot accept responsibility for return of unsolicited manuscripts, although all care will be exercised in handling them.

Amazingly Easy Way
to get into ELECTRICITY

Don't spend your life waiting for $5 raises in a dull, hopeless job.
Let me show you how to prepare for a real job and how to make
real money—in ELECTRICITY, the live, money-making field.
Getting into Electricity is far easier than you imagine!

12 Weeks of Practical Shop Training

Come to Coyne in Chicago and learn Electricity the quick and practical way—by actual shop work on actual machinery and equipment. No useless theory! The average time to complete the course is only 12 weeks. You work on real dynamos, switchboards, armatures, auto and airplane engines, transmitting stations, etc.—everything from door bells to power plants—in full operation every day! No previous experience necessary.

FREE Employment Service to Students

When you graduate, we'll do all we can to help you get the job you want. We employ three men on a full time basis whose sole job is to help secure positions for our students. Also we'll help you to earn while learning. Some of our

PREPARE FOR JOBS LIKE THESE
Here are a few of the splendid positions open to Trained Electrical Men:
Power Plant Operator
. . . $40 to $60 a week
Maintenance Engineer
. . . $250 to $600 a month
Armature Winding
. . . $45 to $75 a week
Auto Ignition
. . . $45 to $65 a week
Contractor — Dealer
. . . $3,000 to $10,000 a year
Motor Inspector
. . . $200 to $300 a month
Electric Lighting
. . . $40 to $70 a week
Signal Engineering
. . . $50 to $75 a week

students pay a large part of their living expenses through part-time work we get them.

COYNE Is 32 YEARS OLD

Thirty-two years is a long time. No school or business could continue that long unless it were rendering real service and getting real results. Yet Coyne has been located right here in Chicago since 1899. Coyne Training is tested — proven by hundreds of successful graduates.

What Graduates Say About Coyne

"One week after graduating, I started my electrical job," writes Leland Hinds of Indiana. "After graduating I was home only two days when appointed Engineer in a light plant in South Dakota," writes George Bagley, of Canada. "Two weeks after graduating I received a splendid job. The main consideration given my application was that I was a Coyne Trained man," reports Harold Soucy of Illinois. "I wish to thank your Employment Manager for securing this position for me," writes Albert Yagon, "he sent me out to this Company the first day and I was employed there immediately." And I could go on quoting from hundreds of letters of successful Coyne Trained Men. What they have done, you should be able to do!

Get The Facts

But get all the facts! You can find out everything absolutely free. JUST MAIL THE COUPON BELOW FOR A FREE COPY OF OUR BIG ELECTRICAL BOOK, telling all about jobs . . . salaries . . . opportunities. This does not obligate you. JUST MAIL THE COUPON!

NOW IN OUR NEW HOME
This is our new fireproof, modern home wherein is installed thousands of dollars' worth of Electrical equipment of all kinds. Every comfort and convenience has been arranged to make you happy and contented during your training.

COYNE ELECTRICAL SCHOOL
H. C. LEWIS, President
500 S. Paulina Street, Dept. 81-41, Chicago, Ill.

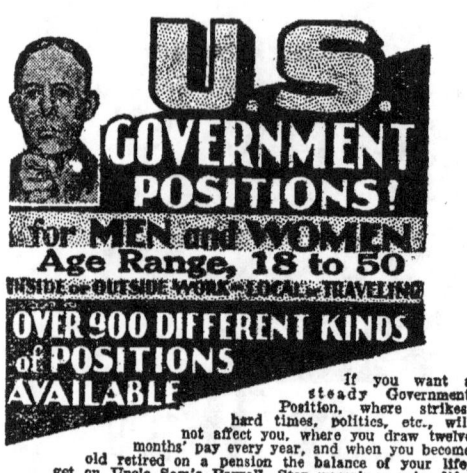

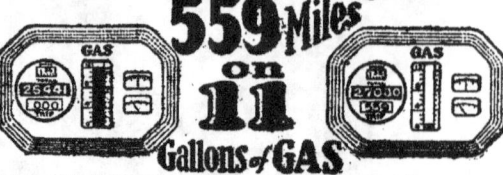

I will train you at home
to fill a
BIG PAY
Radio Job!

I will give You my new 8 OUTFITS of RADIO PARTS for practical Home Experiments

If you are earning a penny less than $50 a week, send for my book of information on the opportunities in Radio. It is free. Clip the coupon NOW. Why be satisfied with $25, $30 or $40 a week for longer than the short time it takes to get ready for Radio?

Radio's growth opening hundreds of $50, $75, $100 a week jobs every year
In about ten years Radio has grown from a $2,000,000 to a $1,000,000,000 industry. Over 300,000 jobs have been created. Hundreds more are being opened every year by its continued growth. Many men and young men with the right training —the kind of training I give you—are stepping into Radio at two and three times their former salaries.

You have many jobs to choose from
Broadcasting stations use engineers, operators, station managers and pay $1,200 to $5,000 a year. Manufacturers continually need testers, inspectors, foremen, engineers, service men, buyers, for jobs paying up to $7,500 a year. Shipping companies use hundreds of Radio operators, give them world-wide travel with board and lodging free and a salary of $80 to $150 a month. Dealers and jobbers employ service men, salesmen, buyers, managers, and pay $30 to $100 a week. There are many other opportunities too.

So many opportunities many N. R. I. men make $200 to $1,000 while learning
The day you enroll with me I'll show you how to do 10 jobs, common in most every neighborhood, for spare time money. Throughout your course I send you information on servicing popular makes of sets; I give you the plans and ideas that are making $200 to $1,000 for hundreds of N. R. I. students in their spare time while studying. My course is famous as the course that pays for itself.

Talking Movies, Television, Aircraft Radio are also included
Special training in Talking Movies, Television and home Television experiments, Radio's use in Aviation, Servicing and Merchandising Sets, Broadcasting, Commercial and Ship Stations are included. I am so sure that I can train you satisfactorily that I will agree in writing to refund every penny of your tuition if you are not satisfied with my Lessons and Instruction Service upon completing.

64-page book of information FREE
Get your copy today. It tells you where Radio's good jobs are, what they pay, tells you about my course, what others who have taken it are doing and making. Find out what Radio offers you, without the slightest obligation. ACT NOW!

J. E. SMITH, President
National Radio Institute Dept. 1MA2
Washington, D. C.

You can build over 100 circuits with these outfits. You build and experiment with the circuits used in Crosley, Atwater-Kent, Eveready, Majestic, Zenith, and other popular sets. You learn how these sets work, why they work, how to make them work. This makes learning at home easy, fascinating, practical.

Back view of 5 tube Screen Grid A. C. set— only one of many circuits you can build.

I am doubling and tripling the salaries of many in one year and less Find out about this quick way to BIGGER PAY

Radio Needs Trained Men

FILL OUT AND MAIL THIS COUPON TODAY

Lifetime Employment Service to all Graduates

The Shadow of the Vulture

by

J. Allan Dunn

The blinds were drawn but on them, as on
a peepshow, moved a fearful shadow.
"That's it," whispered Houston.
"The Ripper!"

A shadow against the night, a downward stroke of a cruel beak, and the Thing had claimed another human victim. Neither rich nor poor were safe from the blood thirst of this mysterious fiend who left no clues to his identity except a sable feather—but this was enough to start Guy Livingstone, famous criminal investigator, on his strangest and most baffling man-hunt.

CHAPTER ONE

The Tearing Beak

IT WAS one of the main residential streets of the great city, but at this dead hour it seemed deserted. The tall and stately buildings were dark. The ruby and emerald jewels of the traffic lights no longer blinked and glowed. The street lamps had halos about them, and their illumination strove against a slight mist that had come in from the Sound, creeping up the two rivers that flanked the metropolis.

In the middle of the wide thorofare ran railed-off sections of lawn and trees with, here and there, mysterious gratings through which came, intermittently, the rushing of transcontinental trains. Then the whole street seemed to shake to the low thunder; the buildings vibrated slightly on their steel foundations.

On either side there throbbed and flowed the life-serving veins and arteries of the city, functioning like the automatic metabolism of a human body. Conduits, in which were wires that carried power and light and sound, tubes holding gas for a million cook-stoves, pipes for sewage disposal. Mighty channels of cement through which surged the water supply for sanitation, for personal purposes, for manufacture, mammoth corridors where the hidden Niagaras were controlled by powerful valves.

These things carried on their tireless service night and day but, above them, in this part of the enormous caravanserai that is called New York—biggest, richest, and wickedest of cities—the inhabitants seemed to sleep, tired of toil and pleasure alike. There was no traffic on the street or its side tributaries. Life was at ebbtide. Presently it would flow again, but this was the hour when vitality was lowest, courage least, man's ego in retreat.

A yell rang out that ended in a shriek, rose, died away from a howl to a mere whimper of the terror that still gripped the man who had uttered it. He remained standing, clinging to the railings of a parklike space to which he had retreated from the middle of the northbound side of the street. His eyes were distended, straining in their sockets, his wits paralyzed, gripped by primitive horror—still staring at the hideous thing that formed and rose and flitted on the white stones of an apartment house in awful apparition.

His jaws seemed locked, his tongue stiff in a parched mouth after the emission of that shriek. He felt surrounded, submerged by an atmosphere of hate—cold and deadly.

The faint mist moved in slow waves. It veiled slightly, but it did not hide this phantom, this projection of an enormous bird, the shadow of a mammoth vulture. The cruel beak sharply defined—a bird of prey, symbol of death and carrion, unutterably evil and foul. Horrible!

Before his gaze it seemed to rise out of the sidewalk, to grow swiftly in height and spread, spectral and menacing. It was only a shadow, but it suggested, perhaps through some jugglery of the drifting fog and sputtering overhead lighting, life in its invisible original.

It lifted, hovered, faded, vanished. From a side street there came the shrill whistle of the nearest policeman on post, followed by the sound of his running feet.

He saw the crouching figure of the man and crossed the street to him, demanding to know what he was up to.

In gibbering accents the other answered, barely coherent, describing what he had seen, pointing.

"There! It was there—but it's gone now! It's *gone.*"

THE officer regarded him with stern suspicion. He saw beads of sweat on the man's brow and considered him a souse. He could see nothing.

"You're drunk! You've got the jimmies!" he said. "You can't raise a racket like that in this neighborhood. What's the idea? Where do you live?"

"It's true, officer. I'm not drunk. I never touch it. I'm Simpson, butler for Alvin Howard in the next block. This was my day off. I've been in Putnam County to see my folks. Came in on the early milk train. And I saw it, I tell you. I saw it. The shadow of a big bird, with a great beak. It was awful."

He fell to shuddering violently, and the officer considered. The name of Alvin Howard was one to conjure with —a rich and powerful man, allied with the "drys." His butler might well be chary of liquor—the man was plainly shocked—but then, on his day off—

The policeman looked up, as if to sight something in the sky, some belated airplane. But it could not have cast a shadow. There was no moon— and the mist would—

There were other feet, pounding rapidly. Aid summoned by his whistle, racing at top speed. Then a muffled, abruptly ended cry. Officer Halloran whirled.

"That's Burke," he said. "Now, what the divil—"

Burke's whistle now cut through the night and the mist. They could see him vaguely, asprawl on the sidewalk. There seemed something else there.

"You'll come with me," said Hallo-

ran to Butler Simpson. No nonsense now. Come on."

Halloran had his gun out. A hunch of disaster possessed him. These were chancey nights, even in this select quarter. All police were under orders to be on their toes, to shoot, and shoot above the waist, if they suspected crime. The gangster big shots lived in places, under cover, where they might be least suspected.

He grabbed the shivering butler by his arm and urged him to where Officer Burke, breathless and disheveled, stood by a prostrate body.

"What's wrong?" asked Halloran.

"I'm askin' you," retorted Burke. "You whistled, didn't ye? And I fell over this. 'Tis murder, nothing less, and foul murder at that. The poor divil's still warm—and he's been ripped open like a cleaned fish."

The three looked at the body of a man, poorly dressed. His hat had rolled into the gutter, and his pate showed bald, surrounded with gray hair. A common face, made no more prepossessing by the fallen jaw, the stary eyes and the look of utter dismay that death had not yet effaced.

His shabby clothes were disarrayed. Something had ripped them apart, had torn the flesh on his chest and sunk deep into his entrails. He lay in a puddle of his own blood that was steadily enlarging.

Simpson, the butler, hid his face.

"The beak! It was the beak that did it," he cried. "I saw it, I tell you! I saw it."

Then he collapsed, suddenly and violently sick.

"It ain't pretty to look at," said Burke. "You figure *he* had anything to do with this?"

"I don't know," said Halloran stolidly. "I'm holding him. Ring in my box, will ya?"

The street was quiet again now. If anyone had raised a window, peeped through a door, they had decided it was none of their affair. It takes more than a shriek and a whistle to summon New Yorkers from their sleep to the streets. No one responded to the rush of police wagons. This was a grim secret of the dead hour that would be blazoned in the early editions of the tabloids, too late for the dailies, too early for the evening papers to scoop.

Now came the medical examiner and the detectives. No newsmen, no photographers. The mutilated corpse was borne away for official investigation. So, much against his will, was the still shaken Simpson. His story of the shadow of the vulture was mocked at by the police, made much of by the writers. Manhattan was served another mystery, another thrill, another menace.

To all of which, as was not unusual, there appeared no solution.

Simpson was discharged, both by the police and his employer. It was admitted that he was sober, that he bore no weapon, but the austere Alvin Howard abhorred any publicity not of his own providing.

The identity of the dead man remained unestablished and, after a brief space on the autopsy table, in the icy partitions of the city morgue, what was left of that torn body went to Potter's Field.

Some frightful weapon had rent it. There was talk of a modern Jack the Ripper, but the butler's tale, fantastic as it sounded, would not be downed.

The stroke of a beak! The shadow of a mammoth vulture! The peril that flew by night!

Catch phrases, perhaps, but they gripped the imagination.

CHAPTER TWO

The Sable Pinion

GUY LIVINGSTONE, criminal investigator, was playing chess in the living room of his penthouse, designed according to his own plans on the top of the Oriel Apartments. His was not a professional title; he took no fees from clients, not needing to in view of his means. His income was amply sufficient to indulge him in what was more than a hobby, the study of criminal conditions—and criminal incentives—in his native city.

His guest was a former college classmate, the architect of the Oriel Apartments—Edgar Houston, a Beaux Arts man, rapidly becoming eminent. He had imagination in his own sphere but little in that of Livingstone. He had dreams of modern dwellings and the needs of those who would live therein, but the psychology of Livingstone left him blank. His artistry was tied up with the science of thrusts and stresses, the needs of population to confine themselves to concentrated and towering edifices that would leave room for open spaces. An idealism that Livingstone appreciated.

Houston worked for the supreme comfort of the physical man. Livingstone to solve the problem of the content of the soul. He believed the two problems parallel.

They were up forty stories from the street. There was a pleasant wind blowing, and the windows were wide open. Outside was a tiled terrace. A fountain played and the breeze carried its spray to beds of flowers and a miniature lawn. Houston faced the window.

Livingstone had made his move. He foresaw victory, inevitable, nine moves ahead, but did not mention it. Houston studied the board, almost touched a knight, hesitated.

Suddenly he stiffened, looking out into the night, across to where another apartment building reared, equal with their own.

"My God, Guy! "He gasped. "Look! Look quickly!"

Livingstone stood suddenly upright, gazing at where his friend's finger pointed.

Across the canyon of the street he saw the roof of the opposite building, the penthouse upon it. There were the lighted windows of a long, low room. The blinds were drawn but, on them, as on a peepshow, moved a fearful shadow. It seemed that of a great bird. The outstretched head and beak of a carnivore, ominous, frightful. Even across the gap of the street there seemed to come a feeling of evil, an emanation of hatred that took the freshness from the air.

The beak struck down.

"That's *It*," whispered Houston. "My God! The Ripper!"

Across the street the light went out suddenly.

"The game's off," said Livingstone in his curiously even voice. "Don't disturb the board. You had a chance to win. Get my gun out of the top drawer of the highboy. There is another one there. You have no permit, but take it, anyway. See they both are loaded. Make sure of that, Edgar."

He picked up his phone—gave the number he wanted.

"Bristol? I want the superintendent, please. Hullo. This is Guy Living-

stone, of the Oriel, across the way. I'm coming over. I live in the penthouse—"

A voice answered, cutting in.

"Sure, Mr. Livingstone. I remember you. You looked us over one time before you went to the Oriel. What can I do for you?"

"Nothing until I see you, except to tell me who lives in your penthouse."

There was a moment's hesitation.

"Well, the name's on the door. I don't see why not. It's Kirby Norman."

"I'm coming over, Wagner. It looks like something might have happened. Might not. Take it easy. I'll be right there. Meanwhile, you might ring the penthouse on some excuse."

Kirby Norman!

Livingstone and Houston looked at each other as the former repeated the name. Kirby Norman was a Wall Street operator who had made an enormous fortune out of the bear market of October, 1929. His wealth had since been largely placed in obtaining control of the properties whose shares he had once sold for a fall and then bought at rock bottom. He had not confined his activity to trading and holding, he was voting those shares at directors' meetings, creating or passing dividends as he pleased. A big man in the financial world and, some thought, a dangerous one since he was purely a speculator and did not profess to understand nor care for the actual working of the industries he handled.

"If that was the Shadow of the Vulture, the same monster that killed the unknown beggar on the Avenue," said Livingstone, "he was after big quarry this trip, unless, of course, he got one of Norman's servants. He flew high," he added half facetiously.

He was not making light of the

affair, but he never took himself too seriously. Livingstone had already figured more prominently than he cared for, and not altogether with the good-will of the police—in certain cases that had baffled the latter.

There had been, for example, the affair of Claire Stead, thought to have been thrown from an Atlantic liner but proved by Livingstone to have been an emotional suicide. It was a curious coincidence that she had lived at the Bristol, though one never knew what tragedy might blossom and bear its evil fruit under the most restricted roofs.

The Bristol, like the Oriel, was of the modern styled type, even though that type seemed to be modelled somewhat on the dwellings of the Hopi and Zuni tribes, the Indian dwellings at Taos and elsewhere. But where those ran at most to five stories, the Bristol reared towards the stars in forty, with setbacks, used for terraces. Its general style was Gothic and the penthouse of Kirby Norman, perched on top, was not unlike a miniature of some medieval schloss on the bank of the Rhine.

Wagner waited them in the lobby.

"I got no answer," he said. "He has three Japanese, butler, valet, cook. They tell me the first two are off for the evening. The cook, Yama, is practically stone deaf."

"Norman in?"

"No one has seen him leave. He had two guests after dinner, but they both went an hour ago."

Livingstone glanced at his watch. It was eight minutes after one.

"We'll go right up, if you don't mind," he said to Wagner. "I know Mr. Norman slightly, if there is any embarassment."

Wagner nodded as the elevator shot up. His job was not too easy. Nat-

urally he hoped to avoid any notoriety, but, knowing something of Livingstone's operations and seeing the keen look in the latter's deep-set, gray eyes, he was fearful.

They walked through a door at the head of a short flight of stairs on to where the setback, parapeted for safety as well as design, held a narrow, but charming garden space. Here too, were shrubs, slim flower beds, vines clambering upward over the penthouse, a little fountain sending up bright spray. There was no mist tonight for the Vulture. Livingstone looked over the parapet to the setback below. There again were tubbed plants. It was three stories down. He ran his hand over the coping of rough-faced brick. Houston saw him pluck something from a crevice that he rolled between his fingers and then transferred to a gold cigarette case carefully. It seemed to urge him to strenuous action.

Livingstone drew his gun, a thin automatic of foreign manufacture, carried under a police permit. He knocked smartly with the butt of it on the stout door, oak, reinforced with wrought-iron straps. There was no response, though the summons was imperative.

"Try the bell," suggested Wagner. "They've got some sort of device rigged up for Yama. A dropper telltale when he's awake and a kind of bracelet he puts on his wrist if he turns in before the other two Japs come in. They've got keys. But this jigger vibrates over his pulse and——"

Livingstone had set his finger on the bell, and the door opened before Wagner had ceased talking. It was Yama, yawning, half-dressed, inclined to object. Livingstone pressed past him, with Houston and Wagner following.

Yama was somewhat reassured by the presence of the superintendent.

They found Kirby Norman stretched out on a divan in his library. He wore pajamas of some sort of oriental brocade, and their bright colors were drenched with blood.

He was barely dead. Bubbles of crimson froth had not subsided on his lips. He had died suddenly, perhaps—probably—but terribly.

His chest was raked so that bare bones gleamed through the torn flesh. Below that was sheer horror.

HOUSTON turned to the open window, twin casements where drapes swayed slightly in the breeze and the stars looked in calmly. He was sickened, though he had seen sights as bad and many times multiplied in No-Man's-Land. But the air seemed close; it tasted flat and brassy; he sensed the same strange feeling of hate that Simpson, the butler, had felt.

Wagner was frankly upset. There was a decanter and glasses on the sideboard, and the superintendent helped himself to a drink without apology. He needed it. The whole episode was hideous and uncanny, aside from any personal relations it might hold toward him.

Livingstone surveyed the body with the grim imperturbability of an autopsy surgeon. The fearful ravage looked certainly as if it might have been done by a beak, the beak of some fabulous creature like a griffin, or of some prehistoric flying creature like a pterodactyl, held over from lost ages, rather than that of a bird. It had struck downward with tremendous force. Beak or claw, it was some frightful, single instrument with enormous strength behind the blow.

Livingstone had known they would be too late from the second when the lights had gone out and the blow fallen. Yama had switched on side lamps and one standard lamp with a rose-colored, silken shade that now cast a mocking hue upon the dead man's blood-drained face.

Yama had gone to his own quarters. There was only one normal exit or entrance to and from the penthouse. Yama was safely handy. But Livingstone doubted if the creature that had killed so savagely had come in any ordinary manner. He might have gone through those open casements, if Norman had, as seemed fairly likely, been asleep.

It was a matter for the police. Nothing must be touched until they arrived, and even the officers should not touch the body until the medical examiner had reported.

There would not be much difficulty about that report, Livingstone fancied, as he put in his call for Spring 7-3100. He asked, when he got connection, for Inspector Ryan of the Homicide Squad.

He expected Ryan, an old acquaintance—if not exactly a friend or colleague—to be in and was not disappointed.

"This is Guy Livingstone speaking," he said, and Ryan grunted a somewhat sour acknowledgement. "I'm on top the Bristol, in the penthouse of Kirby Norman. He has been murdered. I saw the blow from my own apartments in the Oriel. I and a friend saw the shadow of the killer. It looked like that of a great bird. The Shadow of the Vulture, Ryan. And the body bears out that idea. I'd suggest throwing a cordon round the place. It is only a few minutes since it happened, and the killer may be in the building. I'm having the elevators held until you come. Goodby."

He turned to Wagner and told him to go down in one elevator and tell the night operator to report all the cars out of commission temporarily.

"You can let Inspector Ryan and the rest in without too much fuss," Livingstone suggested. "You can't stop the publicity, of course."

Livingstone went outside on the terrace, with Houston following. The air seemed fresher, sweeter.

"What do you make of it, Guy?" Houston asked him.

"I don't know."

"That shadow? How did it get up here, forty stories above the street?"

"I'm not sure of that," said Livingstone.

Suddenly he stooped and picked up an object from a flower bed. He stared at it unbelievingly. Houston gasped, inarticulate in his first effort at speech.

"It's a feather," he managed finally. "It came from—from—"

"It came from a bird—and a big one," said Livingstone drily as he examined it. "Pinion feather. This will make rare stuff for the tabs."

The feather was planly part of the flight plumage. It's quill was big and strong, the rest of it jet black. Livingstone was not expert enough on ornithology to determine from what part of the pinion it might have come. He held it to the light, sniffed at it, wrapped it in his handkerchief with care. The bird who had owned it had powerful oars with which to glide through the air. He laid the feather and handkerchief on the parapet and weighted it with the gold cigarette case, after he had taken from the latter the stuff he had picked out from the interstice in the coping.

"Ryan'll want all of the feather," he said, "but I'll only give him half of this. I might make something of the rest."

Houston peered at it as Livingstone flicked his lighter to a flame.

"It looks like a bit of string," he hazarded.

"Rope," said Livingstone tersely. "Feather or no feather, I don't think whoever killed Norman flew. He climbed. There are several apartments still unrented here. He might have been hiding in one all day, waiting his chance."

Houston shuddered involuntarily. The feather had got on his nerves.

"A madman," he said.

"There are degrees of insanity," Livingstone answered. "It occurs to me that there may be method in this madness."

"Method? You mean there may be connection between Norman and the poor devil they found gutted on the sidewalk?" asked Houston.

"I rather hope there is, and that we can link it," said Livingstone. "He, or it, as the tabs are going to have it, may have a sheer homicidal nature, kill purely for the sadistic joy of mutilation and the sight of blood—but I doubt it. There is cunning there beyond mere dementia, and pleasure in melodrama."

He lit a cigarette and stood there, lean and tall and silent—as still as if he had been a statue set in the little roof garden, save for the gestures of smoking—looking out across the towers of Manhattan with their glittering spires, wrapt in thought, delving into the problem he had already accepted as his own.

Houston lit a pipe. He could not equal Livingstone's nonchalance. The affair was too bizarre. Houston was not superstitious, but this thing possessed elements that made for gooseflesh until reason managed mastery. It was hard to shake off the weirdness of the almost incredible adventure and its surroundings.

The two Japanese would be held downstairs until the police arrived.

Suddenly there came the clamorous announcement of a police car and a wagon.

"They love to advertise, even at this time of night," said Livingstone, rousing from his reverie. "Here comes Inspector Ryan with his cycle squadron. *And* an ambulance thrown in."

He leaned out far over the coping.

"He's surrounding the building, so far as it can be done," he announced. "Ryan's a good officer, but he's limited by his imagination and the fact that headquarters' methods are confined mostly to fingerprints and photographs, with an incomplete filing and Bertillon system. They'll be fingerprinting and measuring all over the shop in a few minutes. We are both going to get into print, Houston—worse luck—but it can't be helped."

There was little for the medical examiner to say or do, and he made brief work of it. His was more or less of a perfunctory job. He had been called from a party to which he wanted to return, but, case-hardened as he was, he whistled softly as he viewed the victim and then superimposed his own fingerprints over those of Wagner on the decanter as he smelled its contents, tasted them on his fingertips and then took a stiff drink.

"He had good liquor," he said. "Well, there's only one verdict. It isn't suicide," he ended sarcastically. "Even an harikari expert couldn't achieve that. What's that you're twiddling, inspector?"

Inspector Ryan was hard-boiled, but he didn't like the feather. He handled it gingerly and regarded it much as a Haitian would a voodoo emblem. The surgeon whistled again as he listened, closed his unused bag, washed his hands in the dead man's bathroom, emerged and took another drink.

"It's up to you chaps, now," he said to Ryan as he left.

The fingerprinting machine was set up and shot its fine powder into the room, filming everything with a scum of artificial dust that was dispersed immediately by the secondary utility of the paraphernalia. A carefully adjusted current removed all but the powder that clung stubbornly to more or ess oily fingermarks. The experts went to work with their lenses, carrying in their minds records in the Identification Bureau, seeking to find comparison, and failing. The death chamber was photographed thoroughly. The work went through with precision.

Inspector Ryan did not make much of the fragments of string, or rope.

"Might have come from anywhere," he said. "I've seen sparrows packing bits about like that."

"In the spring," said Livingstone. "It's August now. That feather may have come from anywhere, too, inspector, though hardly from a sparrow."

Ryan looked at him with disdain.

"Either of 'em might have been blown here," he asserted. "I've seen heavier things whirled up higher 'n this.

Livingstone nodded. He wanted to get away before the newsmen came, reporters and reel men. They were bound to arrive. He didn't feel like being interviewed.

"You know where to get me, and Mr. Houston," he said to Ryan. "We may be material witnesses but you won't need bail for us."

The inspector nodded, not too cordially. He still twiddled the feather. It fascinated him, although he had tried to explain its presence through natural and ordinary means.

"I'll be seeing you later," he said. "Good night."

CHAPTER THREE

The Fouled Anchor

THE story carried headlines for three days in the most conservative newspapers, and the tabloids reveled in its ghoulish details. They made the most of the feather. The killer was called variously the Shadow of the Vulture, The Midnight Monster, and The Terror that Flies by Night. Its hidden horror was accentuated to the limit. Artist's drawings recalled Conan Doyle's fantastic story of antediluvian survivals raiding New York. The sinister shadow was reproduced in the sable feather. New York shivered and enjoyed it.

But there were no clues—unless the feather and the bits of string might be so accounted. The last were not mentioned. Ryan had dismissed them. There had been no robbery. The Bristol had been searched and the empty apartments particularly closely examined. In two of them window casements were found unlocked, but it was agreed this might not mean anything, since no outside fingerprints were found. No one had been seen escaping from the neighborhood, though one woman swore she had awakened and seen an eerie shadow flitting past her window, in midair. After examination by the authorities it was deemed that she was anxious for the spotlight.

The victim might or might not have screamed. Yama was deaf and had heard nothing, seen nothing, until he answered the door to Livingstone. Sound travels upward. The Bristol was a tall building.

Kirby Norman, it was admitted, might have many enemies. His death had produced swift market fluctuations, relieved many who had been more or less under his yoke, but there was no distinctive motive revealed. The Japanese were eliminated. There was no sign of robbery. Distant heirs applied for the estate. Inspector Ryan doggedly cast his nets and drew blank, raked his stool-pigeons vainly over the coals of his wrath, glared at the morning line-up without result, stubbornly hoping for a break.

One tabloid recalled the achievements of Guy Livingstone and suggested it might prove fortunate that he was automatically in on this case, which he might solve, as he had solved others the police failed to clear up.

"In which happy event, not too unlikely," the trenchant editorial paragrapher commented, "it might be well for the police commissioner to study the methods of Mr. Livingstone, rather than the time-worn and too often futile gestures at present used, gestures well-known to every criminal, and so regarded."

Livingstone was far from pleased.

"The newspapers, especially certain types," he said, "are apt to make too many gestures themselves, at the wrong moment. This sort of thing might destroy any usefulness on my part. It emphasizes my identity, and—while, in this case, I am pretty certain that this monster works alone—if he had a mob, they would have me trailed day and night and try to bump me off the moment I seemed 'getting warm,' as the children put it. However, I talked with Ryan this afternoon. He gave me what he may consider his blessing, I suppose—asked me if I had found anything, acknowledged he had not and wished me luck. He knows, of course, that he will be called in at the death, or as soon as I may get on a definite scent. I'll need some help, Edgar. How about it? A dangerous job, with a creature like this at large."

"Get me a permit for that second gun of yours and I'm with you," said Houston, relighting his pipe.

"Good man," returned Livingstone. They were in the main room of the latter's penthouse in the Oriel Building once again, half sitting room, half library-study. Across the canyon of the street the top of the Bristol loomed dark. No one had leased Norman's vacant lodgings, haunted by tragedy.

"We haven't got much to go on. We may get more, before we get started," Livingstone added gravely.

"Meaning?" asked Houston.

"Meaning that this type of killer is not readily glutted. He is like a man-killing tiger that has once tasted human blood. He'll strike again—and soon. I should like to find a link between that first victim and Kirby Norman. I still think there may be one, though the wish may be father to the thought. Ryan insists the man murdered the first time through impulse. He can't stir up any motive for the second killing. Nobody identified that first poor devil. Not many tried. But I must look up the record in the Identification Bureau. They are thorough there. May be a mark or so to help—especially if it's a tattoo mark."

He seemed musing rather than making conversation, and Houston said nothing, though he did not follow the reasoning. He knew that Livingstone's mind was waving tentacles, spinning webs, reaching out in all directions to get some definite lead, something that might be joined to another.

"The main thing," Livingstone went on," is to track this beast to its lair and destroy it. We don't know what it looks like. Only that it casts a mysterious shadow that shows a distinct beak. It occurs to me that this likeness to a vulture might have been more or less accidental, incident to light conditions, the first time and, since then, reading the papers, enjoying the notoriety that feeds his mania, or its mania, if you prefer it, since the creature can hardly boast a soul, it deliberately poses to project that image. If not a beak, then it is a weapon that throws the shadow of one—a weapon the autopsy surgeons cannot define. They think it has a sharp point, but is not otherwise edged."

"Have you any idea?" Houston ventured. Livingstone shook his head.

"Too many. But I am going to get that monster, Edgar. If I have to play decoy myself."

HOUSTON knew it was no use to attempt to try to dissuade his friend from any hazard, however perilous, once he had set his mind upon it. Nor was he lacking himself in a spirit of adventure that, so far, had seen no service outside of the Great War. And Livingstone had invited him to take part in this one. He might be able to protect him.

"The Vulture seems to pick his own victims," he hinted.

"Quite right, I hope. Only two, so far. But it is sure he did not get to the top story of the Bristol in a random hunt. That is why I want to build a theory that his two victims are in some way associated, to insert myself in that association. It's all working in the dark. The vital thing is to land him. Undoubtedly he has some unusual hideout. Ryan's system is thorough enough in combing the town. This man is no gangster. He has no mob, no affiliations to protect him. The underworld will not shield him, and the Norman estate has offered fifty thousand dollars reward."

"It doesn't look very promising," said Houston.

Livingstone grinned at his friend.

"I never heard *you* complain about a stiff problem at chess," he said. "This is much the same thing, only much more exciting. The stakes are higher, the penalties greater, and we play with living pieces instead of wooden or ivory ones. Moreover, their moves are not restricted. But—it's a great game. It beats architecture, to my mind, though it may not be so profitable. But most of our work will come after your office hours, Edgar."

"I'm taking a vacation. It's coming to me."

Livingstone chuckled.

"It may not turn out to be the ordinary man's idea of a vacation," he said. "I've got a little laboratory work to do. It doesn't take much apparatus, outside of a microscope and an enlarging camera. I could wish, though I had some other place to do it than here. Those news chaps are still considerable of a nuisance. They seem to think I've got something up my sleeve and could give them a scoop, if I wanted to. They are a pest."

"Why don't you come to Larchmont for a few days?" asked Houston. "Stay at our place. Mother and Edith are always delighted to see you. You need not announce where you've gone. We'll just slide out."

"That's an idea and a half," said Livingstone. He did not notice that Houston watched him a little narrowly when he mentioned his sister's name. Livingstone was curiously unconscious in a matter where a most attractive girl frankly showed her regard for him. He was too centered on other things to consider sex, though he liked Edith and admired her mother. He went on enthusiastically.

"I'll take you up, Edgar. Norman kept his yacht, the Roamer, off Larchmont. A reporter told me yesterday it was still there, part of the estate. Skipper's on board. I want to talk with him."

"You've got a definite lead," accused Houston, "and you're holding out on me."

Livingstone shook his head.

"I've got a hunch," he said. "And a hunch is a definite natural phenomenom wherein the subconscious stores things one notices automatically, often through deliberately acquired experience and observation. Then along comes something that assembles all that is filed, brings it into the conscious mentality. It's a biological process. I don't like deduction. The analytical, bookkeeping, mathematical end of this game never did appeal to me, Edgar. I'm after a real lead, so we can get some action. Out in British India when they want to get a tiger who has been waylaying mail-carriers, en route, and carrying off a villager once in a while, they use live bait. Usually you sit up in a tree and pot Stripes when he prowls round making up his mind to jump the goat you've got tethered there at the foot of it. It's not very sporting, but it gets rid of a man-eater. Sometimes. Sometimes he sniffs at the goat and goes off for something that doesn't smell or taste so strong. If you could set out a human being for bait, he wouldn't hesitate. Then—it's bullet against claw and fang! We'll never get this beast without live bait, Edgar. And it will have to be to his taste. Probably you'll have to do the shooting."

"God forbid!" cried Houston earnestly.

"I've seen you shoot," said Livingstone. "You've got natural coordination. You're a bit squeamish, sometimes, as you were with Norman's body, though I don't see why you should be, after No-Man's-Land—unless it is because of No-Man's-Land—but I'm willing to play little Bill to your William Tell. If you want to get used to that gat in a gallery, I've no objection, but I'm looking to you to back me when we get going. I wasn't in the trenches with you because they shoved me in the Intelligence Service, but I've played doubles with you in tennis; you've been number four on the same team at polo; I've seen you tackle and bring down your man after he got through the field with the ball in the last five minutes of the second half—and I've seen your target records. I don't know of anybody I'd rather have behind me than you, Edgar. We may both be amateurs in this game, but I've seen plenty of amateurs who could give the pro's odds and win."

Houston flushed under the praise. It was true enough. He had made good in sports. He had won his decorations in the war. And he could shoot.

They gripped hands, looking into each others' eyes, grinning in friendship.

Suddenly they separated. The lights in the room seemed to have dimmed. Again the air seemed to grow stale, and a shadow to pass beyond the open window, dimly veiling the night.

Livingstone rushed outside to the terrace. So did Houston. They separated searching for the intangible. Each realized this must be pure hallucination and yet—"

Livingstone fancied he saw a low hedge of shrubbery waving and darted toward it. There was nothing. He gazed over the parapet. Like the moment in Poe's 'Raven,' there was 'darkness there, and nothing more.'

The terrace ran around the penthouse. They rejoined, somewhat sheepishly. It seemed absurd. They went in.

There, on the table where the chess stood with its scattered men there lay across the squares of the board a sable feather, a pinion plume!

They looked at each other.

The Oriel, like the Bristol, was built in a towering series of setbacks. Someone might have climbed up there, an acrobat, or a sailor. Or something might have flown there. The air in the room had a metallic flavor on the tongue.

Livingstone again lifted the feather, held it against the light, now burning brightly, sniffed at it.

"This feather is dyed," he said. "I'll keep this one."

The telephone rang sharply, and Livingstone answered it. His face seemed to stiffen, and his eyes narrowed as he listened.

"Inspector Ryan speaking. Livingstone?"

The detective's voice sounded strained.

"This is the latest. The Vulture has got his third. In Central Park. Yes—ripped! Dead for more than an hour when we found him, in the bushes. Well out of the lights. Dragged there. Looked like a drunk. But it wasn't a souse. We've got the body, but it won't be so easy to hold it. Even for us. It was Frith. Joseph R. Frith!"

Livingstone involuntarily repeated the name.

"*Joseph R. Frith!*" International banker and world power.

"The Vulture set his trademark on him all right," Ryan went on. "Killed a dog, too. Police dog. Seems Frith took the pooch for a walk every night. Last thing, in the park. Fool thing for a billionaire to do, but he did it. Dog's throat was torn out. And Frith was robbed. He never carried much money, apparently, but his watch is gone. You want to meet me at the morgue? We need all the help we can get, Livingstone. I'm admitting that frankly."

"I'll give you all the help I can, Ryan," said Livingstone. "But I'd rather work independently. I've got something, I think. Can you tell me about where they found him?"

"I'll send you up the copper who discovered him, if that'll help any."

It might," said Livingstone laconically. "Thanks."

He hung up. Then he picked up the feather again and put it away in a section of his private safe.

"I'll examine that later, at Larchmont," he said. "We'll go there tomorrow, Edgar?"

"Fine!"

Ryan's voice had sounded pretty desperate. He knew what the tabs would make of this, that he might be the scapegoat. Norman had been an important enough figure to be eliminated. Frith would be worldwide news. Foreign bourses would be affected.

"Frith is a yachtsman also," Livingstone said. "He owned a big cruiser.

Norman's Roamer was almost a tender to the Albatross. It was only a sixty-five foot auxiliary ketch. But Frith sailed on it, and Norman on the Albatross. I've been aboard both when they were there. I imagine Frith used Norman more than Norman used him, but it's a link, Houston, a definite link."

"You think these murders have anything to do with a market raid?" asked Houston.

"That's a sound question, but I doubt it. But you are not far off the lead. I don't think there was any actual conspiracy in these murders. The Vulture, however, seems to have known the habits of both Frith and Norman only too well. We'll get in my car and run out to the park with the officer, when he shows up."

"A pretty cold scent by this time?" ventured Houston.

"You can never tell. We may find where the killer went to earth. At least no one seems to have sighted his shadow this trip. Unless we saw its aura just now."

Livingstone spoke half jestingly, but his meager jaw was grimly set.

"Funny Frith was robbed," he said. "It makes a new angle. I must call the Identification Bureau."

Again Houston failed to follow the fast shuttling trend of Livingstone's active brain. He tamped his pipe, relit and smoked while Livingstone telephoned, got his number and talked.

"Fouled anchor on right forearm," he repeated. "Mermaid on upper arm, marred by vaccination marks. Small red and blue dragon on left lower arm. Underneath initials E.G.M. You might make a note of that, Houston."

His friend saw that he was on the scent. Livingstone's eyes glittered as he lit a fresh cigarettes and inhaled it, blowing perfect smoke rings and watching them as if he sought to find a cryptic answer amid their vaporous circles. At last he spoke, absorbed, half dreamily.

"There's a definite purpose back of this Vulture, Edgar," he said. "May be a persecution complex. An individual, solitary Red, unallied to any party, with maggots of his own breeding in his rotten brain, sired by misunderstood reading of Marx and Nietzsche, and the like. Nietzsche was a philosopher. He would be amazed to see what crimes are committed in his name. His teachings are new wine, too strong for intellects like those of the Vulture. That's more theory. We'll get going. There's your gun. You may not need it. Take off your vest. It's a hot night. Shove the gun down in the slack of your stomach. It's not a fat man's draw. Button your coat. You've got your permit. I don't know we're going to turn up anything but I don't think we'll waste our time entirely."

A motorcycle panted below, came to a standstill.

"That'll be the flatfoot," said Livingstone. "Here's where we go."

CHAPTER FOUR

In the Vulture's Talons

THEY did not turn up anything definite that night. The city first, and then the nation, buzzed with the news of Frith's death. The police commissioner threatened a turnover. Editorials fulminated over the upset of law and order, mulling over previous arguments. Wall Street was convulsed, and foreign credits staggered. Presidential and monarchical committees conferred to reestablish them.

Before they left for Larchmont the next day Houston played Cerberus for his friend, stemming the clamorous army of newspapermen, who came with notebooks, cameras and microphones, craving an interview.

The police commissioner was being harassed. These mysterious and weird murders had upset the world. Inspector Ryan claimed he had a definite clue, but he had said that so often that the reporters frankly laughed at him. For the want of a counter sensation they styled Livingstone the American Sherlock Holmes and Houston his Doctor Watson, similes that left Livingstone cold and Houston furious.

"You wouldn't crowd in on Edison, if he were working out a problem," would you?" Houston demanded of the rampant reporters. "No, I don't know what leads he is following. I *do* know that he's busy and that when you advertise his activities you limit his achievements."

That afternoon they sneaked out through the service entrance of the Oriel, took a surreptitious taxicab to the depot and a train for Larchmont. There, for twenty-four hours, Livingtone was inviolate and invisible after his greetings to his hostess and her daughter. He refused food, but smoked incessantly, taking cold showers, stalking through the rooms of his and Houston's connecting suite, wrapped in a loin cloth, a Cuban cigarette between his lips, his brows close-knit.

On the second day, at four in the morning, Houston, restless, made more awake by the smell of fresh coffee, went into Livingstone's bedroom to find him bending over a microscope, water boiling over a Sterno and powdered coffee concentrate stewing in it.

Have a cup?" asked Livingstone. "Needed it. Family's asleep. We'll go off to the Roamer this morning, Edgar."

"After you've had some bacon and eggs," said Houston stoutly.

Livingstone laughed. He had relaxed. He shoved over to Houston the shreds of hemp he had found on the coping, also the feather.

"You can chuck the vulture's plume in the wastepaper basket," he said. "It's synthetic. Turkey feather dyed. Melodrama. Grandeur complex on the part of our killer. He's going to be ours, Edgar, though it may not be so easy to land him. But we'll get him. That string, as you called it, is cordage, bought mostly in shops that furnish ship and yachting supplies. Light but strong. Used for halyards, lifts and lazylines. Given a sailor with a grapnel that might be fendered with rubber hose to prevent noise—also slipping—he could cast that up to catch on a coping, climb the knotted cord from setback to setback.

"There's a nautical side to this entire thing, Edgar, though that doesn't complete it. But, if the skipper of the Roamer is available, we may clean up. I want a shower, a hot one this time, a shave, and a drink. Then breakfast."

He was the ideal guest at breakfast, apologizing, jesting with Edith Houston. By agreement with Houston, nothing had been said of the problem on hand, and his hostess, Houston's mother, ignored it, though the girl's eyes sparkled and she showed evidence that she might have been deeply interested in the affair. Tacitly it was ignored, and the talk sparkled on other subjects.

Houston had a small sloop and a membership at the yacht club that arranged for the use of a launch in which they went off to the auxiliary ketch, Roamer, her sails furled and covered, her ropes coiled, awaiting a buyer. But the captain, Olaf Neilsen, was still aboard, with the Japanese boy who acted as cook and steward. Their wages had been paid to the end of the month. The two deck sailors employed by Norman were ashore, with nothing to do but gossip and hope for a new job.

There was also a mate, since Norman had done no actual sailing himself, but the man had taken over a new position. Neilsen was not over cordial.

"I have seen your name," he acknowledged to Livingstone. "I take it you ain't regular police. They've been running me half crazy. You'd think I'd killed the boss, or know who did it. And the newspaper guys are worse. What do you want?"

"To find out who did kill Mr. Norman and Mr. Frith," said Livingstone. "I suppose you're interested."

"He's bugs," said Neilsen, "whoever he is. I've told all I know, I figure. They talked me deaf, dumb and blind. Mr. Norman wasn't so easy to work for, but we got along all right. I've handled the Roamer three years. We won the Canada Cup and were second in the Bermuda handicap. It was a good berth, as they go. He wasn't a real sailor."

Houston, at Livingstone's nod, produced a flask at which the eyes of the skipper brightened. It was a good-sized flask—and the contents were satisfactory.

"What can I tell you?" he asked, after the second round.

"You've been in charge three years," said Livingstone. "Many of the crew with you that long?"

"No. We ain't in steady commission except through the summer. My job's on yearly contract, but I get a winter one. So did most of the men who were regular. But Mr. Norman was sort of short-tempered. He didn't understand shipboard. We had plenty changes."

"Ever have a man aboard with tattoo marks like these?" asked Livingstone and handed the skipper the notation Houston had made of the first victim of the vulture. Neilsen studied them briefly.

"Sure. Stimson. He was a Limey. He knew his business, but he was a busybody. A sea lawyer. Always stirring up trouble. Nosey. But he was a good hand, and we kept him two seasons. What about him?"

Livingstone was discreet. He did not say that Stimson would nose in no more, that he was under lime in Potter's Field.

"He got in the police records," he said, "but he's not suspected of these murders."

"Not *him*," said Neilsen. "He had no real guts. What else, mister?" he asked as he took his third three-fingers.

"I'd like to know the personnel of your crews for, say three years," said Livingstone, while Houston, spurred to keen interest by the information on Stimson, struggled to follow his friend's procedure.

"I'm a bluewater man, or was," said Neilsen. "I keep a smooth log. I can tell you that."

He produced his records, gave a running commentary of the men. Most of them had been fired for more or less trivial offenses by Norman.

"Mr. Norman was nervous," said Neilsen. "He had various kinds of crowds aboard. Might be a pleasure outfit, and it might be stiff business.

Here was this chap Blackman. Mate. And a good one. A strange cuss. Always reading about pirates. Said Norman was one and Frith another. I'll bet he had his master's ticket and lost it. A bit old for this game, but good. I've been glad I had him, plenty times, when we were outside and I needed sleep. Educated. He got fired by Mr. Norman because the boss said he was listening in through the open skylight one time Norman had the big boy aboard. I mean Frith. The one who was killed the day before yesterday—By God—he was killed the same way Norman was!"

"In some respects," said Livingstone. "Not in all. The police think he was taken for what he had on him. Go on! What happened to Blackman?"

"I don't know. He was a mysterious cuss." Neilsen took another drink, loosening his tongue. "Maybe he *did* listen in. Winters, he used to get a city job. He had some sort of pull at the Hall. Landed some connection with the waterworks."

Houston saw Livingstone very deliberately rub out the ash on a half-smoked cigarette, light a new one. He saw him veil his eyes.

"Saved his money, Blackman did," Neilsen continued. "He might have listened in on Frith and Norman, at that. I know after Norman fired him, he made a pile in stock and stepped high and wide along Broadway. Came down here once talking about buying him a yacht. Asked me if I'd be skipper. Then he disappeared. They said he lost it all in the big slump. And some said he was dippy. Anyway, I ain't seen him for a year."

"What did he look like?" asked Livingstone.

"Not so much. Sort of squat. Eyesight wasn't so good. Might have had trouble passing the board, if he'd wanted a ship. Someone said he p.`d up his last command on account of his eyes. Clean-shaven, broad-shouldered, strong as an ox."

"Good seaman, aloft and below?" asked Livingstone casually.

"A-1. Not much chance going a-loft on a hooker like this, but we broke the throat halyards one time off Martha's Vineyard, and he went up the hoops like a monkey. Smart sea-man. Bow-legged as a chimp!"

Livingstone deliberately yawned.

"Who else?" he asked.

Neilsen finished his record, and the contents of the flask. They left him well on toward noon.

"Well?" asked Houston. Living-stone smiled.

"It begins to look like Blackman," he said. "But it's one thing to name him and another to find him. We'll drive in to New York after lunch. I want to talk with the city engineer."

"Waterworks?" asked Houston.

"Congratulations, Edgar! Water-works."

But he would not go into details, and Houston did not press him.

THEY had luncheon at the house. Livingstone was preoccupied, and Edith pouted slightly. Mrs. Houston made c o n v e r s a t i o n, complaining about the hoboes who seemed to have returned with depression. There had been two beggars that morning, one quite persistent about getting some sort of work.

"I let him clean the windows," she said. "He was very nimble—and grate-ful."

"Did he wear glasses?" asked Liv-ingstone.

"No. Not while he worked."

"Did he happen to be bow-legged?"

"I did not notice," she answered stiffly.

"Had two good arms?" queried Liv-ingstone.

Mrs. Houston bridled a bit.

"Certainly."

"I beg your pardon," Livingstone told her. "I get absent-minded at times. He couldn't have been much of a nimble window cleaner with only one arm. How about getting into town, Edgar? We'll be back for din-ner, Mrs. Houston. It is rather press-ing business, but it will give us an appetite and make me more volubly and properly appreciative of your hospital-ity, after I have got it over with."

His bow and smile disarmed her, as it had influenced many. He smiled at Edith, and she smiled back with her lips, but not her eyes.

"You won't go into too much dan-ger?" she asked.

Livingstone looked at her with new eyes and new understanding.

"Account of Edgar?" he asked.

"Partly. I wouldn't mind the dan-ger, if it weren't so second-handed," she told him. "It's about the Vulture, isn't it? I'd like to be in it myself."

They locked glances for a moment and then she dropped her lids.

"You know," he said to Houston, "you've got a mighty fine sister, Edgar! More ways than one."

"I've often thought so," said Hous-ton tersely. "So have others."

Livingstone looked at him sharply and then got into the car behind the wheel and started the engine. He drove swiftly along the roads, through traffic, downtown.

They started back, armed with blue-prints of New York's conduit system for water supply. He did not explain to Houston why he had obtained them.

Not until many minutes after they returned to Larchmont.

That was at dusk, with dinner ready to be served, but kept waiting.

"Edith is late," said Mrs. Houston. "She went bathing and then to make a tea call or so. But she should have been back by now. She will be, by the time you two are dressed."

They went upstairs to change. Livingstone's room gave on a vine-covered porch in the back, overlooking the old-fashioned garden. His dinner things had been laid out by the Houston's colored major-domo. He put down his blue-prints, humming, well satisfied. His hunches, his clues, were linking together.

Suddenly his humming stopped. He could hear Houston in the shower of the companionate bathroom. Livingstone's face was a mask as he picked up a black feather with a note thrust on it, pierced by the stiff quill. The message was in pencil, the writing tolerably educated.

"Lay off and belay. I've got the girl. Your girl and your matey's sister. Leave me alone, and I'll leave her alone. But I've got her. And you can lay to that. In a safe place, mister, where you nor all the cops in New York can find her."

A madman's note. A mad sailor's note—not to be trusted, save that he had got Edith, meant to hold her—God knows what else his crazed mind might at any moment dictate to him to do.

And she had said she wished that the danger of the Vulture was not so second-handed, that she would like to be in it, herself.

She was in it, with a vengeance.
Blackman!

Livingstone had almost decided that already. Now he knew it. The ex-mate, the reader of pirate yarns, eavesdropped by the cabin skylight at intimate conferences between Frith and Norman, both buccaneers themselves—temporary son of fortune, losing all and avenging himself on the men he thought had misled him, killing Stimson because he knew too much—had seen Blackman lurking and listening—

This madman had Edith Houston in his vulture's clutch and held her as hostage—for the present.

He wanted to get away. He was afraid of Livingstone. It was he who had climbed the setbacks of the Bristol and killed—climbed the Oriel and stayed his hand because Houston had been with Livingstone.

Rabid—believing himself exploited, thinking his miscomprehended idea of the talk of Frith and Norman was a deliberate injury against him. This maniac had Edith Houston in his secret hideaway—Edith! In his mind he could see her brunette, vivacious, intelligent. This flood of sickening emotion—more intense than shocked solicitude for a friend—

Did he love this girl?

"Edgar!"

Houston came out, dripping, a towel about his middle, summoned by the rasp in Livingstone's voice. He read the note.

"My God! What can we do?"

"Do? *Get* her. And get Blackman. He says all the cops in New York can't find her. But *I* can—without the cops. Essentially without the self-advertising cops. Edgar, you'll have to tell your mother. Stay with her, if it's best. Though I can use you."

"You don't know her, Guy. The hard work will be to keep her back. I'm with you."

"Then shove on a dressing-gown and go down to her. Hurry."

Houston found Livingstone bending over blueprints when he got back upstairs. "Look here, Edgar," said Livingstone. "See these lines of water conduits. They run close to where Blackman killed Stimson. See, there's an opening to the street. Few citizens know about them. But yeggs from Sing-Sing have used them—miles of mains—from the Catskills south. Mahopac. Croton. Here's another 'out,' right close to the Bristol. Another within fifty yards of where Frith was killed. Tiers of them. Conduits, forebays, the supply regulated by valves. Valvemen every so often. That's what Blackman was, in all probability. Some of the tunnels are not used now except in emergency. Some in course of construction, some condemned by political plays for new expenditure. A labyrinth under the heart of the city—that's where Blackman has lurked; that's why Ryan couldn't turn him up. *And why we can."*

CHAPTER FIVE

Catacomb Lair

ON THE way in Livingstone briefly told Houston the process of his linking up the clue furnished by the rope fragments, confirmed by Nielsen aboard the Roamer.

"The thing now is to get Blackman," he said. "To find a bow-legged, short-sighted, one-armed man who is hiding out in the unused conduits of the waterworks."

"One-armed?"

"Of course, one-armed—at least to all appearances. He wears a steel hook on one arm—that may be removed upon occasion—partly for disguise and partly for a hideous weapon. I don't think he's lost a

hand. It will be a curved weapon in a leather socket strapped to his arm, perhaps held in place by his own clenched fingers. That's the beak, Edgar. He thinks Norman and Frith fooled him deliberately. He is intelligent, but not sufficiently so to overcome the vain glory of his own ego. His tales of pirates have inflamed him to use the steel hook. Furnished him glory in the newspaper stories about him. In his twisted way, he thinks he is vindicated, and that Frith and Norman deserved to die. But he's got the taste to slay, to do things more depraved. We'll get him, Edgar. If you get the chance to shoot the monster before I do, shoot straight. If he sights me, he will stalk me. He thinks I am in love with your sister—and that's the first sane thought he's had for months —or *I* have. What's this—"

'This' was a traffic cop on the New York end of the Long Bridge, his face smiling half apologetically, behind him a sergeant of detectives, known to Livingstone. The latter saluted swiftly.

"Kind of had a notion I might see you, Mr. Livingstone, though I wasn't especially lookin' for you. I'm watching some of Wop Spirito's gang, who have copped some cars and are makin' a getaway after sprayin' Edam Schmier's outfit—or *trying* to make a getaway. Inspector Ryan figured you was out of town. Been tryin' to get you. Wants you to call him up. You see, we got the guy that bumped off Frith and Norman, and the punk."

"You've *got* him?"

Livingstone's jaw sagged with surprise, but he clamped it tight again.

"Sure. *With* the goods. O.K. there. Move the traffic."

Livingstone shifted gears, drove to the University Club.

"I'll call Ryan from here," he said

to Houston. "See what he's got to say."

"I'll wait outside," Houston returned. "I'm a member, but this shack never did give me much of a thrill."

"Yeah," said Ryan smugly over the wire. "We got him. The boob didn't figure we'd cover Pennsylvania and New Jersey. He hocks Frith's watch in Philly, the sap! Got twenty on it, and it's worth half a grand. We get the description, and we turn him up. 'Lefty' Logan! *With* the pawnticket under his mattress. Can you beat that? So you let go wrestling with the case, Livingstone, and get a good sleep because we've got it in the bag!"

"Fine," answered Livingstone. "Fine! That's marvellous work, Ryan. I congratulate you. You've got a confession?"

"Not yet, but we *will* have. Lefty's a junkie. *He* says he was looking for a place to flop, and falls over the stiff. *He* says. So he riffs him and finds out later he's all over blood himself. He ain't doped up so he changes his duds and hits the rattler to Philly on the spare jack he finds on Frith. He should have gone to Shanghai. We got him. He'll come through, if we ask him often enough, and long enough, and hard enough— after we introduce him to the goldfish. Not only Frith, but Norman and the punk."

"Sure," said Livingstone. "Great work. But take my advice, Ryan, and don't show him the goldfish until you hear from me."

"Eh? Why not? We've got the guy, I tell you."

"Without doubt, inspector. But this is just a tip, a hunch. If I were you, I wouldn't show him the goldfish— just yet. Wait until morning."

Ryan hung up, perplexed and a little uncertain where he had been triumphant. Two or three times before when Livingstone had spoken to him in that tone, with a certain curious emphasis to it, he had found out, sooner or later, that it was worth while to stop, look and listen.

He touched a buzzer, chewing his cigar unlit.

"Put that gee below the line," he ordered the officer who answered his summons. "Yes, I mean Lefty Logan he roared with a jerk of his head toward the door of the 'goldfish room.' Take him out o' there and take him downstairs. I'll see him tomorrow. Tell Jerry to stall the press boys on your way out."

Jerry, Ryan's personal telephone operator and door guard, looked in with an anxious face.

"The boys are raising Ned, inspector. They say they know you got Frith's murderer. They want to get a look at him and a picture. They're figuring on featuring him as the Vulture."

"Well, tell those wisenheimers that there's nothing doing. I'm lining things up and I don't want it spoiled by the papers tipping it off. There's nothing to give out. Lefty is being held, and that's all there is to it, so far as they're concerned. Soon as there is something I'll spill it."

The door opened again and the dean of the evening newspapermen entered. Ryan had been bellowing. Now he roared louder.

"What d'ya mean musclin' in on me room without bein' asked. Get the hell out."

"You've got to give us a break, Ryan. The early editions—"

"To hell with the early editions! You heard me?"

The other knew when he had a beat or when he was beaten. He knew Ryan. When that worthy's face got mottled like a head cheese and his eyes glared that way it would be easier to lead a stampeding bull on a length of parcel twine.

"Yeah," he said. "I heard you. I heard you the first time."

"There's something screwy," he told his brothers of the fourth estate. "Ryan's stalling. Covering up. One of us better stick around all the time. I'm wise to the inspector. He's acting just like the man who got a bear by the tail and dassen't let go. All we can use now is that Lefty Logan is being held in connection with the Frith Case. I've seen Lefty a couple of times. He's a dope, and if he's a Vulture, I'm the original Golden Eagle. Let's drift up to the I.B. and see what we can get on Lefty, up to date."

LIVINGSTONE'S face was as grave and grimly determined as that of Houston, brother of the girl who had in some way been spirited off by a madman.

Neither of them dared dwell upon what might happen—what might have already happened—to Edith Houston.

They had already discussed the only avenue of consolation.

"He must have had a car of some sort," said Livingstone. "He was on the roof the other night, clambering up and down with that steel hook of his, his rope and grapnel and his infernal sailor's handiness. He overheard us, of course—trailed us to Nantucket, watched there. He must have some money. Perhaps he got to Frith's wallet before the other chap Ryan's holding. But I think he must have drugged Edith. Got her close enough

on some excuse. He's got the cunning of an inflamed brain. He'll know some way of getting into the water conduits that isn't in plain view. They are always enlarging them with increased watersheds and civic needs. They told me at the Civic Engineer's office that the tunnels are run and lined before they start work on the dams. They've got to keep ahead of the call. The city can't grow any faster than its water supply warrants. So—here—" he produced a folded blueprint and opened it up—"This looks like our best bet. They're excavating here, you see, right on the line of the new subway and building water mains almost parallel, for once economizing on one tearing-up of the streets. I think— I hope—" Livingstone's voice faltered ever so slightly for a syllable or so— "we'll find her there, unharmed, perhaps still in a stupor. *And him.*"

Houston concentrated on the print. It was concise but took in the important section in fine detail.

"This main, chalked red, is active," went on Livingstone. "It's closest to the road surface. There are two galleries under it—one completed, held for emergency, the other unfinished. And, for some reason, the work has been held up on it—some trouble about contracts and court injunctions. Here's a forebay—that's a reservoir fed by the mains to get pressure—not used at present. Eventually all the conduits will be part of the interlocking system. So —my hunch says that here is where we may find him. He could have lived here for weeks without being discovered. There are only a few watchmen, political plum jobs—old men who sit on a chair all night and go to sleep, patrol their territory once with their old eyes half open and their deaf ears closed. A few valvemen on the active main, and that's all. An ideal lair."

Houston had not much to say. Architect that he was, he marveled at Livingstone's comprehensive grasp of the subject, his concise exposition of it. Houston was eager for action; every moment of delay was agony for him.

"Let's take a shot at it," he said briefly.

"Right."

Livingstone swung his roadster west and south. There was the safety of the girl he now knew he loved and also his silent vow to rid the world of this monster. He believed fully that, although Blackman might have murdered, so far, with an idea of reprisal for loss, that impulse to slay might spread like a growing ulcer in his fevered brain.

He had badges from the Civic Engineer, also a letter that would pass him through valve stations, if necessary. He had given one badge to Houston. He felt closer than ever to his friend, with the newborn emotion he had realized for his sister. What a blind fool he had been to have passed up happiness! He could remember times when Edith had shown obvious pleasure in his company, had been keenly interested in his aims. And now—perhaps—it was too late!

He wove his car through the traffic with precision. Once or twice expert taxi drivers regarded him grimly, but with reluctant admiration. He clipped the lights as a star athlete beats the gun.

It was growing dusk. The workers of the city had swarmed, like ants, to the subways and elevated roads, filled the surface cars. In this region of Manhattan, now being changed from all likeness to its former contours where blocks were being razed to widen streets and establish parks, where great canyons were being dug in the earth, the monsters of excavating machines stood silent. The depression was on. No overtime was being paid out; terms of contract were extended; the work lagged.

The pulling down of dwellings left broad spaces where only a few lanterns shone white or red and watchmen lit their pipes to start their perfunctory vigils. It was a place of deepening shadows.

Here and there you could look down into the bowels of the foundation rock of Manhattan, slimy and wet, save where they had been regularly encased. There were arches of cement, girders of rustless steel, dark tunnels and, under the mother arteries, man-made, for man's purpose. Almost a city beneath a city, save that here would be few inhabitants, except when the new subway would whirl thousands through the artificial caverns. Somewhere in these untenanted catacombs would they find the monster—and the girl?

Livingstone parked the car where there was a barrier across a side street and two ruby-glassed lanterns were beginning to shine brightly in the murk, like the eyes of a dragon. He turned his own lights to parking, felt that his gun was easy in the place he preferred to carry it—as he had advised Houston—under his waistband, and led the way to where a gloomy chasm yawned.

A police officer called to them. They stopped, and the man on post came up. Livingstone prepared to show badge and pass, but the patrolman saluted.

"Still on the sidewalks, Burton?" asked Livingstone.

"Yes, sir. They didn't like the way I handled the Solano case."

"They wouldn't," said Livingstone. There had been a pay-off there—hush-money that Burton, in his zeal and honesty, had almost uncovered, a most unpleasant and accusing skeleton, if once revealed.

"Anything I can do for you, sir?" Burton asked. He had once been a detective of the lowest grade, and he still had hopes, though of late they were growing dim.

Livingstone considered. He was glad that Ryan thought he had the original of the Shadow of the Vulture, glad no officers were in on this night's work. Many of them were efficient, but they were hidebound in their methods and too obvious. Burton, he thought, had the making of the type of detective that was needed. He was brave, ambitious, brainy.

Livingstone showed his badge.

"My friend and I," he said, "are going exploring. We might possibly use a little first or second aid. We're going down there, through to the water mains under construction. You might keep your ears cocked, Burton."

"I'll do that, and my gun too,' said Burton with another salute as the two walked away. He had instinctive qualifications for detective work though he was only a tyro, handicapped in many ways. And he had an ardent admiration for what Livingstone had done—an adamant belief that if Livingstone were police commissioner, miracles would happen. Livingstone would have laughed at him. Crime was important, inclined at times to be paramount, and yet it was but a section of the problem that New York Police had to wrestle with—and did, with a conspicuous results.

CHAPTER SIX

The Flood Trap

TWICE they showed badges. Once they produced the pass. After that they were unmolested. The man who asked to see the signed authority was a night foreman who gave them warning.

"I suppose," he said, plainly a little uncertain of their rank and intentions, "I suppose you know there may be a test of C. Gallery tonight, if they've got through with the gatework. They tested the lights this afternoon. All the emergency ladders ain't in place, though. They run out of material, they claim. And the valves on Nineteen B are wrong some way. They leak or something—hard to handle—back up. The air's faulty. I'm just warnin' ye," he added, impressed at once by their manner and indifference, not knowing that they were forced to ignore all odds, to discount their own ignorance.

Livingstone, indeed, swiftly recalling his map, saw additional perils looming and partly understood them. But they were not the main issue.

The descents were hazardous, by iron ladders connected with heavy steel trap doors or else leading to control rooms that, where they explored, were vacant. The valves looked like the skeleton of some strange creature. Compressed air hissed in some spots; in others lights glowed and vaguely dispersed the gloom. Always, in control room or conduit, there were the heavy emergency trapdoor exits, with emergency ladders, spidery things that seemed unstable. Nothing seemed quite complete.

Was their quest hopeless? Anxiously they traversed the cement corridors, seven feet high, troughed in the middle of the floors, coffin-shaped, ominous.

Livingstone had a powerful electric torch which opened their advance, spraying the void before them. The cement was as yet unfinished, showing where the wooden forms had been taken away. Sockets for electric lights protruded overhead with, here and there, a bulb inserted. They could not tell where the switches were, nor did they care—too intent on their purpose.

The conduits angled sharply now and then. They lost true sense of direction. It was a maze. There were openings on either side of the main passage they traversed, where water might pour in, or out. Overhead gaps were blanks of blackness.

Suddenly, well ahead, they saw a widening space that Livingstone, in a whisper, proclaimed a forebay. Here half a dozen conduits connected and the ceiling vaulted high. They could not see all of this, but there was light from electrics that flung confusing areas of darkness and semi-darkness.

Livingstone clutched Houston by the arm; they crouched close to the rough side of the cemented channel, their hands on the butts of their guns. Tense, with bated breath, they watch it—

There—on the far side of the forebay—the ominous portent! There was being cast—the Shadow of the Vulture, growing, enormous!

Then they saw the form of a man, moving fast, the shadow ahead, looming in front, losing precision as he broke into a run. Faint glints came from the figure, from the end of an arm, from his face, as he turned, crouched, and then leaped forward.

Houston fired. The confined spaces of the conduit and the forebay multiplied the report of the gun to sonorous thunder. Livingstone held his release, seeing the figure leap upward, clutch and cling to a ladder, race up the rungs like an ape and disappear.

They raced forward to the forebay and heard a mocking laugh, echoing and echoing. Now both glimpsed a shape against a square of vague illumination that abruptly disappeared as they fired together—and heard their lead

slam against the steel of a closing trap door.

They had seen their quarry—lost him!

A glint of light showed again above, a mere crevice that glowed as if the trap had been slightly lifted—they could imagine the Vulture thrusting his hook into a ring, heaving with his sailor's strength, augmented by his madness.

A voice came down, the Vulture's, not mocking, like his laugh, but grating, virulent, surcharged with hate.

"You fools! Friends of Norman and Frith, are you? They ruined me and paid the penalty. And you sought to trap me. I know you, Livingstone, and your mate. I have listened to you, watched you, followed you, *trapped you!*

"Now you will die, like the rats you are. Drown, damn you, drown! I've got your girl, Livingstone—your sister, Houston. *Ha ha!*"

The voice lost lucidity, its tone held a maniacal streak of fiendish triumph.

"Think of what is happening to her, when the water is in your throats, in your lungs! You thought to clip the Vulture's wings. You'll wish you had fins—and gills—but, here's a feather for you!"

The thin line of light vanished. Again they heard the clang of metal as the trap slammed down.

And something softly slithered, brushing Livingstone's cheek as he grasped it.

It showed in the ray of his torch, a sable feather, like a sinister token from the black pinions of Death. It was a melodramatic gesture, a false feather, dyed, an imposter.

But it might well be an omen of fate, a prophesy of their own ending.

Livingstone clutched and grasped it, crushed it, flung it from him.

"What was it?" Houston asked.

Livingstone did not answer, but swarmed up the iron steps and strove to lift the trap. It was sealed against all his effort. He dropped down.

"There was a ladder back where the conduit angled," he said. "We may reach it first. He won't know for sure which way to go. We have surprised him. He might have thought us only inspectors, if—"

"If I hadn't fired," said Houston bitterly. "I know. It was a long shot and rotten lighting. I shouldn't have chanced it. Now—what's this?"

There was a hissing, seething sound, growing to the noise of many waters, reverberating, manifest as torrents poured into the conduit. With frightful swiftness the water rose, bubbling, laced with foam, above their ankles, forceful, lifting, grasping.

"Come on," cried Livingstone. "We've got to get to that ladder, or—"

He did not need to voice the alternative. They were rats in a trap, soon to be swept off their feet, to be slung against some grating, choking and drowning—unless they reached the ladder.

THE water gained with terrific force and rapidity. It surged about their knees, sucked at them, making them stagger to maintain their balance. Livingstone held his torch high, raying the deluge. The tide mounted to their waists. Houston was swept from his feet, and Livingstone grabbed for him and held him, steadying him against the torrent until Houston got his grounding. Staggering, gasping, they made their way.

It was up to their chests, eddying, raging when, at last, they saw the ladder and Livingstone caught a rung. Houston clung to him, washed out in the stream like a rag.

"I've got a grip," said Livingstone.

"Climb up me. Get my belt. Come on."

The surge ceased swiftly. Either Blackman believed they were drowned or swept like sewer rats far down the conduits, or he feared some interference from having turned the valves.

Livingstone tried the steel door fearfully. It gave, and they crawled through, sopping but eager. Their guns had been well greased. The water would not have affected them.

Lights were showing sparsely in this gallery.

"Come on," Livingstone cried once more, "we'll get him yet. This way."

It was a gamble, but he felt that the Vulture could not be far away. He would think them both disposed of and be apt to move freely. The empty forebay was still a natural center of assembly and distribution. The Vulture was liable to make for it. Livingstone believed he had the girl, drugged or bound, hidden somewhere in the recesses of the upper tiers.

He feared the Vulture's latest, present mood—the delirium of power and triumph over having trapped the pair, which might well run riot—extend his lust for revenge with Edith as the victim.

The thought spurred him; it seemed to quicken his senses—to be guiding him unerringly to where the girl was hidden.

When they came to where the conduit divided at acute angles, Livingstone took the right-hand fork without hesitation, telling Houston, who raced close beside him, to take the left. Intersections might bring them together again, or it might not. Two hounds were better than one. Livingstone felt he was on the right scent, but he might be wrong. Houston was dependable. He could shoot straight—and would.

The cement corridors showed vast and vacant, seeming to ooze moisture that made their padding feet, clad in sneakers, sound squoshily in their strides. The floor was slick, and Livingstone found himself skidding. Lateral passages showed, cavernlike. The place suggested some secret subterranean temple. The two were far apart now, but each selected a passage leading inward, making for the central forebay.

Houston's rubber soles betrayed him. He slid, seeking balance, and his feet struck a slight projection in the floor that nearly brought him down on hands and knees. He managed to recover and then stepped back into an archway, standing stock still, his gun ready.

Ahead of him, where he had stumbled, a trap door was rising slowly and heavily in the bottom of the water alley. It was a door barely large enough to let a man through.

The steel lid lifted. Through it came a gush of brilliant light, illumining a weird and sinister figure.

It was that of a man with a hat jammed down on his head, a blood-red scarf wrapped about neck and chin. He wore glasses that flamed with reflection. Through the lenses showed mad, glaring orbs that looked cautiously about. The left arm ended in a claw, a hook of steel. The light caught that. He emerged slowly from the trap like a hermit crab coming out of its shell, seeking another abode.

The Vulture!

If it needed it, the hideous shadow that the crouching figure flung proclaimed identity, shouted it. Moisture that gathered constantly on the ceiling of artificial stone fell in slow, large drops upon the Vulture, and through them Houston saw the projection of the hideous bird that the umbra of the murderer cast. His hooked arm, half extended, threw the shape of head and beak. As he rose the shadow grew,

purple-black, the Shadow of the Vulture, the shadow of death.

In some places this gallery was still open to the sky, where ladders ultimately would be set. Now, through these gaps, rain began to fall. It caught the glare of light that poured through the trap about the Vulture's ascending menace.

Houston stood in the arch. Here was their quarry but, for a few seconds Houston stood gripped in the sheer horror of the scene. The monster hesitated, suspicious and vigilant, but with an indescribable air of gloating upon the face.

It did not seem human. The lenses to the glasses were thick and convex, they looked like the projecting eyes of some fearful sea creature that had found its way up from the ocean slime to man's territory.

Houston shook off the temporary paralysis. His finger itched upon the trigger of his gun. He began to squeeze it and the handle grip that would release the slug to destroy this fiendish thing.

But——if he shot, if he destroyed, they might never find his sister—until it was too late! There came a shout, reverberating, multiplied by echoes, blending with the roar of swift explosion.

Livingstone was running toward them, his gun belching flame and lead.

Blackman—the Vulture—had laid the trap flat with the floor. Now his body jerked. A bullet from Livingstone had struck his hook as he flung up that arm, either in an offensive or defensive gesture. Now he stooped and thrust the hook into a ring in the trap and started to swarm down the ladder, through which the light still poured.

Since Livingstone was firing, Houston fired too. The rain was increasing; the light was poor, the target none too good. But be believed he scored, on Blackman's neck, close to where the body joined it, through the scarlet muffler. A shot from Livingstone struck the glasses. They were torn from the killer's face, and blood showed, streaking down his high-bridged nose as he dropped lower, and the steel door slammed above him.

Livingstone leaped to the trap, but it was not to be budged. The Vulture had not been hurt too badly to secure it from beneath.

"I found her," said Livingstone. "I've found Edith. He had her stowed away under empty cement sacks in a sort of bin where the contractors built a store room. She'll come too, soon. He had her tied up and gagged, damn him!"

Houston repeated the oath.

"And now he's got away, after all," he said. "We hit him, but—"

Livingstone held up his hand for silence.

Beneath them, booming louder and louder, there came the sound of a muffled Niagara. Blackman would not, could not, have turned on that flow. He was down there, wounded, seeking, as they had done, only a little while before, to find an exit, or a hiding place, striving to get away, half crippled.

There was no let-up in the flow, as there had been with them. They could hear it surging underfoot.

"That's the end of the Vulture—and his shadow. Thank God," said Houston. "The last of Blackman."

"I hope so, most devoutly," said Livingstone.

Through the opening overhead a ray of white light sprayed down, the rain showing in it like silver threads. A voice came in a hollow shout.

"This is Officer Burton, Mr. Livingstone? Is that you?"

Livingstone shouted back in the affirmative.

"Then get out of this. You said you were going down there. It's dangerous."

Another voice, a strange one, called. "We're making tests, tonight. Better get to the forebay quick."

The voice shouted directions that Livingstone did not need. He led the way for Houston, and they climbed to the upper gallery, still in the course of construction, to where Edith Houston was just coming out of her drugged swoon. Livingstone took her up in his arms. There were cement steps at hand that led to a valve station—as yet unfitted—and the open air.

It was good to feel the wind and the rain on their faces after the labyrinth of conduits, with their resurrection from that catacomblike place back to life and —for Livingstone and Edith—love.

There were watchmen, a water inspector and also Inspector Ryan with a squadron, dismounted now from their motorcycles, whose headlights pierced the stormy night.

"I'll take Miss Houston to my car, if you don't mind, inspector," said Livingstone, without idea of delay in the matter, police or no police. "She's been through a hard experience. You know her brother?"

"Go ahead," said Ryan. "Where's the chap you went after? Did you get him?"

Half resignedly, Livingstone gave over his precious burden temporarily to Houston.

"Take her up to my apartment, old chap, will you? There's nothing much wrong with her, thank God. I'll be up in a few minutes.

"I think we got rid of him," he told Ryan. "We tried our best, after he almost got us. Here's what happened."

Ryan listened attentively.

"I thought over what you said to me about waiting for morning before we grilled Lefty Logan," he said to Livingstone. "I figured you had something up your sleeve and were going to try and turn a trick. So, when Burton called me up and said you had gone down into the conduits and that you told him you might need first or second aid before you got through, I didn't waste much time getting down here with a squad.

"You were lucky, at that," he went on. "Blackman, of course, turned the valves the first time but *he* got caught in a flush from the central waterworks. They use these conduits for relief. There's been heavy rain upstate; the reservoirs are too full. Burton telephoned through to the central station; he had brains enough for that," he added rather grudgingly, "or they might have got you in B gallery after all, before you could get out of it."

Livingstone grinned at him.

"The main thing was we *did* get out and left the Vulture behind us, inspector," he said. "It'll make good reading tomorrow when the public knows how you figured out where to find him."

"What's the big idea?" asked Ryan gruffly. "What do you mean *I* figured where to find him?"

"I never did like publicity, Ryan," Livingstone answered. "And I believe it is the task of every good citizen to aid the police in every way. It won't hurt the force right now to have it announced that you've run down that monster. No reporters around yet, or mike and cameraman, thank the Lord! But they will be. Have one of your men get me a taxi before they show up, and then, Ryan, I'll make a bargain with you."

Ryan grunted, as if he had suspected some sort of catch. But he was grateful. He could see promotion, praise, publicity ahead.

"When you get what will be coming to you for this job," said Livingstone, "do me a favor and don't have Burton overlooked. You can take my word for it he's got plenty of brains, Ryan, or he wouldn't have saved my life by that telephoning. Also, inspector, he gave you the chance to be in at the death of the Shadow of the Vulture."

He had his hand on it now—on the
short-barreled Colt he had planted
in the easy chair.

Death Alley

by Frederick Nebel

*Strike—mob meetings—killers' guns
lurking for the wealthy magnate who
had denied Labor's demands. And
only one man suspected a different
motive behind those bold murder
traps, dared follow his hunch down
a blood trail to a deadly rendevouz
of danger—and death!*

CHAPTER ONE

Death Ride

MAX SAUL, humming "The St. Louis Blues," prodded the catch base of the Mauser's butt, drew out the magazine, slipped in eight nickel-cased bullets, jammed the magazine back into the butt and jacked a shell into the chamber.

Cardigan said, "Now for God's sake, Max, watch your step. Last week Pat O'Hara was one of us and tonight he's pushing up daisies. This client Ludwig Hartz is a nice enough old guy but he's got that going-places-and-doing-things complex. Even at a time like this."

Saul slid the flat automatic into his hip pocket.

"Once a yama-yama girl told me I'd live to a ripe old age. She said I had wonderful eyes too."

Cardigan ignored the humor, went on in a deep, blunt voice.

"If I thought Brodski was behind that kill, it would be all right. But I don't. I don't think this mill strike has a thing to do with it. Bush fell on Brodski because the dumb Polack instigated the strike and once made a crack that he'd blow Hartz's head off—and because Brodski has no alibi. But that's not enough, Max."

Saul chuckled.

"I know, I know, Steve. You've got Mrs. Hartz on the brain. And that nice-faced lounge lizard Everett."

Cardigan swore. He strode to one of the windows—a big man, a hard party, rangy in the framework and good-looking in a rough, male way. The St. Louis summer night sky was overcast. Motor cars whirred past on Lindell Boulevard.

Cardigan pivoted.

"Why the hell shouldn't I have her on the brain?" he demanded. "She's twenty years younger than Hartz. The night after Pat was killed she and Everett told Hartz they were going to see The Mikado. On a hunch—I was all worked up about Pat's death—I tailed them. They went out to Sherick's gambling joint, the Ritz, in the county. They were known there. And I saw Clara Hartz cornered by a big guy who frightened her. He faded when Everett appeared. She got a look at me but I made believe I didn't see her."

"Why didn't you tell papa Hartz?"

"I'm no snitch—unless it gets me somewhere. Hartz is dead against gambling and if he knew she went out there it would be just too bad for her. She's worried. She'll come to me. And it's damned lucky for her she wasn't out there a night later—when that machine-gun mob raided the place and got away with a hundred thousand.

Saul said, "And damned lucky for you—the way you used a fake police badge to get in there." Saul put on his straw hat. "Well, toodle-oo, Steve."

"Watch yourself, Max."

"You know what that yama-yama girl said."

Saul went out.

Pat O'Hara was dead. Dead and shoving up daisies. He'd taken unto himself six slugs from a super 45. He must have had a flash of intuition in the limousine carrying him and Ludwig Hartz, the milk magnate, through Forest Park, that unholy night. He'd thrown Hartz to the floor of the car, yanked at his gun—and then taken the lead smack in the chest as the mystery car sped past. Brunner, the chauffeur, had jammed on brakes, smashed a mudguard against a tree—and fainted. Hartz had roared for help.

Detective-sergeant Bush had nailed Brodski, leader of the milk strike.

Everybody blamed it on the strike. Everybody but Cardigan——and he was only toying with a vague idea. The Cosmos Agency had sent out Max Saul from New York, to replace O'Hara, as assistant to Cardigan, the regional head. Either Cardigan or Saul had been with Hartz at all times since the murder.

Cardigan was pouring a pony of Bourbon when the telephone rang. He finished pouring, downed the drink neat and crossed the room rasping his throat.

"Hello," he said into the mouthpiece. "Oh, hello, Mrs. Hartz. . . .No, nothing particular. . . . Yes, I could. When? . . . . All right. The northwest corner of the Hotel Case lounge. I'll walk right over."

The thumb of the hand that held the instrument pushed the hook down slowly. Cardigan replaced the receiver and chuckled grimly to himself.

A self-operated elevator took him down six floors to the lobby of the apartment house. He passed out onto a tiled terrace, strode down broad flags to the sidewalk and turned west on Lindell Boulevard.

He had gone perhaps a dozen yards when a stocky man stepped from beside one of the trees and fell in step beside him. The stocky man's right hand was in his pocket and the pocket bulged.

"Just keep walkin', sweetheart," he said.

"Where?"

"You'll see."

Cardigan's hands doubled but he kept walking. The hair stood up on the nape of his neck. Two girls and a man passed him going east. They didn't notice. The stocky man was in step with Cardigan, but a bit to the rear and to the left of him.

Ten feet further on a lank man stepped from the shadow of a parked sedan.

The stocky man muttered, "Get in that bus."

"Look here——" Cardigan began.

"Get in, get in," snarled the lank man, motionless. "You've got a date."

Cardigan looked down at the stocky man. It was a face he had seen before but for the present he couldn't place it. He was shoved into the rear of the sedan. He dropped down beside a man in shadow who smoked a cigar. The stocky man got in front beside the motionless chauffeur. The lank man climbed in beside Cardigan.

The red cigar-end moved. "Oke, Bunt."

The gear lever clicked. The big sedan moved away from the curb, swung into west-bound traffic, crossed Kings highway and hummed out along Forest Park.

"Well," said the man behind the red cigar-end, "we had a long wait, *wisenheimer*."

The stocky man in the front seat turned around.

"That's him, Gus. That's him all right."

Cardigan said, "I've seen you before."

"Honest?" mocked the stocky man. "Have you now?"

The man behind the red cigar and his lank companion suddenly frisked Cardigan of his gun.

The lank man grinned.

"Why don't you try to get out of this with your police badge?"

Cardigan started. Then he leaned back.

"Oh," he said slowly. "I see." Then his voice rushed on. "What the hell's the idea of this party?"

THE lank man jabbed a gun in his ribs. "The night before that raid at the Ritz you muscled your way in on a fake cop's shield! You were a scout for that mob! Tom Sherick remembered the shield number. You went home in a taxi. The guy drove you home remembered the address. And you paid your fare. Did a cop ever pay taxi fare? Yah! And we found out there was no such shield number on the cops!"

The car turned right into Union. Cardigan looked around at the shadowed faces.

"So help me, I had nothing to do with that." The stocky man in the front seat was the one who had let him in the Ritz. He remembered now.

"That was a fast one all right," the lank man said. "But this is gonna be a faster one."

"Ride?" Cardigan asked

"What do you think?"

Cardigan began to perspire.

"I think," he said, "you guys are off your nut. O.K., I used a fake badge. But I'm a private dick. I was on a tail. It was the only chance I had of getting in, so I used it."

"You think up fast ones, don't you?" the lank man slurred.

The man behind the cigar laughed out loud. The man at the wheel giggled. The lank man rasped a harsh chuckle from his throat. The car sped on. It turned left into Delmar, weaved through traffic; past street cars, past traffic cops. While a gun kept pressing into Cardigan's ribs.

"Listen," said Cardigan, "I'm on the up and up. Take me to Sherick. Let me talk to him. I can square myself. I'm getting a raw deal here."

"And right in the belly," the lank man said.

Cardigan heaved in the seat. The man behind the red cigar-end moved, struck Cardigan across the head with a gun-butt. Cardigan groaned and slumped back in the seat. Through glazed eyes he saw store-windows streak by. He heard the honking of the horns, the shrill blast of traffic whistles.

Then the store windows were left behind. Sounds of the city petered out. There were occasional houses, then fewer and farther apart. The warm night wind blew against his hot face. Fields began to flow past. The big car droned on complacently, doing fifty-five on an undulating ribbon of cement. It boomed through a small settlement, left that behind in two minutes; swept past fields again and patches of dark woods.

"What is it?" Cardigan muttered. "A pitch from the St. Charles Bridge?"

"You'll see," the land man said.

"Listen," Cardigan urged. "For God's sake, listen! Give me a break. I tell you—"

"You can't tell us anything," the lank man said.

The man at the wheel, leaning out, said, "It won't be long now. Right around that bend."

There was a dark forest on the left of the wide bend, and the wind carried a dank smell of marshes.

"That path's right up here, ain't it?" the driver asked.

"Yeah," the stocky man said. "I'll say when."

Cardigan said in a thick voice, "For God's sake—"

"Lay off!" the lank man snarled; then in a quiet tone, "You and Abe go with him, Louie. We'll drive on and turn around and pick you up in ten minutes."

The car was slowing down. Presently it stopped.

"Hop out, Louie," the lank man said.

"Right," said the stocky man, swinging from the front seat.

The man with the cigar threw it away and opened the rear door. Louie ran around the back and waited. The lank man prodded Cardigan with his gun and Louie and Abe hauled him out and rushed him across the road, down a path that bored into the dark, matted forest.

"So it's lights out," said Cardigan, bitterly.

Louie said, "For you, sweetheart."

They moved along the edge of a black pool on damp, soggy earth. Cardigan dragged his feet, tussled between the two. But they held him up, saying nothing, hauled him deeper and deeper into the woods.

Cardigan fell between them, dragging his knees on the wet earth. They could not walk with him that way, and they stopped. Louie cursed and struck Cardigan with his gun.

"Get up!" he snarled.

Cardigan hung a dead weight between them, breathed hoarsely, muttered. "If you heels want to give it to me, go ahead!"

Louie nodded. "Let's, Abe."

"We oughter go in further."

They redoubled their efforts, dragged Cardigan on the muddy path. His legs were straight behind him, his hands clawing at the mud.

Louie cried in a low voice. "Look out, Abe! That's water! We go left here—ain't it?"

Cardigan suddenly heaved his weight and twisted violently between them, breaking from Abe's grasp. He fell to the right, dragging Louie with him. They shot down the muddy bank, plunged into black water, while Abe clawed for a footing and Louie cried, "Help!" in a frightened voice that a mouthful of water promptly smothered.

Cardigan kicked out into the black water. He did not see Louie. He did not see Abe. It was black as pitch in those woods.

Louie cried, "Ugh—don't shoot Abe!"

"Where the hell are you?" Abe snapped.

"Here—I'm here—gimme a hand—"

Through the black water swam Cardigan, getting rid of his coat. The voices of Louie and Abe grew fainter. Cardigan swam into gnarled roots. He grasped them, drew himself beneath them, felt his feet touch bottom. He clawed up a muddy bank and burrowed into thickets.

He did not wait to listen, but stumbled on his way, sometimes on solid ground, sometimes in knee-deep bogs. He fell and rose again and kept putting distance between himself and the two gunmen. He kept on fiercely, blindly, slushing through mud, spitting mud from his lips, choking and hacking and grunting and cursing.

He did not know it, but an hour passed before he fell headlong on a dry hump of earth. He lay gasping for breath, mud from head to foot, his brain almost bursting from the exertion. Then something inside him snapped and he relaxed with a sigh.

Gray daylight was breaking when he stumbled out on the state highway. An eastbound produce truck pulled up and gave him a lift.

The driver looked at him curiously. "You're messed up a bit, ain't you, bud?"

"I was on a wild party," Cardigan said. "I'd appreciate a butt, brother."

CHAPTER TWO

The Widow Talks

CARDIGAN ducked into the apartment house through the service entrance and reached his apartment without being seen. Muddy and bruised, he looked a ruin. He scuffled an envelope that had been slid under the door, picked it up and threw it on a console. He went to the bathroom and soaked himself in a hot tub. Dressed, he looked better.

He went to the console for a cigarette, lit up and then picked up the letter he had dropped there. It was apartment house stationery. A note was inside.

A Mr. Bush of police headquarters called at 10:30 and left word you should come right down.

Adams.

That was the night porter.

Cardigan scowled thoughtfully and took a drag at his butt on the way across to the telephone. He rang headquarters.

"Bush. Give me Bush if he's there. . . . Hello, Bush. Cardigan. I . . . What! . . . Sweet cripes! . . . I'll be right down."

He dived into a coat, grabbed a hat and went downstairs. He taxied to Twelfth and Clark. Bush, leaning over a flat-topped desk, looked sidewise over his right shoulder as he barged in. "Oh, you," he said.

"What the hell, Bush?"

Bush shuffled four lead slugs in the palm of his hand, then threw them dicelike on the desk and snapped thumb against fore-finger. He was a short, compact bald man. His tie was unloosed. He looked haggard from long hours.

Cardigan picked up one of the four slugs, turned it round and round, then dropped it back among the others. His wide mouth was tight, his heavy brows bent over his staring dark eyes.

Bush signed. "Them guys sure meant business this time."

"How—how is Max Saul?"

"Was unconscious the last I seen him—three this morning."

Cardigan made a fist, looked at it narrow-eyed.

"And poor old Hartz—"

"Back of his nut all smashed in. Three times in the back of the nut. Saul took one. Brunner, the chauffeur, got one through the heart and the car smashed. They were coming home from Hamburg Hall. It happened on South Grand, near Longfellow. Why the hell couldn't you get down here before this?"

"I had a date."

"All night?"

Cardigan's lip curled.

"Keep your wisecracks under your jaw, Bush."

"Don't get hot."

"I suppose you're blaming this on Brodski too."

"Quit the razzberry. I'm going to bust this case, Cardigan. Hartz threatened to chuck every striker out of a job. In hard times like this that's a wild statement. Look here, Cardigan." He got up and shoved his pug nose almost against Cardigan's chin. "Ever since the O'Hara kill you've been giving me the razz. What the hell have you got on your mind?"

Cardigan turned and walked to the door.

"What hospital is Max Saul in?"

"You listen to me, Cardigan." Bush tramped after him, faced him again. "You get this. You've been jazzing around ever since O'Hara got bumped off. You've been acting superior and horse-laughing me every chance you got. And I don't like it. I've got more law in my little finger than you have in both hands, and if you slop around here much longer I'll fix you so you get shoved out of the city."

"What hospital—"

"You're just a wisecracking Mick that thinks the bureau's made up of a lot of hicks. I'm just as clever as you are, kid, and I'm backed up by authority. Last night Hartz and his chauffeur were rubbed out and your partner's in the hospital. It's damned funny that you shouldn't have been with Hartz on the two times he was fired at."

Cardigan darkened.

"We worked in shifts, fathead. On alternate nights."

"That's funny, ain't it?"

"It'd be funnier if I pushed you in the mouth."

Bush glowered.

"You stay the hell out of here, Cardigan. I'll handle this case—in my way."

"O'Hara was murdered, Bush. Don't forget that Pat was the best friend I ever had. I'll get the guy that did it. I'll get him, Bush, and I'll give you the pinch—and make you like it."

A wily light came into Bush's eyes. His tone changed.

"Be a good guy, Cardigan. You've got something up your sleeve. What the hell is it? Remember, it pays to stand in good with the bureau."

"I stand in good with the bureau. I don't stand in good with you. And look at me weep over that."

"Be smart, be smart!"

"Nuts for you," Cardigan said, and went out.

At the desk downstairs he found what hospital Saul had been sent to. He taxied out, a tight feeling in his throat. Trouble was piling on his head. First O'Hara. Then Hartz and the chauffeur. And Max in the hospital.

Saul's face was pale; dark circles were under his eyes. Cardigan sat down on a chair beside the bed, laid his big brown hand on Saul's, pressed it once.

"How's it, kid?"

"I feel—you know—sort of lousy."

"Yeah."

They looked at each other.

Cardigan said, "I feel rotten about this, Max."

"Don't be a goof. I'll get over it. Let me feel rotten. It happened so fast. Six shots—and then we swerved. The car passed so close we almost scraped mudguards. We had both spotlights on. One of them swung around when we swerved. I saw a guy's face in the other car, Steve. It wasn't six feet away. He was grinning. A gold tooth flashed."

Cardigan looked at his hands. He didn't want to tell Saul about the ride. The nurse came in and told him he couldn't stay any longer.

"Let me know if you want anything, Max?" Cardigan said.

HE WENT downtown and spent three-quarters of an hour eating breakfast and reading the morning paper. Then he walked to his office in Olive Street and found Miss Gilligan, his secretary, sorting mail. She was a pop-eyed, gum-chewing girl with no looks but a great amount of vitality.

"My God!" she said. "The papers! Did you see—"

"Like a nice girl, get the boss on long distance."

He spoke with Hammerhorn in New York.

"Well, since you read it in the papers there I don't have to explain. . . . Max ought to pull through, the doctor said, but he'll be on his back for weeks. . . . Where was I? On a date. . . . Now don't ask foolish questions, George. . . . What?" He scowled at the instrument, then growled, "You're the second guy today made a crack like that. I was with Hartz night before last. Last night was Max's night. . . . . Well, you get this, George. I don't have to take talk like that from you. Make another pass like that and you and your job can go to hell. Despite which I'll get the guy killed my pal O'Hara. . . . . I'm not getting hot-headed, but don't you. If you think you can handle the St. Louis end better than I can, pull your pants out of that plush chair and come out. . . . . Oh, well, all right, all right. . . . Sure, George. Good-by."

He banged the receiver into the hook and shoved away the mail Miss Gilligan had placed on his desk. He was sore. He had to admit that it looked crummy, his having been off the scene on the two occasions of murder. The ride still simmered in his brain, but he had no intention of reporting it to the police. He handled his own troubles. Besides, bigger things weighed him down. Hartz was dead. Max was out of commission. The papers were roaring with headlines.

He called a county telephone number.

"Is this you, Mr. Sherick? . . . Well, my name is Cardigan, the St. Louis head of the Cosmos Detective Agency. I'm the guy your sweet young things took for a ride last night. I'm back in town and O.K. Use your head, Sherick. If I wasn't a swell guy I'd turn you up. Only take a dose of something to clear your brain, look up my reputation and think over what a boner you pulled. And thank your stars I'm a swell guy. Good-by."

He hung up, felt a little better, took his hat and went out. He taxied to Longfellow Boulevard and Clara Hartz's house.

Mrs. Schmidt let him in. She had been long with the Hartz menage, as housekeeper. She steered him into the large Teutonic living room. She tried to say something but began crying instead and went out.

In a few minutes Clara Hartz came downstairs. She wore a black jacket over black pajamas. Her face was pale, angular, with a strange cool beauty. Cardigan didn't move from the shadows of the living room. His low voice said, "I'm very sorry, Mrs. Hartz."

She lifted her chin and lowered it again without saying anything.

Cardigan went on. "I'm sorry I didn't show up last night."

"I waited two hours."

"You said over the telephone it was important."

She remained statuesque—cool, remote. "It was—about the Ritz the other night. I was worried. I wanted to ask you not to tell Ludwig. Or anybody. The suspense—knowing you knew—and your not saying anything—"

He crossed suddenly to her, his big brown jaw grim.

"Who do you think murdered your husband?"

She had greenish eyes, large—slightly Oriental, cool as ice.

"I wish I knew," she said in her flat voice.

"Do you think the strike caused it?"

"I don't know."

Cardigan's gray eyes glittered. Beside her smooth cool beauty he looked immense, shaggy, threatening. But her eyes never wavered.

"Remember," he muttered, "my friend Pat O'Hara was murdered first. That hits me deep and way down. I'm going to get the murderer—even if I have to cause a lot of heartache."

One of her arched eyebrows rose

slightly, but otherwise not a feature changed. For some vague unknown reason Cardigan suddenly hated her. She was so cool, so collected. He was a man of blood and fire, bitter against circumstances, and her attitude touched him like a bar of ice.

"I don't suppose," she said, "that your telling anybody about Mr. Everett and me at the Ritz will gain you anything."

Cardigan scowled. "I'm not a scandal-monger."

The doorbell rang and a minute later Ralph Everett came in. He was a tall, slim man of thirty, with silky blond hair, girlish blue eyes and pink cheeks.

"Oh, hello, Cardigan."

Cardigan grunted.

Everett said, "Dreadful—murder," and lit a cigarette. "Sorry about Saul, Cardigan."

It was an uneasy meeting. Cardigan saw no remorse here. The death of poor old Hartz did not seem to stir them. A year and a half ago Clara had married the fifty-year-old milk magnate. And for the past year Everett had been welcome in Hartz's household. Hartz had never shown any suspicion.

"Have the police got anything out of Brodski?" Everett asked.

"No. And they won't," Cardigan said bluntly. "I don't believe this strike has anything to do with it. The strike merely proved convenient for somebody else to try murder, and have it blamed on the strike."

"But Detective-sergeant Bush—"

"I know Bush," Cardigan cut in.

Everett shrugged and looked at his watch, nodded at Clara, "I have to catch a train for Cleveland."

"I wouldn't," Cardigan said.

Everett looked at him, startled. "Why not?"

"I just wouldn't. The best thing for you to do is stay right here in town."

Everett bristled. "Why?"

"Because I'm telling you. And I'm being frank with you—both of you. Stay here in town. The press is aching for news and if you pull up your stakes I'll give them a little."

Everett came closer.

"You mean about the other night?"

"Judge for yourself. And maybe if I work back I can find out about other nights."

Everett gritted.

"You would like to break a scandal, wouldn't you?"

"Not unless you force me to. And don't stick your nose in the air, either, Everett."

"You as much as insinuate," Everett snapped, "that I had something to do with Mr. Hartz's death!"

Cardigan wagged a finger.

"Just stick around St. Louis."

Clara Hartz turned away, swivelling slowly on one heel. She walked out of the room and went upstairs.

Everett muttered, "You've a nerve coming here and humiliating her!"

"And you've got a nerve leaving her and trying to go to Cleveland." Cardigan picked up his hat, touched Everett's arm. "But don't," he said.

Everett paled, cleanching his hands. "You're a louse—like all private detectives," he choked.

"Like Pat O'Hara, I suppose. Like O'Hara, who got in the way of a lead party to save Hartz! You lily-livered nice boy! Hartz thought you were a swell guy—the old fool! Why, you—"

He gave it up suddenly. He strode out of the room, through the large foyer, into the street, his cheeks burning. He didn't like wavy-haired nice boys and he didn't like Oriental-eyed icebergs. He had let emotion get the better of him. He felt he had acted like a fool.

CHAPTER THREE

Written Evidence

NO funeral parlor for Ludwig Hartz, since he had not wished it that way. He lay in state in the great living room of the great brick house. Mourners came and went. Clerks, stenographers, even some of the strikers. Relatives sat about in hushed groups. Clara Hartz was in the drawing room, stunning in black, looking tragic in a cool, icy way.

Cardigan was there, standing in the foyer, a dark, shaggy-headed man, watchful though in the background.

Bush came in, his hard bald head shining. He went to the coffin, looked grim, then said some condolences to Clara and elbowed his way back toward the door. He spied Cardigan and came over.

"What are you doing here?" he grumbled.

"No law against it. I see you had to let Brodski go. You certainly paraded a lot of guys through the shadow-box this morning. Good copy, Bush."

"Be funny!"

"Any new clues?"

"You?"

"Here's a promise, Bush. I'll get you a pinch—a real, honest-to-God one. You've been nosing it around that as a dick, I'm last year's summer cold. So I'm going to get you a pinch and make you swallow those words, right on the front page."

"Baloney!"

"You're a nice guy, Bush, only you're a sorehead."

Bush swore and went out, jamming on his hat.

Everett, passing through the foyer a couple of minutes later, stopped and said tensely, "Don't you think it would be the decent thing if you went somewhere else?"

Cardigan said, "I see you didn't go to Cleveland."

Everett's lips twitched. He turned and went off stiffly.

A messenger boy appeared in the front doorway. A man-servant signed for a letter, carried it through the crowd to Clara Hartz. A minute later Clara appeared in the foyer. Cardigan saw the letter in her hand, the white look on her face. He watched her go upstairs.

His eyes narrowed. He looked around cautiously, backed up toward the stairway. He looked up, saw Clara's heels disappearing around the curve above. He turned and climbed quickly, quietly. He reached the top in time ot see Clara standing in a doorway at the front of the upper hall, her back to him. Her head was bent. She was reading something. Then he heard the sudden crackle of paper as she went into the room.

He darted into the bathroom, closed the door, listened. A few minutes later he heard footsteps come down the corrider, descend the stairs. He left the bathroom, walked quickly to the front of the corridor, entered a large bedroom. He crossed to a writing-table, ran his eyes over an assortment of cards, letters, telegrams; touched nothing. There was an ivory-colored metal waste-basket beside the desk. He knelt down, saw bits of torn paper, collected them quickly, held them in his closed hand and returned to the bathroom.

On black-and-white tiles he pieced together a message written on plain white linen paper. The writing was heavy, black, oblique. It said:

Dear Mrs. Hartz:

My sincere sympathy. But as I said at the Ritz last Wednesday night, don't let this tragedy make you forget your obligation to me, in case you decide to leave St. Louis.

D. D. McKimm.

Cardigan remained on one knee for a long minute, frowning at the letter. Then he gathered up the pieces, shoved them in his pocket and went downstairs.

The undertaker was closing the casket.

Cardigan went downtown in a taxi, strode into his office and said to Miss Gilligan, "Darling, call County 0606. Ask for Mr. Sherick."

He went on into his office, slapped his hat on a hook and sat down at his desk. A minute later Miss Gilligan chirped, "All right."

Cardigan pulled his telephone across the desk.

"Hello, that you, Sherick? . . . This is Cardigan. . . . Oh, I'm feeling great, but outside of that I want to see you. . . . No, I'm not going out there. I can't spare the taxi fare and besides I don't like that scatter of yours. I'm naming the place, Sherick, and you're going to meet me. . . . Now don't talk that way. Your sweet young things took me for a ride and you'll play ball with me or I'll throw you to the cops. . . . Never mind what I want to see you about. You come right in here and see. You know my apartment on Lindell and I'll expect you there at eight tonight—sharp. . . . Never mind, Sherick. You heard me. You did a dumb thing by sending your

hoods after me and you'll come in or else——"

He hung up and stared hard at the telephone. He took out the bits of paper, pasted them in order to a letterhead. He read the message over and over.

"H'm," he murmured. "Obligation."

AT a quarter to eight that night he stood in the center of his living room holding a gun in either hand and looking around the room with keen speculative eyes. The gun in his left hand was a Colt automatic. The gun in his right was a special Colt revolver with an abbreviated two-inch barrel.

His eyes settled on a dull-colored mohair easy-chair and he strode toward it, sat down and shoved the revolver down between the arm and the cushion until it was concealed. With an easy upward motion of his hand the gun appeared. He shoved it back again, grunted with satisfaction and stood up. He slipped the automatic into his coat pocket.

He took a drink of Bourbon and looked at the little folding clock on the secretary. At eight o'clock he heard the elevator down the hall open, and a minute later there was a knock on his door.

Tom Sherick was a mountain of a man beneath a wide-brimmed Panama. The man beside him was small, thin, pale-faced, and he carried his hands in his pockets. They stood in the doorway.

Cardigan said, "I didn't expect the wet-nurse."

"Willie goes where I go," Sherick said heavily, his little eyes quivering with suspicoin.

Cardigan stepped back and Sherick

and the pale-faced man trooped in. Sherick went all the way across the room, but his companion closed the door with a kick of his heel and remained in front of it, his big wet eyes sinister.

Sherick stopped, turned, mopped his neck and face with a handkerchief. His pale eyes had fire smouldering in their depths. He gestured with his handkerchief.

"What the hell, Cardigan, what the hell? I had every reason to believe you was a scout for that mob. What do you want? Cripes, what do you want?"

Cardigan sat down on the arm of a mohair easy-chair. "Never mind the apologies. And damper down your loud mouth. I expected you alone. You had to bring along this snot and complicate things."

"Willie goes where——"

"O.K., he's here now. And you're here. And you're the guy I want to have a talk with."

"Well, talk!"

Willie drew in his lower lip and then let it fall out again, where it hung wet and shiny.

Cardigan said, "I want the lowdown on a bird named McKimm."

"Mc—who?"

"McKimm. He hung out around your place and he was known there. What's his racket?"

Sherick stopped mopping his big face. His little eyes narrowed.

"How should I know? Hell, is that what you got me in here for?"

"Just that."

Willie made spitting sounds with his lips and Cardigan looked at him. "Cut out spitting on my carpet."

Sherick started tramping up and down the room, mopping his face again.

"This is funny," he said. "This is funny as hell, Cardigan."

"Says you!" bit off Cardigan. "Don't stall around when you know you've got to come across. You spring, Sherick, or by God I'll throw you to the cops for that ride!"

Willie took three forward steps from the door. His coat pockets moved and as he stood with his head down between his narrow shoulders, a sullen glassy look in his eyes.

Sherick threw an apprehensive look at him, licked his lips with a rapid motion of his tongue, jerked his pale harried eyes at Cardigan. Cardigan's eyes were flickering from Willie to Sherick, and the skin tightened on his jaw so that little muscles bulged beneath it.

Sherick rasped, "What the hell are you tailing McKimm for?"

"That's my business, Sherick, not yours. Yours is to tell me what his racket is and where I can call on him. I want to know that and the cheap snot over there with the two rods doesn't make me change my mind!"

Willie snarled, "For two cents——" His pale face rose, showing dark circles beneath his killer's eyes.

"Be quiet, Willie," Sherick said; then he snapped at Cardigan, "This is all a lot of crap!"

"Remember, Sherick, I was taken for a ride in the city of St. Louis. Not in the county, where you have the big shots smeared to lay off you. You'll tell me what I want to know——"

"Damn it, Tom!" rasped Willie feverishly. "This guy is askin' for a bellyache!" A sudden look of frenzy leaped into his eyes and his two guns came out of his pockets.

"Willie!" cried Sherick.

Willie panted, "The horse's neck's got it comin' to him!"

"Willie, put away those rods!"

A moan came from Willie's throat and he stood shaking and opening and closing his mouth slowly. Inch by inch his guns lowered until they hung at his sides.

Cardigan said, "Hell, Sherick, you're dumb to carry that hophead around with you."

"For God's sake, shut up!" cried Sherick.

Cardigan ran a hand across his forehead spreading cold sweat that had appeared there in shining beads.

"But you've got to tell, Sherick," he said, grimly. "I've got to know. And I want the truth—and then I want you to go out of here and keep your mouth shut."

Sherick began coughing into his handkerchief. His face was red and streaked with sweat. He looked harassed and cornered, and his jowels shook. He glared at Cardigan with hate and venom but with fear also. While Willie stood quivering like a bird dog held back, his lips wet and his eyes shining as though filled with tears.

Sherick stammered, "He—he gambles some. He used to be the silent owner of that gambling joint in East St. Louis—The Gold Casino. He went broke. Clean broke. I gave him a job, but he didn't keep it long. I don't know what he's doing. He used to come out sometimes and hang around."

"Alone?"

"Well, with a couple of pals sometimes."

"Who are they?"

Sherick groaned.

"What's it about, Cardigan? Gee, what's it about?"

"Who are the guys?"

"Oh, hell. Jack Gos and Billy Dessig."

"O.K. Now where does McKimm hang out?"

Sherick almost choked, but he got it out. "He's staying in a room over Lou Abatti's speak—down by the river. And damn your soul, Cardigan!"

Willie cried, "Tom—Tom, for cryin' out loud, let me give this punk a bellyache! You hear, Tom!"

Sherick jumped, grabbed Willie's arm.

"Willie, don't!"

He tussled with Willie, hurled him against the wall, took away the guns and thrust them in his own pocket. He held on to Willie, rushing him to the door. Willie cursed and moaned, and Cardigan opened the door.

"Remember, Sherick," he said. "Keep your mouth shut."

When he had closed the door he said, "Whew!" and stood wiping perspiration from his forehead.

CHAPTER FOUR

Killer's Street

CARDIGAN climbed out of a taxi at Marion and Broadway and headed toward the Mississippi. A warm river mist hung pendant in the dark streets, and infrequent street lights had needle-pointed auras of wet radiance. Cardigan's footfalls were loud, purposeful, clean-cut in the dark alleys through which he strode.

He passed a run-down billiard parlor where the curt click of balls could be heard, and the heavy voices of men. There was a boat horn braying on Old Man River somewhere beyond the house-tops. Cardigan turned a corner, passed a cigar store where a radio bleated. He turned another corner and followed a cobbled street that went slightly downgrade. Halfway down he lingered. An alley dead-ended here into the cobbled street. Fifty yards up the alley crouched a two-story red brick house with a drop light outside a door flush with a broken flag walk. Some cars were in a parking space this side of the building, and back of it was the Mississippi. Insistent was the muffled beat of a jazzband's drum.

Cardigan entered the alley. Under the drop light was a sign—black ungainly letters on white,

THE HONKYTONK

He pushed open an old wooden door painted a nightmare green. He went down worn wooden steps to a foyer where a slash-mouthed girl took his hat and gave him a check. The place was damp and hot. The old building throbbed with the beat of the jazz-band. Up two steps was the dance-floor. The bar was in the basement. It was a French bar—small and narrow with stools in front of it.

Cardigan pushed in. There were no bottles in sight. He ordered Bourbon straight and the barman produced it from underneath the bar. Three drunks were in a huddle arguing about the Browns and the Cardinals. The lights hanging from the ceiling quivered with the beat of the jazzband.

Cardigan drank, looking around. The Bourbon was thrice-cut. He felt his arm prodded and he turned around and looked at Sergeant Bush. The Metropolitan dick was sucking a home-made cigarette. His hard straw hat was tilted over thinned-downed eyes.

"Hello, sarge," the barman said.

"Gin," said Bush, still looking hard at Cardigan.

"You getting collegiate?" Cardigan asked.

Bush downed gin straight without taking his eyes off Cardigan. He said, "You're doing a hell of a lot of running around, Cardigan. What's on your mind?"

"Right now—a certain nosey shamus named Bush."

"Be funny!"

"Go to hell!"

Bush lowered his voice grimly.

"Listen, you. I seen Tom Sherick come out of your apartment house before. Tom and a punk of his named Willie Martin."

Cardigan scowled.

"Haven't you anything else to do but watch my place?"

"What's between you and Sherick?"

"I never saw Sherick."

"You're a liar! I was parked down the hall and saw him and the hood come out of your apartment."

Cardigan cursed under his breath. He faced Bush squarely. "You dirty flatfoot," he ground out. "Have you been tapping my wire?"

"Never mind, never mind—"

"Why the hell didn't you stop Sherick? Hadn't the guts, eh? Nah! He had his hood with him—that hop-head. That's why! Bush, you're a dirty sneak. You're a disgrace to an otherwise fine detective bureau. With swell guys like Holmes and Murfee, I don't know why you were put in charge of this case."

Bush reddened and his jaw hardened.

"What did you want with Sherick, Cardigan? You better tell me, because if you don't I take a squad and go out and find out myself!"

Cardigan's lip twitched.

"You stay away from Sherick, Bush! If you go out there he'll get the idea I welched. And I've never welched on any guy."

"You got something on Sherick," Bush muttered.

"I haven't. That's just another of your weak-minded ideas."

"You got something on him and you made him come across about somebody else." Bush nodded passed Cardigan's shoulder. "Hello, McKimm."

"Hello, Bush."

Cardigan looked in the mirror back of the bar and saw the reflected image of a tall, stony-faced man who smoked a cigar. It was the man who had cornered, frightened, Clara Hartz that night at the Ritz. He went to the bar and brooded darkly over a drink.

Cardigan threw a half-dollar on the bar. He whistled, left the bar, got his hat and went outside. Bush was at his heels. Cardigan opened the door of a waiting taxi and Bush said, "I'll go with you."

Cardigan turned a withering look on him.

"Not on my money Bush!" He climbed in and slammed the door. "Broadway," he said to the driver.

The cab swung around and got out of the alley. Looking back, Cardigan saw Bush climb in another. Cardigan leaned forward.

"Here's a two-dollar bill, kid. Drop me off up the street and then take a ride out to the north end. There's a tail back here I want to drop."

"Jake."

Cardigan looked back and saw another cab following.

"Swing left at the next street," he said. "Don't stop. I'll jump and walk to Broadway. You keep going."

"Jake."

The cab swung left sharply. Cardigan leaped off and slammed the door. He darted into an alley. He saw the second taxi shoot past, with Bush sitting on the edge of the seat.

CARDIGAN retraced his steps and entered the Honkytonk. He did not check his hat. He reentered the bar and saw McKimm still standing there, a felt hat yanked down over his eyes, his hands toying with an empty glass. The bar was crowded now with jabbering drunks, and the jazz-band pounded. Cardigan ordered a drink and paid for it on the spot. Under his hat-brim he watched Mc-Kimm in the mirror back of the bar.

Five minutes later McKimm threw a couple of bills on the bar, waited for change. Cardigan turned and went into the foyer. The hat-check girl had her back to him. She was talking on the telephone. There was nobody else in the foyer. It was noisy with the sound of the music.

The swing-door from the bar opened and McKimm came out. Cardigan lifted his coat pocket. McKimm's eyes narrowed and his lips tightened hard on his cigar. Cardigan nodded toward the exit. McKimm hesitated, stony-faced. Cardigan moved his lips and went closer.

McKimm turned and went up the stairs. Cardigan crowded him outside. There was no taxi.

"Walk fast," Cardigan said.

He drew his gun and pressed it in the small of McKimm's back.

"What's this?" McKimm growled.

"Get."

They walked through the black alley, turned up the cobbled street. Cardigan flattened McKimm again a house-wall, made him raise his hands. He frisked him, took a gun from an arm-pit holster while his own gun pressed hard into McKimm's stomach.

"Now walk again," Cardigan said. "Put your hands in your pockets and keep them there."

"Didn't I see you with Bush?"

"Get along, get along."

Their footfalls echoed in the quiet dark street. Four blocks further on Cardigan stopped a taxi and crowded McKimm in. Cardigan gave his address on Lindell.

McKimm started.

"What the hell's this?"

"Shut up."

They struck Broadway, turned left into Olive and bowled through the darkened business district, past the Post-Dispatch Building, across Twelfth Boulevard and up the hill. At Channing they left the car tracks, hit Lindell and went over the hump past the University.

Cardigan spoke to the driver.

"When you reach the address, a driveway swings through the basement garage. Take it."

McKimm sat in stony silence, his breath audible in his nostrils, his lips clamped on his cigar.

In the basement garage Cardigan backed out, covered McKimm. He thrust a couple of bills into the driver's hand. He motioned McKimm out and took him up in the service elevator.

"Listen, who the hell are you?" McKimm muttered.

"Get out," Cardigan said at the sixth floor.

He marched McKimm down the corridor, unlocked the door.

"Get in."

He followed McKimm into the apartment, which he had left lighted, and kicked shut the door.

McKimm turned and looked at him stonily. "Who the hell are you?" he asked again.

"Pat O'Hara's partner."

McKimm remained stony.

"What is that supposed to mean?"

"Sit down in the straight-backed chair, honeybunch. We're going to play school. I'm the teacher and you're the pupil."

McKimm sat down, said, "The floor is yours."

Keeping his gun and eyes trained on McKimm, Cardigan fished in a vest pocket, drew out a folded piece of paper.

"Catch it," he said.

He threw and McKimm caught it.

"Read it," Cardigan said.

McKimm unfolded the paper, squinted his eyes. Not a muscle in his face twitched. He looked up with his stony expressionless eyes and said nothing.

"Now what about it?" Cardigan said.

"What about what?"

"In your notes, there, what the hell do you mean by the word 'obligation,' McKimm?"

McKimm looked at the note again, folded it, tossed it to the open secretary.

"I don't know what you're talking about."

"I'm in a lousy mood tonight, McKimm, and I don't want wisecracks for answers. I saw you accost Mrs. Hartz at the Ritz the night before it was raided and you didn't look pleasant. And she looked scared. I'm on your tail tight as a tick."

"And you can go to hell."

Cardigan hefted his gun.

"What was the obligation?"

"Just what it said. Maybe I should have used 'debt.' A little debt. That's all."

"Debt for what?"

McKimm stood up, his lips still tight on his cigar, barely moving when he spoke.

"To hell with you!"

"Sit down!" Cardigan took three steps and punched McKimm in the chest.

McKimm sat down, his eyes hard as marbles.

Cardigan backed across the room, got hold of the telephone with one hand. He gave a number. He got a connection and asked for Mrs. Hartz.

"Hello, Mrs. Hartz. Cardigan. I want you to come over to my apartment immediately. . . . I'm sorry, but I'm giving orders. You'll do wise to come over, as fast as you can. . . . Yes. Thank you."

He hung up.

Visibly McKimm's lips didn't move, but they must have, because he was saying, "What the hell kind of a merry-go-round are you on anyway?"

"I'm reaching for the gold ring."

McKimm's eyes remained round and hard and inscrutable.

WHEN the brass knocker on the outside of the door sounded, Cardigan did not move. He called, "Mrs. Hartz?"

"Yes."

"Come in."

The door opened. Everett was there, pink-cheeked and wavy-haired. The angle of the doorway at first prohibited his seeing McKimm. He saw Cardigan, however, and the gun in Cardigan's hand.

"What's the meaning of this?" he snapped indignantly.

"I didn't expect you," Cardigan said, with a wintry smile.

"Do you think I would let Mrs. Hartz come to your place alone? Really!"

Cool and white-faced in her black cloche hat and black wrap, Clara Hartz came in first. She saw McKimm. She looked at him with her Oriental eyes, looked away. Everett closed the door. Then he saw McKimm. He seemed to grow an inch, and his white hands doubled. His blue eyes radiated sudden blue fire but he kept his mouth shut.

Cardigan said, with a touch of bitter sarcasm, "Do I have to go through with introductions?"

"What do you want?" asked Clara Hartz in her flat voice.

Cardigan pointed to the secretary. "Read that letter."

She crossed the room, picked up the piece of paper McKimm had refolded. She read the lines, shrugged, let the note slip back to the desk. One of her arched eyebrows rose.

"Well?" she said.

Everett made an exasperatetd sound, crossed the room, snatched up the note, read it. He flung a look at McKimm. McKimm was stony-faced, stony-eyed. Everett spun on Cardigan.

"What in God's name are you driving at?" he ripped out hotly.

Cardigan ignored him. "Mrs. Hartz, in what way are you obligated to Mr. McKimm?"

"That," she said, "is perhaps my business—and Mr. McKimm's."

"Right now it's mine too."

"On the contrary——"

"You hear!" Cardigan rasped, his face a dull red. "It's my business! It's my business to find out who murdered my partner Pat O'Hara! It's my business to know what kind of business you had with McKimm!"

"Look here, Cardigan," snapped Everett, starting toward him.

"You keep your oar out of this—and stay back!"

Everett cried, "You have no right to question Mrs. Hartz! No right at all!"

"Mrs. Hartz," said Cardigan crisply, "answer my question."

She sighed. "I suppose I'll have to. Well"—she drew in a breath—"I owe him an amount—of money. I've owed it for a little more than a year. When Mr. McKimm operated the Gold Casino, a gaming place, I played there. Rather steeply. I was foolish. He took my I.O.U.'s because he knew Mr. Hartz was quite wealthy. It was unfortunate. I found out that Mr. Hartz was rigidly opposed to gambling. I never had much money to spend. Plenty of charge accounts for legitimate purchases—but no allowance. I shouldn't have, but gambling is one of my weaknesses. I couldn't get the money. The debt is still standing. That is all."

"How much?" asked Cardigan.

She let her long-held breath out. "Fifty thousand."

"What of it? What of it?" snapped Everett.

Cardigan ignored him. Cardigan's face was brown and grim with red burning beneath the brown. He was staring at McKimm. He saw the first flicker of emotion in McKimm's face. He saw McKimm's big hands gripping the sides of the chair, saw an unholy glitter growing in McKimm's eyes.

"Now I suppose," came Clara Hartz's flat, casual voice, "you'll have something else to give to the scandal sheets."

Cardigan's voice was low, ominous. "That kill's the thing, Mrs. Hartz—the murder of my partner. I tell you again I'm no scandal-monger—not just for the sake of scandal. But this goes deeper—This goes way down deep. Or I miss my bet. I miss my bet if the killer of Pat O'Hara, Ludwig Hartz and his chauffeur isn't in this room right now."

She looked at him suddenly. She saw the fierce intensity in his eyes. She followed the direction of their burning, implacable stare. Fright leaped into her eyes. She let out a stifled little cry.

McKimm raised his hand, ripped the dead cigar from his mouth. "Who the

hell are you staring at, Cardigan?" he roared.

For the first time his mouth opened, his lips ripped back across his teeth. A gold eye-tooth flashed at the left corner of his mouth.

Cardigan flung at him, "I'm staring at you, McKimm! I'm staring at the guy that murdered three men and put a fourth in the hospital!"

Ignoring Clara and Everett, he took three hard steps across the carpet, his gun trained on McKimm's chest.

"Oh, my God!" breathed Clara. "No—no—no!"

"Max Saul's living, thank God," Cardigan said. "And he'll remember that gold tooth, McKimm. And you'll remember how the spotlight on Hartz's car swung around as it swerved. You used this strike as a cover-up. You're broke. You need the money. You figured to get your debt out of Hartz's legacy to his wife."

"Is this true, is this true?" cried Clara Hartz.

McKimm heaved to his feet, agony bursting on his face, guilt bare and unadorned in his eyes.

"Sit down, McKimm!" barked Cardigan.

McKimm roared, "My God, Everett—"

A gun boomed.

Cardigan felt a slam somewhere in the back and he started to pitch forward. Clara Hartz screamed. McKimm jumped and grabbed Cardigan's gun, ripped it free. He smashed Cardigan in the jaw, sent him reeling backwards and followed him, ripping his own gun from Cardigan's pocket.

Everett stood shaking and horror-stricken, a smoking automatic in his hand.

"Ralph, what have you done?" cried Clara Hartz.

Cardigan landed in the mohair easy-chair with a bang, his heels flying, his head jerking back, the chair itself tilting backwards, banging against the wall.

McKimm towered with a gun in either hand. "I'm leaving," he clipped and backed swiftly to the door.

Everett shook. "My God, McKimm, don't leave me!"

Clara Hartz pressed hands to her cheeks, stared thunderstruck at Everett. "Ralph—Ralph—"

"Shut up!" Everett screamed at her.

He shook like a man with palsy and backed up beside McKimm.

"You'll—have to take me, McKimm. I just saved—you."

Cardigan snarled, "Yellow as I always thought you were! Leaving the woman to take the rap, eh?" His face was ferocious, bitter, his shaggy hair stood on end. Pain burned in his back, but he was a hard party.

CLARA'S calm was gone. She was flushed, wide-eyed, gripped with terror and wild bewilderment. She saw McKimm's gun move upward. She choked and whirled and spread her body and her arms in front of Cardigan.

"No you won't!" she panted. "I see now. I see it all. You murdered Ludwig to get that money—through me later. And you, Ralph—oh, how could you! You told him of Ludwig's movements. You urged me to divorce Ludwig. I wanted to. I didn't love him. I loved you. But you didn't want me —without his money. Oh, Ralph—Ralph!" She began sobbing hysterically.

Everett looked like a lamb shorn. His dignity, his haughty manner, were gone. He shook and looked wild and desperate.

"I gambled," she cried. "I was weak. God knows I was weak! And I have no excuse. I'm a fool—a terrible fool!"

McKimm clipped to Everett, "Come on."

McKimm opened the door, stepped into the corridor, looked up and down. Doors closed elsewhere. Voices were excited—then silent.

Glassy-eyed, Everett backed through the door, confirming his guilt, leaving the woman who had loved him. She sobbed brokenly.

Cardigan had his hand on it now, on the short-barreled Colt he had planted in the mohair easy-chair before Sherick's arrival. He whipped it up. The blunt muzzle belched flame. Everett jerked and his eyes popped wide. Then he screamed and fell backward, clutched at his chest.

McKimm bolted for the staircase.

Cardigan jumped from the chair, whipped quick words into Clara Hartz's ear.

"That door over there hides an in-a-door bed. Get in there. Close the door. Hide behind the bed. Stay there."

He ran to the corridor door, looked out. A man in a dressing-gown was standing near the elevator.

"Get a doctor," Cardigan said, indicating Everett.

He started down the staircase. Doors were opening and closing, and far below someone was blowing a police whistle. Cardigan reached the lobby as he saw McKimm bolt through the front door. He went through the door a split-second later and saw McKimm crossing Lindell.

A small crowd had gathered in front of the apartment house. Some autos had stopped. People were scattering at sight of the men with the drawn guns. McKimm began running west on Lindell. Cardigan reached the opposite sidewalk and ran after him. Pedestrians ran for shelter. McKimm looked back and fired, missed and crashed the tail light of a parked car.

Cardigan raised his gun but a darting pedestrian got in the way, yelped with fright, flung himself flat on the sidewalk. Cardigan leaped over him. McKimm turned south into Euclid, stopped, turned and waited for Cardigan to swing around the corner. His gun belched and echoes hammered.

Cardigan staggered to the curb, kept his feet, fired and saw McKimm reel but keep running. He fired again and saw McKimm swerve drunkenly. He ran after him unsteadily and McKimm turned and his gun blazed and Cardigan stopped and fell down. Half-kneeling, he raised his gun and watched McKimm jolting across the street. He fired and the bullet tumbled McKimm across the curb. But he got up and staggered on.

Cardigan got up, sweat pouring from him, pain tightening his jaw. He limped across the street. He fell down on the opposite sidewalk and saw McKimm down twenty yards further on. McKimm's gun boomed. The shot snarled against the pavement near Cardigan's head. He leaned on his elbow, looked down his gun, fired.

McKimm whipped over, tried to get up, collapsed. His gun rang as it banged down to the pavement.

Cardigan toiled to his feet, gritted his teeth, staggered toward Lindell. He drew in great breaths. He made himself walk almost steadily. He looked grim and shaggy and he could feel blood crawling beneath his clothes.

There was a crowd in front of the apartment house. He pushed through it, and people saw him and exclaimed but nobody tried to stop him. The lobby was jammed. The elevator was in use, so he took the stairway up. People were jabbering in the corridors. He barely noticed them. His feet were like gobs of lead.

He reached his floor and found a crowd there. He spotted a couple of uniformed cops. He plowed through the crowd and te cops turned and grabbed him roughly.

"Leggo," he muttered.

They tightened on him.

"You damned flatfeet, leggo!"

Bush appeared in the doorway.

"Oh, it's you, Cardigan!" Bush looked baffled and angry. "Let him go, boys."

The cops let go and Cardigan reeled into his apartment. A doctor was bending over Everett.

"I knew you were up to something tonight!" Bush growled. "Now what the hell did you do?"

"This guy on the floor shot me in the back. McKimm is lying over in Euclid near West Pine. I guess some of your cops have got him by this time."

"What'd this guy shoot you for?"

Cardigan sagged to a chair.

"McKimm killed my pal Pat O'Hara. He killed Hartz and the chauffeur. He wounded Max Saul."

"Somebody said they heard a woman scream here."

"They're nuts. It was Everett. When I cornered McKimm here Everett let me have it in the back. He was in with McKimm. He wanted to get rid of Hartz too."

"You're lying, Cardigan!"

"Go to hell, Bush! Let me alone awhile."

"There was a woman here!"

"There wasn't. I got McKimm here and then I got Everett here."

An ambulance doctor and two men with a stretcher came in. The doctor bending over Everett looked up and shook his head.

"He hasn't a chance," he said.

Cardigan, fast losing consciousness, saw the white door across the room open. He shook his head. He did not want Mrs. Hartz to come. He believed that this thing could be settled without her. He knew she had been tricked by Everett. He knew she had nothing to do with the murder of his partner. He remembered that she had put her body in front of him against the muzzles of McKimm's guns.

But she came out—statuesque and white-faced.

"So," growled Bush, with a scathing look at Cardigan.

She gasped and ran across the room. Nobody else had noticed Cardigan sagging. She reached him and put her arm around him. His eyes rolled as he looked up at her. He smiled.

"You've—got—guts," he muttered.

CARDIGAN came to a day later in a hospital room. He turned his head and saw Max Saul sitting in a wheelchair. He licked his lips. A nurse got up and looked at him.

Max Saul grinned, "He's O.K., nurse."

"Yeah," said Cardigan. "I feel like getting up and playing kick-the-wicket or something."

"I'm sore," Max joked. "You're getting all the headlines, Irish."

"How did Everett and McKimm make out?"

"They didn't. They brought McKimm here on a stretcher and I identified him. Everett cleared his conscience before he went places. And cleared Clara Hartz too. It was Everett put the idea in McKimm's head that if Hartz should die Mrs. Hartz would come into a lot of money. Everett figured he would have, too—through marriage to the widow. I think I said once that guy was a lounge-lizard."

Cardigan closed his eyes. "It's tough on the woman, Max. She saved my life."

"She took it all standing up, Steve. And she's been telephoning every half hour about you. Bush started to yammer but Captain Bricknell dampered him down."

Another nurse came in with a vase of roses. Cardigan frowned. "Now who sent those?"

"Mrs. Hartz."

Cardigan relaxed and closed his eyes.

Max Saul said, "That's what I'd call a bed of roses, Irish."

A nurse wheeled him out of the room and on the way down the hall he hummed The St. Louis Blues.

Snowy Ducks for Cover

by

Erle Stanley Gardner

There had been a struggle and Harley Robb had received several wounds from a thin-bladed knife. It was a messy job.

Maybe Snowy Shane didn't play the detective racket exactly according to police rules. But in tracking a killer he knew how to find the short cuts—even when all the evidence pointed in the wrong direction.

IF MOLLY O'KEEFE had been what is known in the vernacular as a "swell looker," Frank Sheridane would never have consulted "Snowy" Shane. For Sheridane was fully as keen a business man as any of the criminal lawyers who handled the big-time murder cases; and it needed no expert in mental arithmetic to reach the conclusion that the more fee for Snowy Shane, the less for Sheridane.

But Sheridane liked to win his cases. A death penalty verdict was as inconvenient for defense counsel as it was fatal for the client. Hence, he consulted the chunky little detective and put his cards on the table. Snowy Shane called the turn with neatness and despatch.

"Bum looker, eh?"

"Not so hot, why?"

"Just wondered. You'd have gone before a jury and trusted to a few. tears if she'd been a mamma."

"Yeah, maybe. Anyhow, I'm here. It's up to you."

Snowy Shane had acquired his nickname for a bushy crop of gray hair which silvered his head with a grizzled mane. His eyes matched his hair, steel cold, with the glint which comes from frosted grass when the sun first strikes it. He was a fast worker, and the police would have none of him. He didn't play the game along orthodox lines, but took shortcuts whenever he felt reasonably certain of his ultimate goal.

He picked a pipe from his pocket, regarded the polished bowl lovingly, crammed in moist crumbs of fragrant tobacco and grunted.

"What you want me to do?"

"Get her out, of course."

"Is she guilty?"

The lawyer grinned.

"She tells me she isn't," he confided.

"Humph," grunted the detective. "If she ain't, who is?"

Frank Sheridane knew the ways of the chunky detective, knew just how far he could be trusted. He bit the end from a cigar, struck a match, and rotated the tobacco between his fingers as he applied the flame, making certain the cigar would burn evenly.

"Harley Robb, president of the Mutual Morehomes Building & Loan had been dipping into the funds, using them for speculation. He was short something over a million."

Snowy Shane nodded.

"He was exposed by someone, forced to sign a confession. That confession has every earmark of having been written under a great emotional strain. It's all in his handwriting."

The lawyer took a folded paper from his pocket.

"Original?" asked Snowy Shane.

"No. A copy. Here's what is says."

"I, Harley Robb, President of the Mutual Morehomes Building & Loan have been embezzling the funds for speculation. I admit my guilt. I had no accomplices. I alone am to blame. Harry Robb."

"That confession was sent by special messenger to the chairman of the advisory committee. Naturally he went at once to interview Robb. He took a detective with him. They found Robb dead—murdered."

Snowy Shane grunted.

"Sure it wasn't suicide?"

"Yes. He was stabbed. There'd been some sort of a struggle."

"Who was the chairman of the advisory committee?"

"Arthur Sprang."

"Who loses the money Robb took?"

"Lots of people. Sprang for one; my client for another. She will lose all of her savings."

The white-haired detective toyed with a pencil. His cold gray eyes regarded the lawyer contemplatively.

"Clues?" he asked.

"There weren't any."

"Why pick on the jane, then?"

"Because she was the last person to see him alive, so far as the police can find out."

"Tell me about it."

"The murder happened some time around midnight. Robb had been at the office, giving the secretary, Molly O'Keefe, some dictation. He seemed distraught, nervous. She went home shortly before twelve. She says Robb was still in the office.

"The confession reached the chairman of the advisory committee around one o'clock in the morning. A messenger had been summoned over the telephone, ordered to take an envelope that would be found pinned to the office door, and deliver it to the address shown on the envelope.

"That envelope was found pinned to the door, delivered. It contained the confession. Sprang was home and in bed when the message was delivered. He summoned a detective and they went at once to the office of the company, found the door locked, forced it, found the body of Robb.

"There had been a struggle. A chair or two was smashed. Rugs were wrinkled and pitched around into the corners of the waxed floor. Robb had received several stabs. It was a messy job.

"Robb wore a wrist watch. It had been smashed in the struggle. The hands pointed to 11:57. My client caught a street car at 12:15. There was a speck of blood on the outside of the envelope in which the confession was enclosed.

"When they arrested Molly O'Keefe they found a wallet that has been identified as belonging to Robb. It contained something over ten thousand dollars in cash. She had hidden it in the mattress of her bed and then sewed up the mattress where she had slit it to put the wallet in."

THE criminal lawyer regarded the tip of his cigar judiciously. Snowy Shane grunted an interruption.

"What's her story—on the wallet?"

"She says Robb dictated to her, seemed very nervous, asked her how much money she had in the company. She told him around fifteen thousand dollars, money she'd been saving for years. He took his wallet from his pocket, told her to keep it in a safe place, if anything happened to her investment to consider the money in the nature of a repayment; but never to let anyone know she had it."

Shane sighed.

"What's the police theory?"

"That Robb told her of his shortage, wrote out the confession. That she asked him about her savings, that he told her they had gone, along with the rest, that she drew a knife, struggled with him, killed him, took the wallet from his body and beat it."

"Find the knife?" asked Snowy Shane.

"No. They can't find it."

"Any stains on her clothes?"

"No. That's a point in her favor."

Shane shrugged his massive shoulders.

"Looks like she could beat the rap before a jury. If they ain't got nothing more than that, it'll be all circumstantial evidence. She could spiel her piece to the jury and raise a reasonable doubt."

The lawyer made a grimace.

"She's got skinny legs," he said, "and a homely face."

"How old?"

"Around forty-three, looks fifty. And—well, the case is young yet. You can't tell what the police will discover later on. I want to get you started now."

"Huh, want me to beat the police to it, eh?"

"Yes."

"And if you're afraid they'll discover something, it's because you've got a hunch your client's guilty."

"Our client."

"Not yet," said Snowy Shane with a grin.

Frank Sheridane twisted the cigar around and around in his mouth.

"She might be, at that," he admitted. "It's funny that Robb would have given her virtually all the cash he had. If he was carrying ten thousand bucks around in his pocket it was getaway money. You know what these looters do as well as I do. They always keep a bunch of cash on them for a quick getaway."

Snowy Shane squinted his eyes in silent thought for a few moments.

"Funny he could have copped that much swag without the advisory committee getting wise."

The lawyer's eyes narrowed.

"If we can get that thought across to the jury, backed by some evidence, we may save our client."

"Your client," said Shane, cupping the hot bowl of his pipe in caressing fingers.

"Maybe if you could find some facts to work on," went on the lawyer, heedless of the comment, "I could pin a theory."

"When was the room janitored?" asked Snowy Shane, interrupting.

"After the office closed."

"Robb was having a night session?"

"So it seems."

"No one else in the room?"

"No."

"If we could show someone else had been in the room, then what?"

The lawyer heaved a sigh.

"Then we'd stand a chance," he said.

"What you want me to do?"

"Give me some facts to work on. I want you to pull some of your fourth degree stuff and give our client a break."

Snowy Shane grinned.

"All right," he conceded, "let's get started and see what we can do for our client."

The attorney chuckled.

"Knew you'd come around," he said.

Shane bristled.

"It was the fourth degree stuff that turned the trick for you," he said.

And Frank Sheridane, criminal attorney, and, therefore, shrewd judge of human nature, suppressed a smile. With Snowy Shane on the job the battle was under way, and he had been saving that fourth degree comment for just the proper time.

THE president's private office of the Mutual Morehomes Building & Loan had ceased to be a private sanctorum and had become a chamber of death.

A uniformed officer guarded the door, admitted the lawyer only after careful scrutiny of his pass. The rugs were still rumpled back, the gruesome red splotches discolored the floor. A chalked outline showed where the body had lain. The room reeked of the smell of death and the acrid fumes of flashlight powder where police and newspaper photographers had taken pictures of what had been found in the office.

The outer offices housed hushed groups of wide-eyed women employees who discussed the case in whispers. A detective accompanied Sheridane and Snowy Shane into the death chamber, a cigar tilted in his mouth, his eyes weary and watchful.

"Take a look-see," he said, "but don't touch nothin'."

Snowy Shane planted himself in the

middle of the room. His eyes went slithering about, steely cold, watchful, alert.

"Fingerprints, Joe?"

The detective shook his head.

"Nope."

"Find the knife?"

"Nope."

"What kind of a sticker was it?"

"The surgeon says it was a paper knife, or a thin stiletto, the kind a frail would pack."

Snowy Shane grunted.

"Let's go," he said, after a while.

Sheridane followed him to the outer office. There Shane secured the names of the three members of the advisory committee—Arthur Sprang, the chairman; Ernest Bagley and Sidney Symmes. He also secured their addresses.

"Looks sort of gloomy," said the attorney as they descended in the elevator. "I'll go to my office. You let me know if—"

Shane shook his head.

"You'll stay with me. I'm going to see these men. I may want a witness."

The lawyer's eyes lighted.

"Fourth degree?" he asked. "Some of your special kind?"

Shane tamped tobacco into the bowl of his pipe, thrust it into his mouth and gripped the stem with firm teeth.

"Yeah," he remarked, "stick around."

They drove to the home of Arthur Sprang first. That individual was paunchy, red-eyed, pasty-jowled. The shock had left him nervous. He consented to see the pair with the statement that the interview would be brief.

"What time did you get the letter?" asked Shane, his gray eyes gimleting the red-rimmed ones of the heavy man.

"About one o'clock."

"Humph," said Shane and filled his pipe.

The attorney produced a cigar, offerd one to the man who let his eyes shift restlessly, from one to the other.

"Thanks," said Sprang, "I have my own pet brand."

He produced a case from his inside pocket, selected a cigar, bit off the end and spat it explosively on the floor. His hand shook slightly.

"Terrific shock," he said.

Snowy Shane leaned forward, jabbed an impressive finger at the bosom of the chairman of the advisory committee.

"How was he lyin' when you busted in the door?"

Sprang repressed a shudder with a visible effort.

"Sprawled out," he said, and shook his shoulders.

"Head toward the door or away from it?"

"Away from it."

Shane grinned triumphantly.

"That," he remarked, crisply, "is exactly what I wanted to know. Come on, Frank."

And he got to his feet, led the puzzled lawyer to the door.

"But you said you wanted to get some very vital information you thought I might have," murmured Arthur Sprang.

"We've got it," said Shane and slammed the door.

In the taxicab, the lawyer regarded him speculatively.

"Really, Snowy, I don't see just what you gained."

"Shut up," said the detective. "I'm thinkin'."

They journeyed in silence to the office of Ernest Bagley. That individual, thin, dour, very nervous, greeted them with a dry, husky voice, shook hands with big, bony fingers that were cold and dry. He was past middle age, abnormally long of arm, high of cheekbone, thick of lip, hollow of cheek.

"You wanted to ask about the murder, you said, over the telephone?"

"Yeah," said Snowy Shane, plunging into the discussion without any polite preliminaries. "How long you known Robb?"

"Ten years."

"Members of the same golf club and all that?"

"No. I don't play golf. Neither did Robb."

Snowy Shane produced his pipe from his pocket, tamped tobacco into the bowl, regarded it ruefully.

"Any pipe tobacco? Mine's run out."

Bagley shook his head.

"I use cigarettes, roll my own. I can give you some of my tobacco I use in them, though."

Shane nodded. Bagley produced a cloth sack, handed it to the detective. Shane filled his pipe.

"Only had half enough for a smoke," he said. "This'll come in handy."

He passed back the sack. Bagley took a packet of brown papers from a vest pocket, rolled a cigarette. His hand shook slightly.

"Ever have any mutual business interests with Robb?" asked Shane, abruptly.

The bony fingers stopped, midway in their task.

"A few," admitted Ernest Bagley, and the cold caution of his guarded tone was apparent to both of his listeners, trained as they were in the subtleties of human prevarications.

"Profitable?" asked Shane.

Bagley looked up from his cigarette.

"That," I think, "is hardly a proper question."

Shane got to his feet.

"All right," he said. "If you won't cooperate with us, we'll have to reach it some other way."

THE attorney followed him from the office, his eyes puzzled. Bagley watched them with a face that was utterly void of expression.

"A good poker player," said the attorney, as they got into the taxicab once more.

"Yeah," said Shane. "We'll go see Symmes now."

Sheridane studied the squat, powerful man with the steel-gray eyes and snowy hair.

"Shane, do you know what you're doing, or are you just messing around in the dark?"

The detective regarded him with eyes that were wide with surprise.

"Why, of course I know what I'm doing. You said you wanted facts, didn't you? Something you could pin a defense to?"

"Yes," said the attorney, "you give me a peg to hang a defense on, and that's all I want. I'll do the rest."

The detective nodded.

"And you don't see what I'm doing?"

"No. I'm hanged if I do. I presume it's some of your fourth degree stuff, but I don't see it."

"Stick around then," advised Snowy Shane, "and save me a cigar. I'm going to switch from a pipe, after a while."

Sheridane regarded him with thought-filmed eyes.

"You know I've got to have something twelve men can act on," he said.

The detective slumped his head down on his shoulders.

"Yeah," he said, and it was apparent that his thoughts were far away. The taxicab lurched over the streets. The two passengers lapsed into utter silence, each occupied with his own thoughts.

Sydney Symmes was a big, broad-shouldered, frank-eyed man whose skin still showed a pale bronze. Undoubtedly, he had lived much of his life in the open. He had just lit a cigarette, and kept it in one corner of his mouth as he shook hands, muttered a conventional greeting.

Snowy Shane regarded him with eyes that held a suggestion of bewilderment.

"How come you're in the building and loan," he asked. "You're an outdoor man."

Sydney Symmes boomed forth a laugh.

"If you're as good a detective on crime as you've just shown yourself to be on occupations, you'll prove an airtight case on that girl."

Shane shook his head, a fierce, swift, impatient gesture.

"I'm trying to show the girl's innocent."

"Oh," said Symmes, and his manner underwent a subtle change. "I thought you were working for the company."

Snowy Shane let his gray eyes glitter with frosty belligerency.

"You don't want to have this girl convicted unless she's guilty, do you?"

Symmes clamped his jaws in a straight line.

"Miss O'Keefe is guilty," he said.

Snowy Shane grinned.

"Oh well, let's not argue about it. Where did you get your outdoor complexion?"

Sydney Symmes became cordial again. His eyes softened.

"Forest ranger for the government for fifteen years, down in New Mexico and Southern California."

Snowy Shane turned to the lawyer.

"You got any questions?" he asked.

Sheridane frowned.

"I'm listening," he commented.

Shane returned his attention to Symmes.

"Funny you left the service to get into this game."

"No," smiled Symmes, "it wasn't. You see, I was educated as an attorney, but my health gave out and I went into the open. Robb was in my class at college. He often suggested that I should come back to the city. A year or so ago he sold me on the idea. I had a little money. I put it into the building and loan and, through his influence, was placed on the advisory committee."

Snowy Shane rubbed a speculative forefinger along the angle of his jaw.

"The confession must have come as a shock to you."

Symmes squinted his eyes, leaned forward. His fists clenched with visible emotion. His voice quivered.

"That confession is a forgery. The man who says Robb was short in his accounts is a damned liar, and that goes for anyone who says it. See?"

There was no mistaking his belligerency.

Shane got to his feet.

"Sure we see," he remarked, and led the way to the door.

"Wait a minute," invited Symmes. "I meant no particular offense. I was sticking up for my friend, and I got a little hot-headed, I guess."

"Yeah," commented Shane. "You would. That's your outdoor training. See you later, maybe. Good-by."

Sheridane's brow was corrugated as he settled back in the cushions of the cab.

"That some of the fourth degree stuff?"

Shane nodded casually.

"That's it," he said.

"Well," commented the lawyer in a voice from which he strove to keep his impatience, "it doesn't help any."

Snowy Shane stretched out his chunky arms, yawned.

"Uh huh," he agreed. "Let's go back to the office where the murder was pulled. I want to see something else."

JOE KARG, police detective in charge, regarded their second visit with dour disapproval.

"Didn't you guys see enough the first time?" he asked.

Snowy Shane transfixed him with hostile gaze.

"No," he said.

He took a cloth sack of tobacco from his pocket, held his pipe cupped in his left hand, poured in the tobacco, and some of the grains spilled to the floor. He lit the pipe and broke the match in two pieces, flipped it under the table, bent to examine the floor.

"The old bloodhound," remarked Karg with a grin, "looking for tracks."

"Shut up, Joe," said Snowy Shane.

He puffed placidly at his pipe, his eye, meanwhile, peering along the floor as though taking measurements. Sheridane nervously glanced at his watch, took a cigar from his pocket, bit off the end, spat it explosively.

"Listen, Snowy, I've got to get to my office. I can't just stick around."

Snowy Shane straightened. His eyes were gleaming with frosty enthusiasm.

"Joe," he said, "will you ring up Sprang, Bagley and Symmes and tell 'em to come over here right away. I got the murder solved."

Joe Karg jeered at him.

"Yeah, you're the human bloodhound. Murders are open books to you. You give 'em the once over and——"

Snowy interrupted.

"Of course, if you don't want a promotion."

He let his voice trail off into silence. Joe Karg thought that matter over.

"Would I get the credit?"

"You'd get the credit."

The police detective moved to the telephone.

Sprang was the first to answer the summons. He entered the office, puzzled, awkward, ill at ease. Snowy Shane sat him in a chair, taking pains to make him face the window.

"Sprang," he said, slowly and impressively, "someone was in this room last night. Someone who smoked cigars and bit off the ends."

Sprang's glassy eyes stared uncomprehendingly for a moment.

"You mean me?" he asked, a flush suffusing his face.

"I don't know," said Snowy Shane, "but here's the end off a cigar that was on the floor. You smoke your own brand. Let me have one of 'em."

The man handed over a cigar, meekly, questioningly.

Snowy Shane extended his hand.

"Thanks. That's all."

"You called me over here for this?"

"Yes. That's all. The department will analyze the tobacco in the end of the cigar and the one you gave me."

Sprang lurched to his feet.

"Of all the damned fools!" he snapped, and lunged from the office.

When he had gone Sheridane eyed the detective coldly.

"I presume you are aware," he said, formally, "that I was smoking in here a few minutes ago, and the cigar end you have is one I bit off."

Snowy Shane said nothing.

Bagley was entering the room, nervous, furtive, almost cringing in his manner.

"You smoke cigarettes. You roll 'em. Ever spill tobacco?" asked Snowy Shane.

The nervous man blinked his eyes.

"Huh?" he asked.

Snowy Shane pointed to the floor.

"Get down here," he said. "Look here on the floor, grains of tobacco. The same sort that you use to roll your cigarettes. That means somebody was in this room after the janitor cleaned it last night. That somebody smoked the same brand of tobacco you do.

"Now suppose that somebody was the murderer. What'd be more natural than for him to roll a cigarette after he'd done the job? And his hand would be shaking, and he'd spill some of the tobacco, and—"

The nervous man interrupted.

"You lie!" he screamed. "I wasn't here. I know nothing about the murder. I can prove it. You're a double-crossing crook. You planted that tobacco here. You came out to my house and saw the kind of tobacco I smoked, and—"

Joe Karg clapped a hand on the man's shoulder.

"Easy, bo," he said, warningly.

Snowy Shane waved a hand toward the door.

"That's all," he said.

Bagley wanted to remain and talk, but Karg escorted him out. They closed the door and waited some five minutes for Symmes. Karg's eyes were singularly unenthusiastic.

"Hope you don't think you're getting anywhere with this stuff, Snowy," he observed.

Snowy Shane shrugged his huge shoulders.

There was an impatient knock at the door. He opened it to admit Symmes. Snowy Shane sat him in the same chair, facing the window, dropped to his knees and pointed to the broken match.

"Symmes," he said, "you were a ranger in the dry southwest. Did you, by any chance, learn to break matches into two pieces before you threw them away?"

Symmes looked at the match, laughed good-naturedly.

"Hell no. I've heard of fellows who did that. I never did."

Snowy Shane got to his feet, dusted the knees of his trousers.

"Thanks," he said. "That's all. I guess I pulled a boner, Karg. None of these men had anything to do with it."

Symmes grinned, extended his hand.

"No hard feelings," he said. "You detectives have got to do your duty. Call on me any time."

HE left the office. Joe Karg's face showed hostility. "The next time I let a private dick horn in and sell me on a wild theory, you'll know it!" he snapped.

Snowy Shane nodded, gloomily.

"Sorry, Joe."

"And the next time you catch me wasting time on a wild goose chase—" began Sheridane, but Snowy Shane's eye transfixed him with disdainful hostility.

"That'll be about all, Frank. You make mistakes yourself. Come on. You've got one more job."

He led the way to the elevators. Sydney Symmes was standing before the shaft which showed a red light.

"Just in time," he said.

Shane grinned.

"Figured we'd be," he said.

They rode to the street.

"Come up to my office a minute," invited Shane.

Symmes looked at his watch, frowned.

"Only take a few minutes," said Shane.

Symmes consented with a very apparent lack of enthusiasm. Once in the office, Snowy Shane began to talk.

"I got a theory about this case," he said. "Robb didn't cop that coin without some split. The guy he split with was a friend. And he didn't write that confession when Molly O'Keefe was in the office. Remember, she was a secretary, and he'd been dictating to her. If he'd been goin' to make a confession while she was there he'd have dictated it to her, an' made a long statement.

"That's the way those guys do when they kick through. They write a regular smear. I've seen 'em before. But Robb's confession was awfully brief, too brief. And it put too much stress on the fact that he was the only goat. I have an idea somebody made him write out that confession, put the screws on him somehow.

"Then, after the confession was written, the guy croaked him, telephoned to the messenger service and told them to come and get the envelope for delivery."

Symmes smiled, nodded.

"It's good to see someone who really runs trail on a case," he said. "That's the way we used to do it in the forestry service, just run down trail until we got to where we were headed. But how about the time of the murder? The wrist watch shows that it was right about the time Miss O'Keefe left doesn't it?"

"Yeah," said Snowy. "The guy that croaked him set the wrist watch back, and then smashed it. That was done after the murder, not before."

He took out a cigarette case from his pocket, extended it to Symmes. Symmes took a cigarette, struck a match, dropped it to the floor, still burning, picked it up and blew it out.

Snowy Shane beckoned to Sheridane.

"I want to see you a minute," he said. "We'll be right back, Symmes. Just wait here."

Sheridane followed Snowy Shane into the corridor.

"What's the idea?" he asked.

Shane grinned at him.

"That cigarette I gave him was awful. It'll just arouse the tobacco appetite, but he can't smoke it. He'll start in smoking one of his own, maybe three or four, if we wait long enough."

"What'll that do?" asked Sheridane.

"Make a smoke screen," said Shane, and grinned.

"You think he's guilty?"

Shane shrugged his shoulders.

"He'll leave if we keep him waiting," protested Sheridane.

"He can't. The door's locked. There's a night latch that's rigged just opposite from most of 'em. It springlocks a man in, instead of out."

"But I don't get the idea!"

"You said if you could prove some member of the advisory committee was in that room during the night you'd do the rest, didn't you?"

"Yes, and I meant it. That's all the break I want before a jury."

Shane grinned.

"Let's go down and buy some pipe tobacco. I been smokin' odds and ends until my throat tickles."

THEY went to the tobacco store, took plenty of time. Then Shane almost forcibly restrained Sheridane from returning to the office until another ten minutes had passed.

He opened the door of the private office. Sydney Symmes glowered at them. His face was dark with wrath.

"What the hell's the idea of locking me in here and disconnecting the telephone? I couldn't get out, and—"

Snowy Shane walked past him to the ash tray.

It was littered with cigarette stubs. The detective started fingering through the stubs until he found a charred match. It was straight, unbroken. He found another and another, but the third had been broken, then straightened.

"Well?" said Shane.

Symmes laughed nervously.

"To tell you the truth, you got me pretty well flustered up there in that room. I'm going to tell you chaps the real truth. I was there last night.

"I got there around eleven fifteen. Miss O'Keefe had been taking dictation, but she'd stepped into the ladies' room to put on a little make-up. Robb told me he was finished dictating. But he seemed all nervous, wrought up over something, so I didn't stay.

"When I heard of the murder I determined to say absolutely nothing about having been there, for fear some one might think I'd come to see him, found out Miss O'Keefe was there, and then gone out, waited for her to go, and then gone on in again."

"As a matter of fact I do break matches. All the rangers in that section of the country do—or used to when I rode it. You flustered me when you dug up that match. I knew I must be careful.

"But you got me shut up here, and I was nervous, and I got to smoking and breaking matches before I thought of it. I straightened 'em again as well as I could. I'd have burnt 'em up, but I knew wood ash is distinctive, and I had an idea you chaps were watching me through some sort of a peep-hole.

"What I'm telling you fellows is the absolute truth, and I want you to believe it."

He looked at them with steady, pleading eyes.

Snowy Shane nodded his head solemnly.

"You've got me sold," he said.

Symmes heaved a sigh.

"I thought you'd see how it was."

Shane nodded again, smiled.

"Glad you explained, Symmes. You can go. I'll have to report to the officer in charge, but there'll be nothing to it. They may ask you a question or two."

Symmes lunged for the door.

"Good-by Symmes."

"Good-by!"

The door closed. Sheridane glowered at the detective.

"Of all the damned fools! What if he was telling the truth? We could have browbeat him, called in the police, got the newspaper reporters, got Symmes admitting he had told a false story —Hell, with that much of a break I could give this jane a chance at a hung jury, or a cinch on copping a plea."

Shane smiled.

"Stick around," he said. "We could not browbeat that bozo on suspicion. You wait here. I'm going to run over and see Joe Karg."

AND he shot out of the door as a man who is going some place in very much of a hurry. He went at once to the death room, where Joe Karg sneered at him.

"Oh yes," sniffed the officer, sarcastically. "I'll get the credit. I'll get—"

He stopped. Shane was trying to light a cigarette, and his hand shook so that the match simply wouldn't connect with the end of the cigarette until he had steadied it with the other hand.

"Listen, Joe," said Snowy Shane, his voice stuttering with excited eagerness. "It's the b-b-biggest thing in years. I pulled a boner on it!"

"What the hell," asked Karg with interest, "are you talking about?"

"That match. That broken match."

"Hell, you planted all of those smoke clues."

"No, no. That is, Karg, you're

right about me planting 'em, but I had a hot tip on Symmes. When he swore he never broke a match I knew he was lying. I got hold of him after he left here and got him up to my office.

"Well, here's what happened. I got him started smoking, and he broke a match before he thought. Then I put it to him, locked the door, rattled the handcuffs, gave him everything I had, and he confessed!"

"What!" yelled the officer.

"Telling you the whole truth, Joe. Honest Injun!"

The officer was suspicious.

"You've lied to us before Snowy."

"But never unless the lie cleared up a case," protested Shane.

"Well, go on. Then what happened?"

"He thought it over, and retracted his confession and thought up another lie that'd get him out of it. See?"

Something of the detective's trembling excitement communicated itself to Joe Karg.

"What the hell!" he exclaimed. "Why didn't you send for me?"

"Didn't have time. Listen. Here's what happened. He knew Robb was at the office dictating. He hung around until the jane went home. Then he got in and had it out with Robb. He and Robb had been splitting the take. Robb was going to confess. Symmes tried to hold him in line, couldn't. The state examiners were on the trail of the shortage and Robb was panicy.

"So Symmes finally got Robb to promise that Robb would take all the blame in his confession. Robb wrote out that confession. Then Symmes croaked him.

"He set the watch back, smashed it, and dusted. He telephoned the messenger department to come and get the confession and left it pinned to the door. Then he went to bed.

"That was just the way I had it doped. The confession stressed too much about Robb being the only one who was responsible."

Joe Karg's eyes were glistening.

"Never mind what you doped out. What did Symmes himself say?"

"Just what I've told you."

"Then what?"

"Then I told him to write it out. He started, but got cagey, wanted to know if I could guarantee he could cop a plea. Then one thing led to another, and he got the idea he could swear that he'd gone into the building around eleven fifteen to see Robb, that he'd found Miss O'Keefe out powdering her nose, that he'd lit a cigarette, dropped the broken match, and then beat it before Miss O'Keefe came back.

"So that's what he's going to swear to now. He swears he never did confess, that he never was alone with me, that Sheridane was there all the time, and a lot of hooey like that."

Karg took a deep breath.

"If I'd only been there! Then what?"

Nothing. I let him go. I figured I'd let him think he'd checkmated me. Then you could go to work on him."

Joe Karg bit a cigar clean in two.

"Son of a gun! We'll fix that baby. We'll frame a stoolie to dress up like a janitor and swear he saw him hanging around the building. We wouldn't use the stoolie in court, but we sure can use him to make Symmes cave in again.

"Listen, Snowy, will you do something for me?"

"Anything, Joe."

"Well, just duck out of this case. Leave it all to me. You promised me the credit."

Shane was lugubrious.

"I promised Sheridane I'd get the broad free if she was innocent."

"Well, if I get Symmes that's all you want."

Karg looked at the detective anxiously. Snowy Shane thrust forward his hand.

"It's a go," he said.

SHERIDANE and Snowy Shane sat in a suburban hotel where they had registered under assumed names.

"I still don't get the idea," he said. "You told me you'd give me the low down at breakfast."

Snowy Shane glanced at his watch.

"Well, I started something."

"Fourth degree?"

"Yes. I told Karg that Symmes had confessed, and then I ducked you out of town so they wouldn't start quizzing you and have you throw me down."

The lawyer's jaw sagged.

"You told Joe Karg what?"

"That Symmes had confessed."

"Good heavens! Of all the bone-headed fools! Why, that's criminal defamation of character. What'd you do that for?"

Shane shrugged.

"You see, if Symmes had confessed to us, Karg wouldn't have had much credit. Then again, Symmes would need more third degree stuff than we could give him. But, by letting Karg think, on the q.t. that Symmes had confessed, Karg would start working up a case against Symmes.

"Otherwise they'd never have done anything, because they thought they had the case pinned on the broad."

Sheridane sighed.

"You kept me out of it?"

"Sure, swore you weren't even with me."

The attorney sighed again, this time with some measure of relief.

"You lied to Karg."

Shane nodded easily.

"Sure. A dick's gotta lie occasionally. It's part of the game. We all do. I just tell different kinds of lies from the other guys. You've gotta catch crooks the best way you can, not the way you'd like to catch them."

A uniformed bell boy walked into the dining room.

"You said to notify you if an 'Extra' came out, sir. Here it is."

Snowy Shane reached for the paper.

Across the top, in screaming head-lines, were the words—

SYMMES CONFESSES ROBB'S MURDER

Detective Joe Karg forces confession after clever deduction traps culprit in mass of lies. Police release Molly O'Keefe.

The attorney glanced with wide eyes, incredulously at the detective.

"Of all the nervy guys in the world, you're it!"

Snowy Shane made a deprecatory gesture.

"No. It's a simple system. All I had to do was to sell the police on the right idea and let 'em go to it. We could never have broken Symmes down. Joe Karg could, and did."

The lawyer reached for checkbook and fountain pen.

"You win, Snowy."

The detective grinned.

"Yeah," he said, "I got by, but only by the skin of my teeth. You hired me because my methods were unusual. Well, they were unusual enough this time. Just make that check payable to bearer. I ducked for cover after pulling that last fast one, and I'm going to stay under cover until Joe gets his promotion."

The Pullman Murder

by

T. T. Flynn

Bill lifted the clothes gingerly—and then almost dropped them again at what he saw underneath.

In the dead of night a mysterious girl had entered his Pullman compartment, left a blood-soaked bag of strange contents. Now the law hunted him as a killer. No evidence on earth except her's could prove his innocence, yet she had vanished. Why was she going to let him face the murder rap alone?

CHAPTER ONE

The Alligator Bag

SLEEP was torn from Bill Brady abruptly. He found himself sitting bolt upright in the berth, staring with wide startled eyes into the pitch blackness of the train compartment, heart pounding, body tense.

Outside, the long-drawn wail of the locomotive's whistle drifted eerily through the night. The rapid rush of its exhaust blended with the rhythmic clickety-click-click of steel wheels over rail joints. The berth rocked and swayed, cinders stormed against the windows. And when Bill Brady peered through the window he saw wan moonlight falling on the open countryside.

Everything was normal, natural, as it had been when he had gone to sleep. Bill Brady had no memory of a nightmare—and yet something had brought him out of deep sleep abruptly, forcefully.

He was wide awake now, still possessed of that uncomfortable feeling of apprehension. He fumbled for the reading light switch and the light came on.

His glance went around the cramped compartment, half expecting an intruder, for he remembered having left the door unlocked. But he was alone. Everything was peaceful, quiet, as it had been when he turned in to sleep. Everything the same, except—

Bill Brady went rigid, staring at an alligator hide gladstone bag lying on the floor just inside the door. That was not his! It hadn't been there when he went to sleep!

He swung his feet over the edge of the berth into his slippers, stepped to the bag and picked it up. It was heavy, as if well filled. An expensive bit of luggage too, far more costly than his own modest cowhide traveling bag. It had lain on its side, as if tossed hurriedly through the door.

That was what had awakened him, he decided—the door opening, the bag landing hard, the door slamming shut. Sounds different from the rhythmic noises of the train progress which had lulled him to sleep.

He stared down at the bag in his hand, amazed, curious, wary. Something was wrong. People didn't go about tossing bags into strange train compartments without good reasons.

Who had done it? And why?

He set the bag on the berth, reached for the package of cigarettes he had put on the window ledge just before going to sleep. Like many men Bill Brady smoked far too much for his own good; the last thing at night, the first in the morning, and in moments of excitement like this.

But his fingers never closed on the cigarette package. The rays of the reading light fell on them. Bill went rigid, slowly drew the hand back, staring with fascination at his fingers. The skin was smudged scarlet where they had touched the handle of the bag!

Scarlet! Damp! Blood.

Bill gulped as he bent over the bag and examined the handle carefully. His senses, dulled by sleep, shock, surprise, had failed to note what he now saw clearly. The handle was stained with blood. Fresh, undried blood, spattered over the top of the bag also, as if it had dripped from the hand or arm that had carried it.

Bill discovered that his fingers were trembling slightly as he secured the cigarettes and lighted one. His watch showed five minutes to two.

His gaze went with fascination to the bloody top of the bag, and then to the door. What grisly mystery lay behind this discovery in the early hours of the morning? Slowly he turned to the door and opened it, half expecting to find a corpse in the passage outside.

There was nothing.

The outer knob of the door showed no trace of blood. Nor did the floor as far as he could see. His compartment was one of the end ones in the car. He stepped into the passage and looked along its length. All the doors were peacefully closed.

The mystery thickened. Why his compartment? And why the blood on the handle, shouting plainly of some grim, terrible happening?

Bill Brady stepped back inside the compartment, closing the door. His curiosity was mounting rapidly. He eyed the gladstone with fascination, finally yielded to the overpowering curiosity and tried the catches.

To his surprise the bag was unlocked and opened easily. Dainty feminine underthings, folded neatly, confronted him. A woman was involved then! And a young woman, by the looks of those silk undies. Bill lifted them rather gingerly—and then almost dropped them again at what he saw underneath.

PACKETS of bank notes, wedged in solidly, tightly. Hundreds, thousands of bills. Worn, aged-looking bills, secured in bundles by thick rubber bands.

Bill lifted out one of the packages and riffled the ends. Twenties all the way through. Another package lay under the one he lifted out. And when he turned the leather shirt flap, the other half of the gladstone contained another covering of silk undies, with packages of twenty dollar bills packed solidly beneath also.

"Good grief!" Bill breathed, and to make certain he wasn't dreaming he pulled out one of the bank notes and fingered it carefully.

Many hands had done the same thing, by the appearance and feel of that crinkled, smudged rectangle of government paper. And all the others were the same; not a new bill in the lot.

Bill closed the bag and rang for the porter. The white-coated figure was at the door a few moments later, yawning behind a black hand as his eyes rolled inquiringly.

"Have you noticed any excitement in the car here during the last hour?" Bill demanded.

"No, suh," the porter denied, shaking his head. "Car been quiet, like de daid." He yawned again.

"You've been asleep."

"Well, uh, yas, suh. Kinda dozed off," the porter confessed. "Long runs like dis, we po'tahs got to snatch sleep when we kin git it. 'But," he added hastily, "nothin' movin' around de car. I wakes mighty easy, suh. Always do. Somethin' wrong, suh?"

Bill indicated the alligator hide gladstone.

"Seen this before?" he questioned.

The porter peered through the doorway at it, hesitated, scratched his ear.

"I don' jest 'zackly remembah, suh," he admitted. "Powerful lot o' bags come through." And then he brightened. "But yes, suh—I remembahs it now. Sho do."

"Where did you see it?"

"When you git on at Washington," the porter said triumphantly. "Sho do remember. I took it from you an' carried it heah to your compartment." He grinned, pleased with that bit of deduction which obviously should satisfy the white gentleman.

Bill saw there was nothing to be gained by questioning him. He had been asleep, knew nothing.

"A scream woke me up," Bill told

him, not quite truthfully. "You'd better knock on all the doors in the car here and make sure everything is all right. It sounded as if someone was being murdered."

"Goodness goshness!" the porter gasped, rolling the whites of his eyes. "Murdered? You is makin' fun with me. Ain't you?" he added hopefully.

"Rap on the doors," Bill ordered curtly. "Never mind about waking them up. And if you find a compartment that doesn't answer, call the conductor and open it."

The porter moved away, scratching his head uneasily and casting a dubious glance back. Standing in the doorway, Bill watched him go slowly along the aisle, knocking on the doors and asking if everything was all right inside. And presently he was back, beaming with relief.

"Everybody ansuh all right, suh," he stated. "Reckon you musta had a nightmare. Folks gets 'em sometimes on trains like dis. Everything strange, an' all."

Bill had slipped on his clothes by then, realizing there was no more sleep for him tonight. He accepted the porter's statement without argument.

"I must have eaten something that didn't agree with me," he nodded. "Sorry to have troubled you. Here!"

He tipped the man fifty cents, accepted his thanks, watched him go back to the smoking compartment.

Bill stood there, pondering his next step. What should he do? Look up the conductor, tell him the story, turn the bag over to him and forget about the matter? That was the sensible thing. It wasn't his bag, his money, or his business.

He reached for another cigarette, discovered the package was empty, and turned to his bag for a fresh package. As he lifted the cowhide traveling bag away from the wall, a folded slip of paper fell to the floor from behind it.

Bill picked it up. The paper hadn't been there when he set the bag against the wall before turning in.

Take it off the train. Will meet you in the lobby of The Bartlow.

It was a blank sheet of paper, the words scrawled hastily in fine angular writing, that might have been made by a woman. And on the edge were two bloody smears.

Bill saw then where the paper had come from. As the bag had been tossed through the door, the paper had been thrown with it, and it had zoomed lightly through the air, struck the wall, and dropped down where he had now found it.

The mystery thickened, began to flame with interest. Did the writer of the note know him, Bill wondered. Or had the note reached him by chance? Was there deliberate planning—or accident behind it?

He hesitated, and then slowly folded the note and slipped it in his pocket.

NINE o'clock. The air was cool. Bill stepped down from the Pullman in the jostling file of passengers. The porter bobbed his thanks, grinned recognition as Bill tipped him another fifty cents. The passengers were milling around the row of luggage on the platform; red caps were staggering away under their burdens.

Bill spotted his two bags—the tan cowhide and the alligator gladstone— near the end of the row. He beckoned to a red cap, pointed them out, followed the man in toward the station. And as he went his mind dwelt on the thing he was doing. What was he going to find in the lobby of The Bartlow? What explanation lay behind the queer happenings of the night before?

They passed through the exit gate and the crowd of waiting people beyond. Bill said to his red cap: "I want a taxi."

"Yas, suh."

A moment later Bill was conscious of someone falling into step beside him. A voice breathed confidentially into his ear.

"I got a car waitin' for you outside."

It was a thin, scrawny little man with a beaked nose, bright piercing eyes, a hat cocked rather rakishly over one eye.

"You have?" Bill said noncommittally.

"Yeah?"

"I don't know you."

He received a broad wink from one of the bright eyes.

"That's all right brother. I know you."

"Fine," said Bill pleasantly. "Who am I?"

The scrawny little man pointed to the mystery bag.

"That's yours, ain't it?"

"I'm handling it," Bill admitted. "What about it?"

The little man chuckled knowingly.

"Not many like it. An' the initials on the end are O. K.—L. X. D. You're the right party. I got the car waiting outside."

Once more Bill was conscious of being in the grip of preplanned events. But he was wary.

"Who sent you?" he demanded.

"Hell, you know."

"No," said Bill. "I don't."

"Well, you'll soon find out. The car's outside."

"Keep it," said Bill pleasantly. "I'm going in a taxi."

"Not takin' any chances, are you, brother?"

"No."

"You don't know where to go."

"Yes, I do."

"Where?"

"The Bartlow."

"That ain't the place."

"It is for me."

An ugly note entered the other's voice. "What are you tryin' to pull off?"

Bill dropped a hand on his shoulder, and his fingers dug in until the little man winced.

"Beat it," he advised. "I don't like your looks."

"Listen—you'll get——"

"Not half what you'll get," Bill replied, spinning him away with a sweep of his arm.

The little man cursed. People walking nearby looked curiously. The red cap chuckled.

"You sho handles 'em rough, cap'n."

Bill smiled a trifle grimly, looked around to see the little man tagging behind some yards distant. A taxi rushed up to the loading platform as they came through the door. The red cap started to put the bags in front.

"In back with me," Bill ordered.

He tipped the red cap, told the driver to go to The Bartlow, and they rolled swiftly through the crowded traffic of the city. Bill had lost sight of the little man as they left the station. He was out of sight—but not out of mind.

A woman had written that message, Bill was certain. It was a woman he was looking for. That scrawny, beak-nosed fellow with the beady eyes and the furtive confidential air was a false note. Bill had disliked him at first sight, distrusted him as soon as he began speaking. Now he was anxious to see what would happen at The Bartlow. One thing certain—there were going to be many explanations before he surrendered the bag.

The Bartlow was one of the newer hotels, fifteen stories high, smart, cosmopolitan, busy. A porter whisked his bags out of the taxi and trotted in to the desk, Bill following. A dapper clerk behind the desk looked at him inquiringly.

"Room and bath," said Bill.

A card and pen were shoved before him. He registered, tipped the porter, nodded to the bell boy who picked up the bags.

"Wait over there by the corner of the desk for a few minutes."

And while the boy did that, Bill looked around the lobby searchingly, expectantly. It was crowded, people sitting about, coming, and going. A bell boy walked past paging a Mr. Winterbottom. Other guests arrived and were smoothly moved along to their rooms.

Ten minutes of that—and nothing.

Bill finally grew impatient. No one seemed to be on hand to meet him. No one seemed to be paying attention to him, outside of casual, passing glances. He finally spoke to the impatient bell boy again.

"Let's go up."

His room was on the sixth floor. There was no floor clerk. The bell boy went through the usual formalities of putting up the shade, opening the window, glancing in the closet and bath.

BILL tipped him extra for the wait down in the lobby, the boy went out, the door closed and he was alone with the bag. It rested there on the luggage rack, new, impressive—and something of a white elephant now.

The spots of blood were still on the handle and top. He had taken a damp cloth and removed what he could, but the stains were still there. Through the rough leather sides he could visualize the small fortune in bills stowed inside. Bill found himself wanting to

get rid of the bag and its contents. The telephone rang sharply. He answered it eagerly.

"Mr. Fiske waiting to see you in the lobby," a girl's voice said pleasantly.

"Who is this?" Bill demanded.

"The switchboard talking."

"What does Mr. Fiske want?"

"He didn't say," the girl answered.

"I'll be down," Bill told her.

He stood frowning a moment after he hung up. Suspicion grew in his mind. That call was queer. He heard faint voices in the next room; a door closed. Bill opened the door and saw a bell boy passing. He beckoned the youth to him.

"Did you just room someone next door?" he asked.

"Yes, sir," the boy answered, looking at him curiously.

"Who?"

"Two gentlemen."

"Luggage?"

The boy hesitated, pressing his lips together unwillingly.

Bill slid a dollar bill out in his hand. The boy's fingers closed over it.

"They didn't have no luggage," he said.

"Thanks. That's all."

Bill stepped back in the room, looked at the connecting door. His suspicion was increasing. Every small occurence was assuming significance. He stepped quietly to the door, made sure the catch was shut on his side. And then smiling grimly he picked up the bag and went out. If the phone call was a decoy to get him out of his room, so the bag could be picked up while he was gone, someone was going to be surprised.

In the lobby no one came up to him. Bill waited a few minutes, and then stepped to the desk, identified himself and asked where the man was who had called him.

The clerk shrugged.

"He was here a few minutes ago, Mr. Brady. I don't know where he went."

"What did he look like?"

"A short man," said the clerk. "He wore his hat tilted a little to the side. Thin face—that's about all I remember."

No need to guess who Fiske was. A fictitious name, of course. And a plain ruse to draw him away from his room. Little enough luck they'd had at it. On sudden impulse Bill turned to the checkroom window and checked the bag. That would settle matters for a time. The sixth floor hall was empty. His door was locked as he had left it. Bill unlocked it and stepped into the room. And as he turned a man sprang out from behind the door and shoved a gun in his side.

"Hoist 'em!"

Bill's hands went up involuntarily.

The gunman kicked the door shut. He was a squat, powerful-looking man, with a bullet head, dressed neatly in dark brown, a soft hat pulled low over his face. Bill grinned at him, not doubting what he was after, and thinking of the bag safe in the checkroom.

"Make yourself at home," said Bill. He received a scowl in return.

"Where's that bag?"

"What bag?"

"Don't stall. You know what one I'm talkin' about."

"I'm a stranger in town," Bill grinned at him. "I don't know much of anything yet. Not near as much as I'm going to."

"Listen, mister," said the other in an ugly voice, "I ain't here to trade hot air with you. Unloosen that tongue an' tell me what you done with that bag."

"It's gone," said Bill airily. "Far, far away, where the little lilies grow,

and mugs like you draw punches every morning for breakfast. Like this."

The last as his left hand knocked the revolver aside and his right flashed in a beautiful cross that smashed into the lowering jaw beside him. Bill's six feet of solid meat and whipcord muscle carried the explosive qualities of dynamite. The blow lifted the other to his toes, slammed him against the wall. And before he could turn dizzily and bring the gun into action again, Bill was on him with all the quickness and fury of a hunting cheetah.

He caught the gun wrist, his other forearm snapped up under the wobbly chin of the intruder; and the bullet head banged hard against the wall. Despite the feeble resistance, Bill tore the gun from the other's short stubby fingers, whirled him around and jammed the gun in his back.

It had only taken a brace of seconds to do the whole thing.

"Now we'll sit down and talk everything over," Bill said through his teeth. "There's a lot I want to find out from you."

His back was to the bathroom door. He had no suspicion of further danger. He did not see or hear the bathroom door swing open and a tall figure eel out at his back.

The first Bill knew of it was a terrific blow that struck the back of his head. The room seemed to explode into blackness. His grip on the other loosened. He lurched, dropped, knew nothing of the kick that landed on the side of his head.

CHAPTER TWO

Mystery Girl

THE sounds crept through the haze which clouded Bill's senses. Crept through, thrust into his consciousness and he opened his eyes.

He saw the dappled ceiling, the walls rising to it, recognized the hotel room and the sounds that had aroused him. Sharp imperative knocking on the door.

"Wait a minute," Bill called, and was mildly surprised to find the words were little more than a mumble.

He got to his feet with an effort. The back of his head blazed with pain; he staggered dizzily.

The knocking ceased at the sound of his voice. Bill leaned against the wall for a moment and then stepped to the door.

A glance at his wrist watch showed eleven minutes after twelve. He had been lying there on the floor for hours, unconscious. The door was locked, the key on the floor inside. Bill picked it up, slipped it in the lock, turned it and opened the door.

The slender figure of a girl whisked in and closed it. He heard a gasp of surprise; saw her arm make a sudden movement to the pocket of her dark blue suit—and come out holding a small nickel plated automatic.

"Get back!" she ordered tensely.

Bill stepped back before the menace of that gun.

"Who the devil are you?" he demanded.

She was medium height, slender, with a strikingly pretty face under the pert little hat swaggering down over one side of her forehead. Her face was oval, her nose small and well formed, and her mouth just now was a tight red line. Pretty—and strong. A girl to know her own mind. And just now she seemed to. The small efficient automatic was as steady as the wall beside her.

"Watch that gun," Bill warned with irritation when she did not answer at once. "It might go off."

"It might," she agreed. "So stand right where you are."

She had regained her composure, spoke clearly, coolly.

"Is this your room?" she asked.

"It is," said Bill wearily. "And I suppose you came about that bag."

Her eyes narrowed, her lips pressed tighter together.

"Where is Louie?" she demanded.

"Who?"

"Louie."

Bill shrugged.

"Why ask me? If Louie is one of the two thugs who cracked me over the head this morning, I want to find him too."

"What do you mean?" she whipped out.

"What I said," Bill told her. "A couple of men entered this room while I was out. While I was dealing with one of them, the other clubbed me from behind. I've been unconscious since then. Didn't know a thing until you knocked on the door."

Her lip curled the merest trifle.

"Do you expect me to swallow that?"

"I don't give a damn whether you do or not," Bill snapped, feeling the back of his head tenderly.

There was a great bump there, sore, tender; and the hair was matted in one spot with dried blood.

Bill turned his head. "Have a look at what they left. I'd hardly go to that trouble—even for you." The last he uttered sarcastically.

He heard her draw nearer to look, then retreat against the door.

"You seem to be telling the truth, in part anyway," she admitted. "Now what's the rest of it? Where's Louie—and where's the bag?"

Bill faced her again and spoke deliberately. "Get this straight—you nor anyone else gets that until several things are cleared up. First, I want to know why it was tossed in my compartment on the train last night, with the note to bring it here. And I want to know what happened on the train to put that blood on the handle. And after we get that straightened out I want to know why this room was broken into after I had been decoyed downstairs, and why a gun pulled on me when I got back. And last—why is the bag circulating around full of twenty dollar bills? If you want it, start telling."

Her eyes had widened as he spoke, gone wider as he kept on. The tenseness of her face gave way to open astonishment.

"Y-your compartment?" she gasped.

"I said mine."

"That was—your compartment?"

"It was."

SHE stared at him soundlessly for a long moment, and then whispered, "I believe you're telling the truth."

"Certainly I am. Now try it yourself. And make it snappy. I haven't had any breakfast—my head hurts like the devil—and I feel like making it unpleasant for someone. In about two shakes I'm going to telephone the police."

"I wouldn't," she advised calmly.

"Why not? I've an idea they'll be interested."

"They are," the girl said with a wry smile. "What's your name?"

"Brady—William Brady. Bill if you feel like using it. And now yours, whether you feel like giving it or not."

"Joan Stevens," she said promptly. "My right name, by the way. I'm telling it to you because I think we should know each other."

"We should," Bill agreed. "Now the explanations."

"Did you buy a ticket for that compartment?" Joan Stevens countered.

"No. I paid the Pullman conductor. I barely made the train. No time to buy a ticket. I took a chance on getting something, and was lucky. The conductor said the space was sold, but the holder of the ticket hadn't shown up to claim it."

"That explains it," said Joan Stevens calmly. "Well, Mr. Brady, you got the bag and note intended for the man who held that space."

"Oh," said Bill. "Er—who was he?"

"It doesn't matter."

"How did you find me here then?"

"I asked at the desk if he was registered. When the clerk said he was not, I asked if a man carrying that alligator hide bag had registered. It is an unusual one. The bell boy remembered it. I got the room number and name, and thinking he had used a different name on purpose I had the room called several times. It didn't answer. Finally I came up to see for myself. And found you."

"I see," Bill said slowly. He considered. "I still want an explanation of the matter before I step out."

"You won't be through with it for some time," Joan Stevens told him calmly, and she held out a folded newspaper that had been thrust under her arm. "Read that."

It was a noon edition. Black headlines leaped at him.

MURDER IN TRAIN COMPARTMENT
Man's Body Discovered in Pullman Yards

A man's body was discovered this morning in a Pullman compartment of Train 19 after the cars had been switched to the Pullman yard. Death was caused by blows of a heavy blunt instrument and a stab wound in the heart.

The compartment showed signs of the desperate struggle the victim put up for his life. There were no marks of identification on the body and no luggage was found in the compartment. The porter of the car recalled the missing luggage as being an alligator hide gladstone bag. Robbery was apparently the motive. No sounds were heard by anyone else in the coach.

The porter of the adjoining coach told a strange story to police officials of one of his passengers summoning him in the middle of the night and stating that he heard a scream, which sounded like a woman being murdered. He asked the porter to awaken the occupants of the other compartments and make certain everything was all right. That was done, and nothing unusual was found.

The porter further stated that he was shown an alligator hide gladstone bag and asked if he could identify it. He could not and was dismissed. Police have a good description of the man and are spreading a dragnet through the city in search of him. Detective Lieutenant Battley stated that the porter had undoubtedly talked to the murderer, and had been shown the missing luggage. All signs indicate the man's actions were most unusual and probably an indication of a deranged mind.

The conductor stated that the man had leaped on the train as it was pulling out, and announced that he had no ticket and wanted to buy space from the conductor. A compartment was available and was sold to him. The description given the police was of a man over six feet tall, dressed in a gray suit, wearing a soft hat, face slightly lean and nose large. When last seen he was carrying an alligator hide gladstone bag and a tan traveling bag. The police expect to make an arrest in the case during the day.

Bill Brady read it through to the end, the grim certainty of impending trouble closing down about him as he did so.

"They're looking for that bag," Bill muttered, looking up.

Joan Stevens had watched him intently as he read. Her face was enigmatic; her thoughts successfully hidden. And when she replied to Bill's remark her voice was cool and steady.

"Looking for the bag—and you, Mr. Brady. They are going to charge you with—murder."

BILL had never heard the word in that light before. Murder — charged to him! His face was white and set as he rapped out an answer.

"But I didn't kill the fellow! I don't know who he is, haven't any idea what it's all about!"

"Do you think the police will believe that?"

And Bill shook his head slowly.

"I'm afraid they won't," he confessed.

Sudden anger swept him. He said heatedly: "But they'll go a long way toward it if they hear your story! You can clear this matter up! And by heavens you're going to! I—I'll—"

Bill took a step toward her as he spoke, and stopped in his tracks as the small automatic in her hand leveled at him with a threatening little movement.

"Don't lose your head," the girl advised coolly. "I can't help you as much as you think I can. And first, we have to get that bag out of the way. Where is it?"

"In the checkroom," Bill said after a moment. "I had an idea an attempt was being made to get it when I was called down to the lobby. I took it with me and checked it before I came back up."

"Good." There was a note of relief in her voice. "We'll go down and get it. And then you've got to get out of the hotel as quickly as you can. That alligator hide bag will be traced here without doubt. And if they catch you—" She hesitated.

"Yes?" Bill prompted grimly.

"Many a man has gone to the electric chair on less evidence. You have no witnesses as to what you were doing that night. That scene with the porter will damn you before any jury."

And Bill had to admit that she was right. The prospect was ghastly, soul-shaking. The pictures flashed before him—arrest, trial, conviction; the long wait in the death cell, and the last solemn walk to the execution chamber.

A life wiped out, a future left blank, because of something that was no doing of his. He thought of the steamer waiting at the dock, which he was to board in two days for Peru and the copper mines up in the Andes that were to have been his home for three years, before he stepped to bigger things.

"God, what a mess!" Bill breathed.

Joan Stevens put her gun away, as if realizing that she had no further need of it now.

"You see, there's only one thing to do," she said calmly. "Take your bag off the rack there, stop at the checkroom for the other, get it out of sight as quickly as possible and hide. I bought the paper on the street a few minutes ago. The edition was just on the streets. Most people probably haven't read it yet. I think you can get away all right. Where is your check?"

Bill reached in his shirt pocket where he had thrust the luggage check. It was still there.

"You're lucky," Joan Stevens remarked. "If they had found that, the gladstone wouldn't be in the checkroom now. Hurry."

Bill lifted his traveling bag off the luggage rack, picked his hat from the bed. Joan Stevens opened the door cautiously, looked in the hall and then stepped out.

"Lock the door," she suggested. "It may delay things."

Bill did that, and followed her down the hall. Now that the first shock of surprise was over, his suspicions were increasing. The blood-smudged note, in feminine handwriting, and every action of hers so far pointed to her as the wanted killer. Her actions mystified him. Had she shown him the news-paper to frighten him into surrendering the gladstone bag and fleeing, certain that he would not go to the police? Was she planning to vanish, leaving him to face a charge of murder?

Everything was mixed up. One fact only was clear. He had to disappear before the police net closed about him. Otherwise—ruin! Joan Stevens spoke as they came to the elevator bank.

"We'd better walk down."

And walk they did, down into the noise and bustle of the crowded lobby. Bill stepped to the cashier's window, paid his bill, left the room key.

And as he was turning away from the window, Joan Stevens hurried close and whispered tensely under her breath.

"Two detectives are at the desk questioning the clerk! They've either traced you here, or they're taking this hotel in their general search! And I think there's another one standing at the door!"

The cashier's office was around the corner from the main desk. Still farther back was the checkroom, across from the elevators.

Bill suddenly found himself thinking clearly, coolly.

"Bring my bag," he told her.

He went to the checkroom window, tossed the square of numbered pasteboard before the black-shirted attendant. The young man glanced at it, yawned slightly, moved back among his racks.

Bill silently cursed his slowness. But when the alligator bag was thumped down before him, he lifted it casually and turned away leisurely. The dining room entrance was nearby. Bill walked there, waving a bell hop back. And when a waiter sprang to meet them inside the dining room, Bill waved him away also, so authoritatively that the fellow did not question their advance across the dining room.

A waiter hurried through a pair of swinging doors at the back. Bill and Joan Stevens followed him a moment later, into the hot aromatic atmosphere of the kitchens.

A white-hatted chef stared at them inquiringly.

"Where's the back door?" Bill queried.

The chef pointed. They hurried toward it, ignoring the curious stares of the kitchen help. The door let them into the alley, where a pimply-faced dishwasher in a dirty apron and no shirt was squatting on a box, smoking a cigarette and reading a newspaper.

Bill saw him look up, saw his eyes drop to the alligator hide bag in a stare of interest.

"This way," Joan Stevens urged, turning to the right.

And as Bill went he heard the hasty crumpling of the newspaper pages. A glance over his shoulder showed the other reading avidly, and then looking after them.

Bill's pulse began to tick faster. They had been recognized.

That fact blotted out everything else. He did not notice a short, slouching figure step out of the doorway and sidle after them.

CHAPTER THREE

Wanted: For Murder

BILL looked back as they turned out of the alley. The dishwasher was gone.

"That fellow at the door was reading a noon edition—and he recognized the bag!" Bill snapped. "He's gone in to spread the alarm."

Joan Stevens increased her pace, dodging through the people on the sidewalk.

"We've got a chance," she threw at him.

And just short of the corner she stopped beside a small black coupe parked at the curb. A key flashed in her fingers, unlocked the door.

"Get in!" she ordered. "Put that bag down out of sight!"

She slipped behind the wheel, started the motor, and was pulling out from the curb almost before Bill got himself and the bags stowed away in the cramped space. They slipped into the traffic stream and left the region of the hotel.

"Your car?" asked Bill.

"Borrowed it," she answered.

Silence fell between them. Joan Stevens drove expertly, swiftly. They left the crowded business district behind, bowled swiftly along a broad boulevard toward the outlying sections of the city.

"Where are you going?" Bill demanded.

"I want to get you out of sight," she said briefly.

"Why bother about me?"

"You were drawn into this through no fault of your own. I don't want to see you arrested and charged with murder.

"That all?"

"That's all."

"Look here!" Bill burst out. "I still have some explanations coming. What's back of all this?"

A quick sidewise glance at him, and then her eyes went back ahead.

"It hasn't anything to do with you," she answered coolly.

And that was all Bill could get out of her. It left him resentful, suspicious. He would have made her stop the car, let him out, only that seemed no better than the course they were now pursuing. The police were combing the city for him, they had a good description of him now. He was a stranger in the city. The railroad stations, the hotels, boarding houses were probably all being watched, not to speak of the outgoing ships. Chances were he'd not get far before he was picked up. At least while he stayed with this girl he was out of the public eye.

Hunted! For the first time in his life Bill knew the feeling of being wanted. Every man's hand against him. No place to turn. Misery and ruin waiting if he were caught. It took an effort to shake off the feeling of sick despair, and wait coolly for what lay ahead.

The coupe turned off the boulevard, zigzagged through several streets, turned at last onto two strips of cement driveway running back beside a small, modern cottage into a clapboard garage.

Joan Stevens stopped the car at the back corner of the house, beside steps leading into a tiny screened back porch. A hedge, a vacant lot and the next house lay on their right. The girl looked carefully about, then got out.

"Pass me the bags," she ordered.

Bill did so. She put them in the porch out of sight. "Come in," she said.

Bill entered curiously, wondering about the cottage. Modest, respectable, it was a strange setting for the lurid part they were playing. And inside even more so. Kitchen, dining room, bedrooms, living room were like thousands of others in the suburbs.

Joan Stevens led him into the living room, motioned him to put the two bags on the floor. She stepped out of the room, was back in a moment with a black suitcase.

She opened it on the floor, and opened the alligator hide bag also. Tossing the silken garments aside, she began swiftly to transfer the bundles of money into the black suitcase.

"What are you going to do?" Bill queried.

"Get rid of this thing," she said, indicating the alligator hide bag.

That done, she closed the black suitcase and shut the other bag with a snap.

A telephone bell rang in one corner of the room. Joan Stevens answered it hastily. An exclamation of relief burst from her.

"Louie! Heavens! I'm glad to hear you! What happened?"

She listened intently, then spoke rapidly.

"The news story is correct, in part. It was a ghastly trip. Everything wrong. Come out here as soon as you can."

SHE hung up, stood for a moment in frowning thought, then said hurriedly.

"I'm going out for a few minutes. There will be a visitor here shortly. Let him in. Talk to him if you feel like it. I'll put this bag in the bedroom closet. He'll probably want to look at the contents."

She carried the suitcase into the bedroom, returned and picked up the alligator hide bag.

"Take a good look at it," she said with a smile. "This is the last time you'll ever see it."

And Bill met her flash of gaiety with a smile himself. When she looked like that it was hard to believe anything wrong about her.

"Too soon won't be soon enough," he stated. "I hope I never see the blasted thing again."

She went out with it. Bill heard the coupe back along the drive, through the front window saw it turn into the street and roll away. He sat down on a sofa against the wall, alone in the house, wondering what the end of all this was going to be.

Ten minutes passed, perhaps more. Bill was prowling restlessly about the room, smoking a cigarette when he heard steps go around to the back of the house and enter the porch. Then a knock on the back door.

Bill went into the kitchen, looked through the door glass. A stoop-shouldered man in his shirt sleeves, head bare, was waiting outside. Bill opened the door.

"What do you want?" he inquired.

"Gas meter," said the stranger casually.

"Do you know where it is?"

"In the kitchen."

"Come in," said Bill, stepping back.

The stranger walked in, his gaze going keenly about the kitchen. Bill noted then that his shoes were well-shined, his trousers of fine quality, pressed to a knife edge; and he wore a silk shirt and a necktie that might have been custom made. Fine feathers for a meter reader. And now that he thought about it, the fellow had no record book with him.

The stranger had stepped over near the stove. Bill followed him.

"Meter reader, ah?" he remarked. "I'll have a look at your credentials. Where's your book?"

The other had entered with one hand in his pocket. It snaked out now—with a flat, blue-black automatic.

"Here!" he said.

No humility in that voice now. Sharp, grating, sneering. Bill froze at sight of the gun.

"Well!" he said after a moment. "What's the idea?"

And into his mind flashed the thought that the police had caught up with him in some way. Had Joan Stevens betrayed him?

"Stick 'em up!"

Bill's hands raised slowly.

"Turn around!"

He obeyed. The other stepped to him, frisked him quickly, finding no weapon.

"You alone in here?"

Bill shrugged.

"What does it look like?"

"Get into the front of this dump."

In the living room the other stepped back, his eyes darting watchfully about.

"Where's the suitcase?"

"What suitcase?" Bill parried as he stood there, hands in air.

"Don't stall, damn you!"

Bill shrugged again.

"I don't see any suitcase around here."

Footsteps tramped on the front porch. For a moment Bill had the ghost of a hope that the man Joan Stevens had spoken to over the telephone had arrived and might help.

THE door was opened without ceremony. Two men burst in. And at sight of them Bill lost whatever hope had come to him. For one of the men was the thin scrawny little man with the beaked nose and bright piercing eyes whom he had warned away at the railroad station.

And his companion was no more reassuring—a dark-visaged, plump-faced young man with blue-black close-shaven jowls, a sensuous, loose-lipped mouth and a sleek air of cold ferocity. The scrawny one carried a coat over his arm that matched the trousers of the pseudo meter reader. He grinned unpleasantly at sight of Bill standing there with hands in the air.

"How do you like it, you big tramp?" he asked. "Crack him one for the shove he give me in the station, Sam."

"Crack him, yourself," Sam grunted, and spoke to the other. "He won't talk, 'Duke.' I've frisked him. He ain't got a heat, an' there ain't no one else in the house."

Duke drew out a silver cigarette case, put a straw-tipped cigarette between his lips and held a lighter to it leisurely.

"He'll talk," he said.

And Bill's nerves tightened at the cold venom in the words. Duke inhaled, trickled smoke through his nostrils and caressed his blue-black jaw thoughtfully while he surveyed Bill.

"Your heat, 'Shrimp'," he spoke suddenly.

The thin scrawny Shrimp reached under his coat and flashed a .38 automatic.

"Want me to give it to him?" he questioned eagerly.

And again Bill felt the cold drain on his nerves; for if there was ever eagerness for sheer murder in a voice he had just heard it then. That irritated shove in the railroad station had made him an enemy to the death. Thin, scrawny, this Shrimp might be, but he was as deadly as an adder. There was even something snakelike in the cold glitter of his beady eyes.

"No, damn your bloody heart!" Duke refused. "Get careless with that rod before I tell you to and I'll slit your throat myself. Get me?"

Duke spoke without passion, and the threat in his voice was the worse for it.

"Sure, I gotcha, Duke," the little gunman agreed hastily, sobering.

Duke stepped forward leisurely, removing the cigarette from his mouth. His right fist flashed up without warning, smashed Bill in the middle of the face.

"Who said you wouldn't talk?" Duke asked casually, trickling smoke through his nostrils again. They were flattish, almost negroid. He looked out from half-closed eyes.

Bill felt a warm stream creep over his upper lip. He put his hand there. It came away stained with red. His nose felt as if it had been broken. Involuntarily he reached for the handkerchief in his hip pocket. Duke kicked him on the shin.

"Keep your hands out in front of you," he warned coldly.

Bill had never known the rage that swept him like a red tide as he faced the three of them. Little droplets of warm blood fell unnoticed down the front of his shirt. The pain of that blow and the agony in his leg vanished before it. His fists balled, his arms tightened as he swayed into a fighting crouch.

The calm cruelty on the soft fleshy face before him was disturbed for an instant. Duke stepped back.

"If he moves, shoot him in the guts!" he cried.

With a mighty effort Bill conquered the urge to tear down and destroy that natty figure. The idea was insane, hopeless. They had him. He did not doubt they would slaughter him the first threatening move he made. He relaxed. "What do you want?" he asked thickly.

The scrawny Shrimp chortled with satisfaction.

"Slam him again, Duke! It's good for him!"

"Shut up," said Duke.

And to Bill, "Want some more of that, you rat?"

"I can do without it," said Bill.

His eyes were devouring that soft dark face before him. He never wanted to forget it. Some day, some place, there would be a settlement for those blows. He had been angry before, but never with the blaze of hate that was licking through his body now. It was like a consuming flame.

"You'll get plenty more if you don't yap quick," Duke warned him. "We ain't got all day to hang around.

Where's that alligator bag you brought here?"

"Gone," Bill told him truthfully.

"Don't lie, damn you!"

"I'm not."

"Sure he is," the Shrimp spat. "Didn't I see him come out of The Bartlow with that dame, carryin' it? They got in the car with it an' come here."

"I wonder if that dame took it away with her," Duke said with a scowl.

"Not if she had any sense an' read the papers," Sam grunted. He had rolled down his sleeves, taken his coat, slipped it on. "The whole town'll be lookin' for it. Watch 'im while Shrimp an' I frisk the house, Duke."

Duke took the automatic from Shrimp's hand. "Go ahead," he said.

The search was quick and thorough, beginning with Bill's traveling bag. Finding nothing but clothes inside they went into the other rooms. And not three minutes passed before an exclamation of satisfaction sounded in the bedroom. Shrimp appeared with the black suitcase.

"I found this hid in the closet," he said. "Lamp it."

Setting it on the floor he opened it, revealing the packed bundles of bills inside. Duke looked, nodded with satisfaction.

"O. K.," he said. "Let's go. Wipe that blood off your face, fella. And when you go out, don't bat an eye at anyone. If you do—it's curtains."

Bill pulled out his handkerchief, swabbed the blood off his face.

"You taking me with you?" he questioned uncertainly.

"You got ears, ain't you?" Shrimp rasped unpleasantly.

Bill ignored him, speaking to Duke, who seemed to be the leader.

"You've got what you came for. What do you want now?"

The ghost of a smile met that. A smile without humor. A loose-lipped grimace of cruelty.

"It's a surprise," Duke promised. "One you won't get over for a long time."

Shrimp burst out laughing, shrill, rasping promise of what was to come.

CHAPTER FOUR

Casino

BILL walked down the front steps with a man on each side of him and the knowledge that pocketed guns covered him.

A long black sedan stood at the curb. Shrimp got in first, then Bill, and the sleek Duke. Sam took the wheel, shoving the suitcase on the floor beside him. They rolled away.

Nothing was said. Duke stared ahead with an unreadable face. Shrimp hunched in the corner, hand in pocket, beady eyes watching every move Bill made.

With a grim flash of humor Bill thought that even the police would be welcome now. He had a chance with them, more than he could say of these men.

He wondered what lay in store for him. Wondered too what Joan Stevens would think and do when she got back and found him and the black suitcase gone. Or had she meant to come back? Nothing had been said about her. No attempt made to wait for her.

The sedan cut across town, struck a through street, bowled swiftly along it into the country. Beyond the city limits it rushed forward with increasing speed. Now and then off to the left Bill caught sight of the blue expanse of the bay, saw that they were roughly paralleling the shore, drawing closer to it.

Half an hour of that, and the bay was only a few hundred yards away. Cottages scattered along the shore. They passed through one little village. And several miles beyond slowed sharply and stopped, horn tooting imperatively.

Between the road and the bay was a high board fence enclosing an area of several acres. In answer to the horn a gate in the fence opened. They swung across the road and rolled through. A shaggy-haired hunchback with a large grotesque head waved as they entered. Bill looked behind, saw the hunchback closing the gate again, limping as he walked.

Inside the fence were trees, a well-kept lawn, and a large rumbling two-story wooden house that seemed to sprawl all over the place in a confusion of wings, wide porches, gables and windows—An unpainted monstrosity of architecture with a wide cinder parking space at one side.

The automobile stopped on the cinders with a jerk. Bill looked beyond to the beach. The wooden fence ran down to the water. There was a sizable boathouse and a jetty running out from shore. Beside the jetty a sleek power launch rocked slowly on the slight swell. Farther out across the bay a distant trail of smoke drifted up from an outward bound tramp steamer. Duke got out.

"Come in," he said briefly.

Sam eeled from behind the wheel and joined him. They stood watchfully while Bill stepped to the ground, followed by the beady-eyed Shrimp.

A sandy-haired man in a waiter's coat and white apron appeared at the top of the wide wooden steps which led up to the huge veranda before them.

"Watcha got there?" he called.

"A tourist," Shrimp answered, showing his teeth. "He's takin' in the sights."

Duke said nothing.

Sam dragged the black suitcase out of the front seat and they walked up on the veranda. Tables and chairs were scattered over it. Part was given over to a smooth dance space. Wide double doors admitted them inside, into a long wide room, thickly carpeted and filled with gambling paraphernalia. Bill recognized roulette and crap tables, black-jack and poker.

A large bar ran along one end of the room. But there were no customers. The place was dead, deserted. White dust coverings over some of the tables helped the effect. A porter was sweeping at one end of the room. He stared curiously as they walked across it, through a doorway at the back, into a hall.

A stairway on the right took them up to a wide squarish hall on the second floor. It was lighted by a skylight in the ceiling. Doors opened off it. Before one of them a man lounged in a chair tilted back against the wall, picking his teeth. He tilted the chair forward with a thump and stood up, holding the toothpick in a corner of his mouth. A hatchet face, seamed and hard surveyed them unsmilingly.

"Hello, 'Chip'," Duke said to him. "Paddy McGovern in?"

Chip jerked his head silently at the door. The toothpick rolled to the other side of his mouth. His glance went over Bill.

"What you got there?" he asked.

"Plenty," said Duke briefly, opening the door and entering the room beyond. Bill and the other two followed him.

As they went in Bill saw Chip press a button beside the door.

THEY came into a small reception room, having a deep-piled rug on the floor and comfortable leather-covered chairs set against the wall. Duke stepped across to an inner door and turned the knob. The door did not open. He rapped. There was a slight click. The door swung in.

They entered a large, low-ceilinged room, windowless, lighted by indirect fixtures on the ceiling. It was sparsely furnished by several chairs, a long table against the wall, a comfortable couch, two filing cabinets, a bookcase and several small etchings on the walls. At one end of the room was a tremendous bat-topped mahogany desk.

Little curls of smoke drifted in the air, and from an ash tray on the desk a thick cigar spiraled more smoke to the ceiling.

As they entered a husky voice was saying heavily: "Tell him that's all the break he'll get. If he don't like the terms, he can lam out of town. And this is the last warning he gets."

A telephone slammed down on its cradle and the man who had been speaking stood up. Bill had the impression of a mountain of flesh ballooning out of the chair. Great broad shoulders and a thick gross neck; a barrel chest and a still greater middle around which was a belt that almost could have served for a trunk strap—a mighty figure made still vaster and grosser by the addition of fat.

"Hello, Paddy," Duke said.

Paddy McGovern stepped around the end of the desk with a nimbleness that was surprising in such a mountain of flesh. Bill stared at him in fascination. His face was as big in proportion as the rest of his body. A huge, round expanse of dead white flesh. Pale eyebrows tufted over small eyes sunk in folds of fat. A button nose centered between sagging corpse-like cheeks. From a slobbery mouth the husky voice rumbled with surprising volume.

"So you got him," said Paddy McGovern.

"Yeah. And the dough too. It was switched to this black suitcase. He tried to bluff it out. Said it wasn't around. We found it hidden in the house—a little dump out on the north side where he lammed."

"Well, well, well," Paddy McGovern husked. "Lammed, did he? Who punched him in the mug?"

"Who d'you think?"

Paddy McGovern turned to the desk and picked up the cigar.

"Do it again," he said, and tucked the cigar between his lips and watched with interest.

Duke needed no second invitation. His fist ripped at Bill's face. Bill slid back a step, jerked his head to one side; and as the fist grazed the front of his battered face he drove a blow in Duke's natty middle that sank up to the wrist. Duke reeled back, gasping, holding his middle. Pained surprise and sudden fury distorted his face.

Crouching, Bill waited. "The next man who hits me better have a gun!" he threw at them.

"Slip me that rod!" Duke gasped, turning to the Shrimp. And with the automatic he whirled back, snarling. "I won't hit you. I'll cut you down like a rat! Watch out, Paddy! He's mine!"

Paddy McGovern had moved in between them with amazing catlike quickness.

"Lay off!" he commanded harshly. "I'm telling what to do around here!"

And as Duke drew back sullenly, Paddy McGovern turned to Bill. "So that's the way you feel, eh?" he husked.

Bill said nothing. Paddy McGovern's little eyes surveyed him through the folds of fat.

"Smart dick, aren't you?" he asked.

"Eh?" said Bill. "Dick?"

"You heard me."

"I don't know what you mean."

"You will," Paddy McGovern said. "What I want to know now is, what's your game?"

"My game?" said Bill harshly. "My game? Why, damn you, I haven't got any game. What's yours? What's the idea of bringing me here?"

For the moment Bill forgot his helplessness, forgot the waiting guns as his angry words tumbled out. But only for a moment. Paddy McGovern spat a bit of tobacco from the end of his cigar.

"Shut up that loud talkin'," he warned, "or I'll have your mouth bashed in. You ain't in no headquarters squad room now."

Bill sobered.

"You must think I'm a detective," he said.

"You are," said Paddy McGovern, as if that fact was settled beyond doubt.

"I am not," Bill said flatly.

It made no impression.

"What's your game?" Paddy McGovern asked again.

"I haven't got any."

"How much do you know?"

"Nothing," said Bill, scowling.

"Last chance," said Paddy McGovern, narrowing his eyes. "Don't try to make a monkey out of me."

"I don't know what you want to hear," Bill retorted. "Whatever it is, I can't tell you. That blasted alligator hide bag was thrown in my train compartment last night with a note asking me to take it to The Bartlow. I did. Since then things have been happening so fast I don't know what it's all about."

Even as he said it he realized the story sounded weak, evasive.

"Just an innocent hick running around with your eyes closed, eh?" Paddy McGovern said without emotion. "That all you got to say?"

Bill shrugged. There was nothing else he could say.

"Give him the works, boys," Paddy McGovern husked.

They closed in on Bill from four sides—The three who had brought him here and the guard at the outer door who had entered also. Bill drove a blow to the flat face of Sam. Sam rocked back, cursing, whipping back with the barrel of his automatic. The Shrimp catapulted against him, striking savagely. Bill fought him off.

Without warning his legs were kicked from under him. He fell heavily. And they piled on him.

Kicks, blows from fists and gun barrels came from every direction. He struck back, tried to roll over and get up. They drove him down again. The wind was knocked from him. His senses began to swim. He seized a leg, tried to draw himself up.

A kick in the back of his neck drove everything black. If the brutal manhandling kept up after that Bill didn't know it. Merciful unconsciousness had claimed him.

IT WAS dark when Bill's eyes opened. Pitch dark. And wild exotic strains of music were throbbing in his ears. He lay still for a moment, listening to the music, trying to gather memory.

It came back in fragments, and then with a rush. He groaned. Every inch of his body was sore. When he moved little knives seemed to strike at his muscles. His head was a throbbing lump of pain. And he was chilled, cold, damp.

He moved his hand. It splashed in

water. That roused him completely. He struggled up. The pitch blackness was still there. Feeling about, he found that he was sitting in water an inch or so deep, over a concrete floor. Bill staggered to his feet, wondering dizzily where he was.

The music was still there. Not imagination. Muted, exotic, blood stirring. It seemed to come from overhead. Dance music, played by an orchestra. And he could hear the shuffling of feet, the faint sounds of voices and laughter.

Stretching out his hands, Bill groped through the darkness, soon found that he was in a small empty cement-floored room about ten by ten feet. He could not feel the ceiling overhead. The uneven floor was partly covered by a film of water. The walls were damp stone.

He found a door of heavy planking, with no knob inside. It felt as solid as the stone walls when he lunged against it.

His pockets had been emptied. Money, watch, matches and cigarettes were gone. Arms and legs worked all right; no bones seemed broken. Bill squatted on his heels against the door and relaxed.

The music stopped for a few moments, then started again. The gay sounds drifted down mockingly. Up there life and joy, while he crouched below like a rat in a trap. The furious anger was gone. Chill wariness gripped Bill now. They thought him a detective. They had let him see where they were bringing him. They'd never let him get away after that.

A quarter of an hour, more or less, passed. Bill was wishing mightily for a cigarette when he heard steps on the other side of the door. He got to his feet hastily, stepped to one side. And none too soon. A bolt rasped. The door opened. The bright beam of a flashlight preceded a figure through the door.

Bill lunged like an uncoiling steel spring. His arm went around a neck. The light wavered crazily, a gasp of astonishment burst out as Bill hurled everything he had into one mighty effort.

The idea had sprouted full blown on the instant. It worked. The stranger reeled off balance. His body came around hard. And Bill drove the head against the sharp corner of the door frame with crushing force. The flashlight dropped. The dead weight of the body sagged in his arms.

Bill lowered it to the floor, picked up the flash which was still burning. Its light showed a face he was familiar with—the man who had surprised him in his hotel room.

Bill grunted with satisfaction. He had been wondering whether there was any connection between that visit and what had happened afterwards. He listened in the open doorway. No sounds outside. He risked the light, saw a narrow passage that was more like a tunnel. Damp, dark, deserted.

Dropping to a knee he searched the limp form. The heart was beating slowly. The light showed a deep gash in the back of the head, but the skull seemed all right. The fellow would probably live. Bill hurriedly went through his clothes. He found a billfold with money, cigarettes, matches and a watch.

He lighted a cigarette, drew deep on it with appreciation, then looked at the watch. Twenty minutes to ten. It was somewhat of a shock to realize that he had been unconscious most of the day and evening. There was no gun on the body. No matter. He'd do what he could without it. Bill dragged the body away from the door, keeping the cigarettes and the money. No telling how badly he might need the money. They had taken his. He stepped out in the passage, closed the door, found a stout bolt on the outside and slipped it.

CHAPTER FIVE

Rat's Trick

TO THE RIGHT the passage ended in a blank end wall. Fifteen yards or so of it went to the left. Several doors opened off it. Stout locks were on the first two. The third had only a bolt like the one on his door. Curious, Bill pushed it back.

His light flashed into a space half the size of the one he had left. Half the size, because the other half of the room was stacked almost to the ceiling with burlap-wrapped cases of liquor.

He started to close the door, then decided that a stiff drink would help a lot in what lay ahead. He stepped inside. Something moved against the right wall. Bill shot the light there— and caught his breath with astonishment. Eyes squinting against the light, Joan Stevens stood proudly, warily.

"Wh-what do you want?" she demanded with a trace of a catch in her voice.

"What are you doing here?" Bill burst out, and reversed the light so that it shone over his face.

"Brady! *B-Bill Brady!*" Joan Stevens uttered in a little cry of relief. "Where did you come from?" And she left the wall and came to his side in a little rush. "What has happened to your face?" she demanded. "It looks like—like—"

"Like hell, I guess," Bill finished for her frankly. "And it feels the same way. They've been working on it."

"Oh!"

There was understanding and pity in her exclamation. He felt her hand on his arm lightly.

"I'm sorry I brought you to all this," Joan Stevens told him. "Believe me, I had no idea from first to last that it would end this way for you. When I brought you to my sister's house I was merely trying to take you to a safe place. What happened? They told me you had talked. And I laughed at them and told them you didn't know anything to tell them."

Bill patted her hand. It felt small and cold. Like a frightened child's. The authority and dash seemed to have left her for the time being, driven away by defeat and imprisonment. Rough handling, too. He saw a purplish bruise on the side of her face. Somehow it affected him more than all the rough handling he had received.

"They must have followed us to the house," he said. "You hadn't been gone long before they were there. Tricked me. They found the black suitcase and brought it and me here. Tried to make me talk. When I couldn't tell 'em anything they ganged me. Guess I've been out all day. Just came to a little while ago. Found myself locked in a room like this."

"How did you get out?"

"Chap came down to pay me a visit. I met him at the door," Bill chuckled slightly at the remembrance. "He'll be there for quite a while," he added.

"I heard his steps go past," Joan said thoughtfully. "What shall we do now? I have an idea they don't mean to let us get away."

"If they did they'd be fools, and I don't think they are," Bill said. "That means we can't slip up now. They brought us to a roadhouse of some kind."

"Paddy McGovern's place," said Joan. "It's notorious. Everything goes as long as you have the money. He buys protection with big sums. But I think he's gone too far this time."

"I hope so," Bill said, taking down one of the burlap-wrapped packages. He opened the end, pulled out a bottle, snapped off the top against the cement floor, threw back his head and took a stiff drink.

"Gosh, that's rotten stuff," he choked. "But it's got a kick. I feel better. Care for some? Might buck you up."

"No, thanks," Joan refused. "I'm bucked up enough just having you here. I feel everything is going to be all right now. If I can just get to a telephone for two minutes."

"We'll try it," said Bill. "We're down under Paddy McGovern's place. Seepage from the beach was in the room where I was. All we've got to do is get upstairs among the people there. Once we get in the crowd we'll raise so much trouble they'll be glad to get rid of us."

Bill said that, but he didn't think it. He knew well enough that they'd never get away if it could be prevented. They were too dangerous to Paddy McGovern and his men.

They had been speaking in low tones since they met. Both suddenly stiffened, fell silent as a voice came ringing down the passage.

"What the hell's the matter, Jerry? Paddy wants them two brought up right away. Need some help?"

Bill stepped to the doorway, cupped his hands to his mouth, called gutturally: "Yeah."

They heard steps clumping down wooden stair treads.

"Stand back ready to hold the light," Bill whispered. "And watch out. There may be some shooting."

He drew back in the doorway himself, directed the light to the floor, so that its reflection streamed out the door. And waited. The steps hurried along the passage. No light preceded them. A voice grumbled "I don't see why the devil Paddy don't get these lights fixed down here. It's so dark you could run into yourself."

Bill recognized the voice of Sam. A kind of fierce joy came to him at the chance of paying back another score. Silently he handed the light to Joan.

"What's the matter — lost your voice?" Sam asked unsuspectingly as he approached the door. "Or are you in there necking with that dame? She's Paddy's, big boy. Don't forget."

The last, spoken in the doorway, was snapped short as Bill's hands shot out, clamped about Sam's throat, dragged him in. A jerk, a kick with his leg and Sam went down heavily, Bill on top. Gurgling, gasping inarticulately, the fellow fought. And Joan kept the light on them.

"Watch his hand, Bill!" she warned in a tight voice.

Bill had already felt the hand snaking in between them, thrusting under the man's coat. Thought of the gun holstered there whipped him to fury. He jerked the fellow's head up, slammed it down on the cement. And when Sam still struggled feebly, Bill balled a fist and drove it against the point of his jaw.

Rough work, but the only kind to use now. It did the trick. Sam gasped, relaxed where he lay, his head rolling to one side limply. Bill reached in where the hand had been groping. Sure enough, the automatic was there in a shoulder holster.

Bill got up, made sure it was loaded and ready for use.

"This is something like it," he panted. "Now we can talk turkey to 'em.

Let's travel, lady. Give me that light. Chin up—and out we go."

BOLTING the door behind them, they stole along the passage, Bill leading with the light and gun. Ten feet or so from the end a flight of narrow steep stairs led up. Bill took them on his toes to a cramped landing. If there was a door there he could not see it. A tiny circle of light level with his chin drew his attention. An eye applied to it looked over the expanse of the big gambling room, different now from when he had seen it before. It blazed with light, was crowded with people, men and women. Roulette balls were spinning, dice were rolling, table men calling monotonously. A babel of life, action, noise.

If there was a way into the big room it was secret. After looking for a few moments Bill stared up the next flight of steps. There was another cramped landing at the top. Another peep hole there. And Bill's heart leaped as he looked through it. He was gazing into the big sparsely furnished office of Paddy McGovern. And McGovern's husky voice was even then speaking.

"Don't let anyone in but Duke, Chip. I'm gonna be busy for a while. Keep 'em out of the reception room too. Get me? Not a one. But have several of the boys waiting outside. I'll be needing 'em."

Bill could just see the corner of the big mahogany desk several feet away, and part of the figure standing before it. He heard Chip answer

"Sure, I getcha, boss. Say, what are you goin' to do with them two?"

"Make 'em talk," Paddy McGovern husked. "And then they're going out the back way for boat ride in the bay."

Silence for a moment—and the Chip said understandingly "I getcha. I get-

cha. I won't let no one in till you ring an' release the door lock."

He disappeared. The office door closed. A match scratched inside. Bill pressed against the wall before him. There was no hinged door there. But after looking intently he saw a sliding panel. He pushed it to one side. It slid noiselessly. He stepped through into the office.

Paddy McGovern was sitting at the desk, smoking a newly lighted cigar. He heard Bill's step and growled.

"What's the matter? You guys go to sleep down there?"

And he swung about in the chair. Bill slipped to the corner of the desk. Paddy McGovern's porcine jaw dropped as he stared into the muzzle of the automatic in Bill's hand. He stiffened in the chair mutely. Bill showed his teeth in a cold grin.

"You guessed it," he said softly. "They both went to sleep down there."

Joan came to his side.

"See if the big tub of lard has got a gun on him," Bill said to her.

There was no need to warn Paddy McGovern to sit still and quiet. He knew, and did. Joan searched him quickly, found no weapon.

"Look in his desk drawers," Bill suggested.

In the top right-hand drawer she found a big automatic.

"Keep it," said Bill briefly. "And if I have to shoot, start popping too. We won't take any chance with him."

The fat cigar had been hanging loose in Paddy McGovern's slobbery mouth. He took it out, reached over to the ash tray and dropped it. His soft, puffy hand was trembling.

"So you got out," he muttered thickly.

"No. We're still down there," Bill corrected cheerfully. "This is only a big dream. And what a nightmare it's going to turn into. Joan, you said something about a telephone. There it is."

Joan snatched it from the cradle, gave a number crisply. And it was answered at once.

"Louie? Yes—Joan! I was hoping you'd be there! Paddy McGovern's place! Upstairs in his office! Get here as quick as you can with everything! We're holding him with a gun! Yes—good-by!"

She hung up, gave a sigh of relief and turned to Bill. "We'll be all right if we can hold him here fifteen or twenty minutes."

"I guess we can do that," Bill assented cheerfully.

Bill moved around behind Paddy McGovern.

"Where is this back entrance?" he asked. "It might come in handy."

"There ain't no back way," McGovern answered hoarsely without looking around.

"Bad memory, eh? Does this help it any?"

Bill pressed the muzzle of the automatic into the rolling fat about Paddy McGovern's collar and twisted, screwing the flesh. Paddy McGovern winced.

"I'm just looking for an excuse to get rough with you," Bill said mildly in his ear. "I haven't forgotten this morning, McGovern. My face still hurts. When I think about it, I want to drop this gun and get at you with my hands. If I ever start, God help your black soul. They'll have to gather you up with a shovel."

Mild—but Paddy McGovern shivered as he heard it.

"There's a way out," he admitted. "Over there in the corner."

"Show me."

The vast bulk of fat heaved out of the chair. Paddy McGovern lumbered over to the corner of the room where the two high filing cases stood against the wall. He caught one of them, pulled, and they both swung out, revealing a gaping black hole in the wall.

"Good enough," said Bill. "Leave them like that. Sit in the chair there."

"I'd rather sit at my desk," Paddy McGovern growled. "I'm used to it."

"Go ahead," Bill shrugged. "And if anyone starts to come in, tell 'em you're busy."

Paddy McGovern dropped heavily into the desk chair again.

"What are you two figuring on doing?" he husked, looking at them.

"Staying here with you," Joan answered promptly. "And from here you go to a cell. I doubt if you come out in a long time."

"Lots of people have said that," Paddy McGovern sneered.

"You're hearing it right now," Joan said evenly. "You can't buy your way out of this."

"Twenty-five grand cash to forget it," Paddy McGovern husked.

Joan's lip curled.

"Fifty grand. Paid in your hand before you go out."

"Save your breath," Joan advised.

"Honest, ain't you?" Paddy McGovern sneered.

Joan shrugged.

Watching the man carefully, Bill lighted a cigarette, smoked slowly. The minutes ticked by. They were not disturbed. Music sounded faintly below. Paddy McGovern sat still in his chair. He had evidently given up hope of bribing them, had apparently resigned himself to the inevitable.

His hands were in his lip. Bill's glance wandered an instant. The man was unarmed. There was nothing he could do. But he had underestimated Paddy McGovern's resources. Out of the corner of his eye he saw the hands slide gently under the desk top. Too late, he realized there might be a trick.

The door swung open by invisible hands. The lights went out. A buzzer burrrred sharply in the outer room. And there was a slithering sound behind the desk as Paddy McGovern went down behind it. His husky voice shouted.

"Get him, boys!"

There was a rush of feet outside.

CHAPTER SIX

The Water Trap

BILL was already at Joan's side, and he shoved her to the corner where the filing cases were swung out, jerking the flashlight from his pocket. The beam picked out the dark opening in the wall. Joan slipped through. Bill followed, thrust the flash in her hands as the light went on once more. Paddy McGovern's voice bellowed.

"In the wall there! They're going out the back way!"

Joan's feet were pattering down steps, the light picking out the dusty board walls of a descending passage barely wide enough to get through. Bill fired a shot through the opening behind and tumbled down the steps after her.

At the bottom the passage led straight for a few yards, turned in a jog, and led straight again. Joan flitted ahead of him with the light, stopped finally at a blank ending.

Bill squeezed past her, took the light. It revealed hinges, a bar resting in steel sockets. He jerked it out, shoved, and a door opened. And he stepped out into a bank of shrubbery at the back of the house.

The night was bright with moonlight. Heavily curtained windows let no light out of the house. Bill doubled around the corner of the house, saw the

wide cinder parkway near the front. It was crowded with automobiles now.

And even as he looked two figures came dashing out of the front into the light cast by a single bulb burning at the corner of the house. One of them called out.

"Oh, 'Limpy,' seen a man and a woman come around here?"

The hunchback who had opened the gate that morning moved out from between two cars, shaking his head. Bill was already turning back.

"The beach!" he snapped to Joan Stevens.

They ran toward the bay front where the moonlight gleamed on the restless water. And they were almost there when a shout at the back of the house announced their discovery. A gun barked. The bullet whined uncomfortably close.

Bill slackened his steps so Joan could keep up with him, led her to the corner of the grounds, where the board fence met the water. And too late he saw when he got there that a high, closely woven wire fence was strung out into the bay on stout posts.

Guns were barking behind them. A bullet whipped through the sleeve of his coat. He heard Joan give a gasp as lead plowed up sand at her feet with a sullen *plop*.

The boathouse loomed darkly close by. Bill caught her arm, urged her toward it. They reached it unscathed, found a door unlocked, tumbled inside into darkness. Breathing hard, Bill whirled, saw half a dozen dark figures out in the moonlight, running toward them. He shot at one, and missed. Resting the automatic against the side of the doorway he aimed carefully, fired again.

His target wavered, pitched forward to the ground. The other dropped down, began to crawl forward, shooting as they came. The wink and flash of the shots were like vicious fireflies spangling the night. Lead crashed into the boards of the boathouse, tearing clear through.

"Get down!" Bill cried to Joan.

She had already dropped to the floor in the doorway. Her gun barked loudly in the confined space.

Bill felt a cold slap on his left arm, knew that he was wounded there. He dropped beside her. Lead was smashing and whining about the open doorway and through it. Now and then splinters rained down on them. Bill fired coolly, deliberately.

Once as a figure leaped up to run forward, he sent it pitching clumsily to the ground by a carefully-aimed shot. But the storm of lead continued. The trigger of Bill's weapon clicked futilely. And he had no extra clip.

"I guess they've got us," he remarked. "Better try to slip out on the pier. You might be able to swim for it."

"I can't swim."

"Get out on the pier anyway," Bill said grimly. "I'll hold them here at the door as long as I can."

"They'll murder you in a second."

And Bill had no answer to make to that. He knew they would. He waited in silence. He felt a soft hand grope for his. Joan Steven's fingers closed tightly.

"You've been a pretty swell chap, Bill Brady," she said.

"That goes double," Bill answered gruffly.

He had to speak gruffly. There was a lump in his throat when he thought about her. So they waited.

And as no shots came from them the men out there in the moonlight grew bolder. One of them stood up. The rest did the same when they saw he was not harmed. They began to close in.

"Here we go," said Bill, getting to his feet.

AND as he stood there gripping the gun and waiting for the last final scene, automobile motors roared at the front of the grounds. A police siren screamed warningly. Bright headlights swept in and stabbed back toward the beach. And they came on past the big house. Spotlights swept back and forth across the wide lawn, picking out the scattered figures that had paused in their final dash toward the boathouse.

One of them shot at the head car. And then on the night air rose the deadly rat-a-tat-tat-tat of a machine gun. One of the running figures whirled and fell. A second staggered as the spotlight picked him out and the machine gun snarled again. Flashlights bobbed out from the machines, following the running figures. A scattered shot or two, and suddenly it was all over almost as quickly as it had started.

"It looks," said Bill, "as if this was our lucky night."

He stepped out of the doorway and Joan came with him. As they advanced a voice shouted.

"Joan! Is that you?"

A tall, slim figure came running toward them, caught Joan in his arms, and gave her a bear hug. Bill watched it enviously. Joan freed herself with a laugh.

"My brother Louie," she said to Bill. "This is Bill Brady, Louie. He had your compartment on the train and got mixed up in this business without knowing what it was all about. He's had a terrible time. And if it hadn't been for him I couldn't have called you —and—" She left it unfinished.

"Too bad," Louie sympathized, gripping Bill's hand. "And all the thanks in the world to you, Brady. I've been camping by the telephone waiting for news of some sort, with an emergency squad of police waiting to leave as soon as I got in touch with them or they heard from Joan. I didn't know what had happened when I got to the house and found no one there."

"I went out to get rid of the alligator bag the money was in," Joan told her brother. "I was afraid of it. Bill here was in trouble. There was enough circumstantial evidence against him to send him to the chair. The police were looking for him and that bag. I didn't want them to find it around him. You've seen the papers, you know now what happened. My man was murdered in the night. I wasn't sure who did it. The evidence showed Bill did.

"And I must have been followed from the house. My car was crowded into the curb. I was kidnapped and brought here. I wouldn't talk. They threatened to kill me, and then locked me up in the cellar." She shuddered, and finished, "I didn't even know they had Bill until he walked in on me. And was I glad!"

They had approached the machines as she spoke. Uniformed men were herding prisoners together and handcuffing them. And others were lifting the wounded off the ground and bringing them in. Bill saw one form they let lie where it was. His flash showed it to be the scrawny Shrimp.

A brusk officer with the braid of rank on his coat turned to them.

"You Miss Stevens?" he questioned.

"Yes."

"What's happened here? I'm Captain Martin."

Instead of answering, Joan darted to the prisoners and pointed at one of them. It was the dapper Duke.

"Search him," she requested sharply.

As the Duke's pockets were emptied, Joan watched tensely. Stepping forward, she took a leather billfold from the bluecoat's hands. Without speaking she opened it, looked through the sheaf of money inside.

"I thought so!" she cried triumphantly, turning to Captain Martin. "Some of these are marked! They'll convict this man of that killing on train 19! They were gone when I found his body and searched it. Now you have them. I thought the man who killed him and stripped his pockets wouldn't be able to resist keeping it."

"I don't get all this," Captain Martin said gruffly. "I know you're working in the treasury service with your brother here. And he's told me you were getting ready to round up a gang of counterfeiters and passers. But what do you know about that killing?"

BILL swallowed at what he heard. Treasury service! Joan in the U. S. Secret Service! Suddenly everything began to clear up. And Joan went on and answered the captain's question.

"We've been trailing down a stream of bad twenty dollar bills that have been flooding the country. Good ones. Made with hardly a flaw, and aged artificially until they look as if they've been in use for years. No one would ever suspect them. We finally found where they were printed, and picked up one of the messengers who was starting out to deliver a batch in another city. This city. He weakened when he found we had him cold, promised to talk if he got immunity and a thousand dollars. We gave him that in marked bills. He hadn't been with the counterfeiters long, and claimed he didn't know where he was taking the counterfeit money. He was to be met at the station and recognized by the peculiar alligator hide bag he carried the money in. My brother and I decided to let him deliver it, and shadow him. At the last minute Louie had to attend to some important business. He had his tickets, said he'd make the train.

"He missed the train," Joan continued, "and had to take the next one. I thought he was on board. The porter in his car said his compartment was occupied. We had planned not to see each other on the train, so there would be no connection between us. Our man was nervous, said he thought his arrest had been seen. I thought he was stalling, so I handcuffed him in his compartment and left him for the night, taking his batch of money in my compartment.

"But sometime after midnight I heard my door tried. It was locked. I got up and looked out. There was no one in the corridor. After thinking it over I dressed and went to the end of the car where my man was, taking the bag of money with me to be sure it was safe. And I found him—dead."

Joan shuddered at the memory.

"It was horrible," she said. "There he was, handcuffed and crumpled on the floor. He had evidently fought as well as he could. I knew then he had been right when he said the arrest had been seen. And I suppose they had followed us, not trusting him to keep his mouth shut, and probably hoping to get the bag of evidence. I went through his pockets and found that they had been stripped already. There was nothing more I could do there. If I gave the alarm, it meant that everything was out in the open and our chances of getting the men at the other end were gone. I took the handcuffs off of him and left him there. The bag of counterfeit bills I had worried me. I scribbled a note and took the bag into the next car where I thought my brother was. His door was unlocked. I tossed the bag and note in and hurried back so no one

would see me near him. When we got in I waited until most of the passengers were off the train and then left. I thought I was followed. I wasn't sure. I wasted an hour or so trying to find out. And never did. Then I went to the hotel where my note had told my brother, as I thought, to go.

"He wasn't registered there, but I found that a man carrying an alligator hide bag had come in and registered as William Brady. I still thought it was my brother, and tried to get in his room several times. He seemed to be out. I finally went up and knocked. The door opened and I found Mr. Brady here. Already papers were out with his description as the killer. The best thing I could think of was to hide him until I got in touch with Louie."

It didn't take long to tell the rest.

"It's simple now," Joan finished. "Paddy McGovern was distributing the counterfeit money in this territory. I suppose he was passing a lot of it out to his gambling patrons. You can find out by examining their money now."

"We'll do that," Captain Martin promised grimly. "My men have the place surrounded and are holding everyone. You've done a good thing, Miss Stevens. This place has been a sore spot for a long time."

Bill took off his coat as the tense group broke and started toward the house.

"I've got a little nick in the arm," he said, looking at the blood-stained sleeve over his biceps.

"Bill!" Joan exclaimed.

Louie, her brother, uttered something that sounded suspiciously like a snort as he watched the two of them examining the injured arm.

"Looks like you're both wounded," he remarked.

"I'm not," Joan denied.

"In the heart," said Louie callously.

The Devil's Jackpot

by Edward Parrish Ware

Mystery in the Arkansas Pearling Country

A man was running toward them—running raggedly as though the effort cost him too much.

Valued in gold, that rough lump of fresh-water pearl wasn't worth much. Yet four men had been murdered—a girl abducted—apparently to get possession of it. In some strange, baffling way it seemed to hold the solution to one of the most daring crimes ever committed in the Black River country.

CHAPTER ONE

The Death Pearl

JIM LENOIR, of the Lenoir Detective Agency, had been in a reflective mood for the last half hour, and had arrived at length at the rather pessimistic conclusion that another good reason for laying up your treasure in heaven is that there is no safe place on earth to keep it, when the phone rang.

"Chief Miles talking, Jim," came gruffly to his ear.

"Yeah. I'd know that grunt of yours, chief, even in a circus menagerie," he laughed. "What's on your mind?"

"Somethin' besides tryin' to kid somebody!" the old officer snapped back. "You wantin' to take on another out of town case?"

"No. Positively—"

"Wait," Miles cut in. "She's young, and pretty as a picture. You'll change your mind when you see her—"

"I'm not going to see her!" Lenoir interrupted in his turn.

"Yes you are, son," the chief told him with a chuckle. "I've already sent her to you!" He hung up.

And that was that.

At the age of thirty, James Lenoir, after a hard apprenticeship on the regular police force of Memphis, Tennessee, found himself at the head of a busy and prosperous detective bureau. So busy and prosperous, in fact, that he had found it unnecessary—inadvisable even —to accept cases calling for out of town activities unless, of course, they were important enough to carry exceedingly fat fees.

"Damn Miles, anyhow!" he grumbled. "Just let somebody apply to him for a private dick, and he forgets there's any other in town! And, right now, I'm busy as—"

Before he could finish, the door to his private consulting office opened to admit Clara, his secretary-stenographer.

"A young woman from Chief Miles, Mr. Lenoir," she announced in her quiet voice.

"All right, Clara," he told her resignedly. "I'll see her."

The girl came in at once, advanced somewhat timidly and paused in front of Jim's desk. He glanced up—then all his irritation vanished. She was young—scarcely twenty—and possessed of the sort of child-woman appeal that all he-men find irresistable. He promptly agreed with Miles that she was as pretty as a picture—and a mighty unusual picture at that.

"Sit down, please," he requested, noting that the girl was well dressed, though her clothing probably was not very expensive. Becomingly dressed, perhaps would express it better. She had poise, too.

"Thank you. My name is Mora Surrat," she said, sitting down across the desk from Lenoir. "Chief Miles, to whom I went for advice, sent me to you."

"Yes. He just had me on the wire. How can I serve you, Miss Surrat?"

For answer, Miss Surrat opened her pocketbook and took out a lump of something that looked like a cube of translucent soap. It was a hard substance, however, and possessed considerable weight. It might have been a clouded glass marble of irregular shape. She placed it on the desk.

"Do you know what this is?" she asked.

Lenoir took up the lump, examined it for a moment, then nodded.

"I should say that it is rather a large and unusual specimen of fresh-water pearl in the rough," he pronounced, eying the girl with quickening interest. "Am I right?"

"Yes. And it is about the man who

sent me that pearl that I wish to consult you." She hesitated, then went on. "My uncle, Tom Surrat, left Memphis a year ago, located on Black River in the pearling section, and set in to make a fortune. He succeeded to some extent —just how well, however, I don't know. I am his only relative."

She paused again, brows slightly knitted. It was as though she tried to marshall her thoughts.

"And your uncle sent you this specimen?" Lenoir prompted.

"Yes. That was a month ago. Sent it, and wrote me concerning it and others. Said he'd located a bar that was rich in the finest pearls he'd seen on the Black. The one sent me was a fair specimen. And that, Mr. Lenoir, is the last I've heard from him."

"And you have grown uneasy about him?"

"Very. He informed me in that last letter that he would be home within two weeks. He'd cleaned up, as he termed it, and was ready to come back. But he hasn't come."

"Probably he couldn't get away as soon as he expected," Lenoir comforted her. "I shouldn't worry yet awhile. Where was he located?"

"Near a big camp called Jackpot, but the railroad stop is called Black Rock. I understand that the camp is down the river from the railroad town. It isn't altogether the fact that Uncle Tom has not returned or written me, Mr. Lenoir," she went on, "that has frightened me. You see, Uncle Tom is one of the most absent-minded men alive. Has to make notes of the simplest things like dates, things to do, house and telephone numbers, and so on. He might have decided to return within two weeks, changed his mind, and then forgotten to write me about it."

"Then what is it that troubles you," Jim was curious to know.

"It is this, Mr. Lenoir," Miss Surrat answered, a catch in her voice, eyes large with fear. "I am in deadly danger. And that danger, call it a woman's premonition if you will, is connected directly with Uncle Tom and his failure to return or write. Just how it is connected I cannot say—but it is!"

HYSTERIA born of uneasiness concerning a well-loved uncle?

Lenoir could hardly believe so. The girl looked far too sensible for that. He looked at her more closely now, and saw that her sensitive face had trouble in it. Her large blue eyes held shadows of fear.

"Suppose you tell me your story, Miss Surrat," he suggested, his interest warming. "Then we'll see about this danger. What has happened to frighten you?"

"I have been attacked on the street, my apartment has been searched, and I feel that there is always somebody following me around," she replied, her voice lowering, and the shadows becoming now stark fear.

"When did all this take place?" Lenoir demanded tersely.

"At different times since I received the pearl," was the reply. "Three weeks after the pearl came, I returned to my apartment from work one evening and found that it had been thoroughly searched. The janitor of the building could give me no information about it. He had seen nobody going in or out.

"Then, two days afterward as I returned rather late—about nine o'clock it was—two men stepped out of a dark alley and grabbed me. One clasped a hand over my mouth, and the other dragged me into the alley."

She paused there, and her face suddenly went red. Then it became as suddenly white again.

"I was as thoroughly searched as my

apartment had been," she said almost in a whisper. "They—they searched my clothing. Even rolled my stockings down. Then, finding nothing—whatever it was they wanted could not have been money, because they didn't touch the contents of my pocketbook—they fled down the alley and left me lying there."

Jim Lenoir began to feel his blood boil. He was not especially subject to intense feeling over the woes and abuses of other people. He'd heard too many such relations during his service as a sleuth. But he found himself suddenly full of sympathy for the blue-eyed girl before him.

"Go on," he said gently. "About the following. Somebody trailing you around?"

"Yes. I am not sure, of course, but I see the same men—all strangers— close to me wherever I go. At lunch. As I leave my apartment to go to work. When I return. Then, this morning, I received this."

She opened her purse again, took out an envelope and laid it before Lenoir. The detective removed a single sheet of paper on which was printed in penciled characters—

You know what we are after. If you are willing to give it up, have it in your purse when you return from work tonight. Otherwise you die.

"And have you any idea of what they want?" Lenoir asked.

"Not in the least."

"What did Miles say? This part of the case, at least, is his."

"He took no stock in it, but said you might. Do you, Mr. Lenoir?" she asked anxiously.

Jim nodded vigorously. "You bet I do!" he snapped. "I agree with you, Miss Surrat. I think you are in deadly danger!"

Lenoir seized the phone and got Chief Miles at once.

"Hey, chief!" he demanded angrily. "What's the matter with you cheap regulars? Hadn't you enough men to spare one to investigate the Surrat matter? That's your—"

"Hold it, Jim!" Miles bellowed in interruption. "You bet I've put a trailer on the pretty lady. If somebody is shadowing her, then I'll soon know it. But this case, if it is a case, throws back to that damned pearling place, an' that's somethin' you can tie to. She wanted me to suggest somebody to go down there and locate Uncle Tom, so I sent her to you. Now, you go to hell!"

Lenoir, with a grin, hung up. Old Miles, under whom he had served in the past, was as much a roaring lion as ever!

"Miss Surrat," he asked, turning quickly to the girl, "where was this rough pearl when your apartment was searched, and when you were searched?"

She gave him a startled look.

"In the right-hand drawer of my desk at the office where I work," she replied. "I put it there and forgot it. To tell the truth, it doesn't look valuable to me. You—you don't think it's that the men are seeking?"

"Well, no. Not for its intrinsic value, although it may peel out a beauty," Lenoir answered, turning the bauble over and over thoughtfully between the thumb and forefinger of his right hand. "I was just wondering if this thing might not mean something more than just a mere jewel."

"What more could it mean?" Miss Surrat asked in puzzlement.

Lenoir smiled. "I don't know," he answered. "Has your uncle sent you anything more than this from the river country?"

"Nothing."

"He never wrote to you about the location of this fabulous bar he mentioned?"

"Not a line."

"Nor told you he had a cache? A store of pearls hidden somewhere?"

"No more than I have told you, Mr. Lenoir," she was positive.

"Then I am sure puzzled," he told her—and meant it. "The fact that your troubles began after you received the pearl," he explained, "would make it appear that they are related to it. Yes, that is it. This ugly, but probably valuable, bit of stuff must have a bearing on the matter. Shall I keep it for you?"

"You—you mean you will take my case?" she asked eagerly.

"Oh yes."

"But—but, Mr. Lenoir," she stammered, embarrassment dying her cheeks red, "I haven't a cent with which to pay you! If the pearl can be sold you may take that—"

"We won't sell it, or even try to sell it," he broke in. "And as for the fee—well, we'll settle that later. I feel something big and unusual in this thing, Miss Surrat. Besides, you are in need of protection. You shall have it."

THE phone rang, and Lenoir put the receiver to his ear. It was Chief Miles again.

"Jim," he said, "I put Gus Shores on Miss Surrat, and he's down in the lobby of your place now. He just called in to report. Says if there's anybody shadowing the girl he can't make him. You know how good Gus is. If he can't make a shadow, then there ain't none. That pretty girl's yarn is all hooey, if you ask me."

"But I'm not asking you!" Jim snapped. "You're as wet as the Atlantic, chief! Or maybe Gus has gone blind. I'll give you the lowdown later."

He hung up. Ordinarily, he would have heeded Miles, but he couldn't in this case. The girl was in deadly earnest, he was sure, and every word of her story was true. He turned to Miss Surrat.

"Have you a photograph of your uncle?" he asked.

"Yes. A very good one, too. It is at my apartment."

"And the letter he wrote when he sent the pearl? You have that?"

"I think it's among his other letters," she told him. "I don't remember destroying it."

"Good. I shall want to see the photograph and read the final letter, as well as all the others you have from him," Jim told her. "It may be we shall find something in them that will give us a lead. What is your address, please?"

She gave him the address, a small but genteel apartment house on Madison Avenue, and Jim made note of it. He glanced at his watch. It was then four o'clock.

"Going to send you home," he told her, "and send one of my men along with you," he added hurriedly as she gave him a look of fear. "He'll go home with you and stick around until I get there. I'm going down in that Black River country, Miss Surrat, and will leave tonight. Think the root of this matter lies down there, and is connected with your Uncle Tom. While I'm gone you will be well guarded."

"Oh, you are very kind, Mr. Lenoir!" the girl exclaimed, her voice quivering. "I can't thank you."

"And don't need to," Jim told her hastily. "I'm a detective, and this is all in line of business. Just you quit worrying. We'll dig this thing out, never fear."

He pressed a button and summoned Tom Burdick, one of his operatives.

"Tom," he said, after introducing the big sleuth, "see Miss Surrat home, and stick there until I arrive. That will be within the next hour. Got to leave town tonight, and there's some other business before I can take hold of this. Somebody is trailing her, and there's a chance for trouble. So watch your step."

"Right, chief!"

When Lenoir was alone in his office he strolled to one of the windows overlooking Main Street, thinking intently on the strange case just disclosed to him. Also, it must be confessed, considering the lovely young woman who had disclosed it. The rough pearl came in for a bit of thought, too. He wondered just what place the bauble occupied in the tangle. Just what significance it had, if any at all.

Through the open window came the staccato crackle of revolver fire, and Lenoir leaned far out over the sill where he could get a view of the street. A woman's frightened scream came up to him. Then he saw a man's crumpled form on the sidewalk directly below.

At the same instant a black sedan went speeding south on Main Street, ran a red light at the first intersection, then disappeared around a corner toward the Mississippi. There was no chance to see the license number, nor did he get a look at the occupants of the car.

The next instant he was dashing for the elevators. When he reached the sidewalk, Miss Surrat was nowhere to be seen. On the pavement at the curb lay Detective Tom Burdick—dead from three bullets in his body!

CHAPTER TWO

"Don't Buy Any Chips!"

LENOIR raised from peering at the body of his dead operative, and found Gus Shores, Chief Miles' man, at his elbow. The regular's face was pale and grim.

"What happened, Gus?" Lenoir asked, his voice tight in his throat.

"I didn't see so much, Jim," Shores replied. "When I saw the girl come down with one of your men beside her, that was my cue to drop off. Chief's orders. I had just started up the street when I heard the shots. I turned and saw Tom staggering about, going for his gun. He went down. A bird in the sedan jerked the girl into it, and they were off. That's about all I can tell you, except that I got the number of the license tag. It was a Tennessee plate."

"What did the men look like? Can you describe them?"

"The bird with the gat was covered up with smoke," Shores answered. "The one that got the girl was short, heavy, and dark. That's all, Jim. Sorry."

By that time the spot was the center of a big crowd, and the regulars were on the scene. Lenoir left the chase to them, and returned to his office to give orders to his own men. There was nothing he could do in the girl's behalf that could not be better done by the regulars. They had all the city resources at their disposal. He entered his office on the run.

"Mr. Lenoir," he was greeted by his excited secretary. "A telegram just came. It seems very important. Will you read it now?"

He snatched the yellow slip from her hand and continued on to his office. Inside, he let his glance drop to it. Instantly he was on his toes.

JAMES LENOIR, FLATIRON BLDG., MEMPHIS, TENN.

COME POWHATTAN IMMEDIATELY STOP AM WOUNDED STOP BANDITRY ON RAMPAGE STOP FEE NO OBJECT

JOHN COPELAND
BLACK ROCK, ARKANSAS

Lenoir knew Sheriff John Copeland well. He had worked a case for him once, and knew him to be an intelligent, capable officer. He wanted to oblige, but there were other matters now engaging him.

"By God!" he exclaimed suddenly. "Black Rock—Powhattan! That's where the Surrat case is taking me anyhow! Can there be a connection?"

He pressed a button. His secretary came in.

"Wire Sheriff Copeland that I will be there some time tonight," he instructed crisply. "Then get Steve Kelley in here pronto!"

Two minutes later the door opened and a wirey, black-eyed man of thirty came in.

"Want me, chief?" he asked.

"Grab the fastest car you can get and beat it down the river route for Black Rock, Arkansas," Lenoir ordered tersely. "The car you want is carrying a Tennessee tag. Here is the license number. Big sedan. Black. Three men and a girl. If you don't connect, go to Sheriff Copeland's house in Powhattan. Put yourself under his direction. I'll be there as soon as I can. Beat it!"

"Right!"

Just the one word, and Steve Kelley, the best woods-scout, and one of the deadliest men with a gun in the entire country, was on his way. He was Lenoir's right-hand man. When the two worked on the same case, then it was a big case indeed.

"Maybe it's a bum hunch," Lenoir gritted after Steve had gone, "but I want Steve down there anyhow. I'll need him, the way things are starting out!"

He buzzed again. This time he sent for Wade Stone.

"Get over on Madison Avenue," he ordered, giving Miss Surrat's address, "and bring me all the pictures of men you can find. Also all the letters. Step on it!"

Stone was gone. Lenoir then began calling Miles.

"Anything yet, chief?" he asked eagerly.

"Not a damned thing!" Miles bellowed. "We're doing everything we can, Jim! Got things movin' in a hurry. What you think of all this, anyhow?"

"It's by me, chief," Jim acknowledged. "If you get anything, call me at once, will you?"

"Damned right!"

Miles hung up.

Lenoir sat back in his chair, face suddenly drawn and weary. He had fumbled. His client had fallen into the hands of her enemies, and it was his fault because he should have foreseen their move and guarded against it. What was it all about, anyhow? What danger threatened the girl? Why had she been abducted—at the cost of a human life? Tom Burdick had died defending her. It must be a desperate game indeed!

He thrust a hand into a coat pocket for his cigarette case, and felt something foreign there. He drew it out. It was a bit of torn envelope with a few words printed on it in pencil. He read it with growing anger.

Don't buy any chips. This game
is too stiff for you.

One line—but it was enough to make Jim Lenoir see red. It had been hastily printed, he could tell, and had been slipped into his pocket while he was in the crowd about the corpse of Tom Burdick. There was no other explanation. Somebody—one of the crooks in the Surrat case—had spied him there and had slipped the thing to him as an act of bravado.

Then a question suddenly crossed his mind. How did it happen that he was known to the man who had slipped him the warning? This matter concerned itself with the Black River pearling district, and he had never been down there but once. How, then, had he been so easily recognized?

THE only plausible answer was this. Somebody concerned in the Surrat case had seen him and known him during his brief sojourn on Black River. Such persons were few. He was certain of that. Was there a clue in that slip of paper? That warning?

He reversed the paper, and what he saw drew his brows together. The scrap had been hastily torn, and it was from the front of the envelope—the part upon which had been written a name and address. It was only fragmentary, but some part of the address showed. With patience he made out:

eed,

ttan,

rk.

Not much—but it made Lenoir's eyes shine!

That envelope had been addressed to somebody whose name ended in two "e's" and a "d", and the post office had been Powhattan, Arkansas! So the Black River angle was showing up!

The pearl carried by Mora Surrat, a present from her uncle, was a thing of vaster importance than appeared upon its rough surface. That now was certain.

But how could it be? Nothing there, except a hunk of nature's construction, bearing no inscription, no device, no message of any kind.

Unless, indeed, the thing was in itself a message! He had not thought of that possibility before. Could it be a talisman of some sort? Something that would be open sesame for a pot of gold? He took the pearl from his pocket and placed it under a strong microscope, examined every face of it. But he had to give up. There was not upon it even the tiniest scratch.

Again he called Chief Miles, only to learn that there had been no trace of the black sedan. Then his phone rang. He grasped the receiver eagerly.

"Lenoir speaking."

"Chief, this is 4-5."

Lenoir's lean body stiffened, and steely lights shone in his gray eyes.

"Yes, 4-5," he said. "What is it?"

The answer came in a voice sounding somewhat strained.

"I'm at the place on Madison. The girl is here. Just got in. You'd better hurry over."

The voice was that of operative Wade Stone—but the number was not his. Not by a long shot! The number was one any operative of the Lenoir agency would use if trying to communicate danger.

Lenoir was on his feet instantly. Wade Stone was at the Madison Avenue place—and there was danger!

Lenoir was on his feet before the receiver clicked on the hook. In the assembly room was not a soul, as he very well knew there would not be. His men were either on assignment, or working on the Surrat case. Clara, the secretary, was at her desk, her face white and strained. She had heard the 4-5 signal, and knew that trouble was on the wing.

"I'm off to the Madison Avenue place," Lenoir called to her as he reached for the doorknob. "Stone is in trouble there. If Hicks, Adams or any other of the boys come in, send them there on the run!"

He hailed a taxi on the street at the corner, leaped in and gave an order to burn up the pavement. He was obeyed. What had happened he had no idea, but he was fairly certain that he would not find Mora Surrat in her apartment. At least, Stone had not been speaking of his own volition. Somebody, he was very sure, had been standing behind Wade, a gun against his spine, dictating that message. Otherwise Wade would not have given the prearranged number —4-5. That number was a warning to take care.

Lenoir leaped from the cab at the entrance of the apartment building and dashed for the stairs. He purposely made his arrival spectacular. Up to the third floor he raced—then abruptly shed his appearance of impetuosity. Down the corridor he walked at an unhurried gate, reached the door of Number 331, then paused.

What lay behind that door? What danger assailed Wade Stone? Had the girl really been brought there? Well, he'd damned soon know!

He rapped on the panel. The door opened. And the tall, swarthy man who opened it found the muzzle of a 45 caliber gun against the third button of his vest.

"Back right up," Lenoir advised evenly. "And if you want to see mamma again—be careful!"

The tall man was taken completely by surprise. He backed into the room, and Lenoir followed carefully. Inside the door he paused and looked around, then flipped a second sixgun from his hip. With it, he covered the heart of the only other loose party in view.

"Get 'em high—quick!" Lenoir snapped. And the short, roughly clad man across the room beside the window thought better of his urge to draw. His hands went up.

Lenoir kicked the door shut behind him, and grinned at Wade Stone, who sat tied in a chair, a gag in his mouth.

"Quite a little party here, eh, Wade?" he laughed easily—and nastily. "Well, I suppose I was expected to join it and be tied up like you."

He whipped his hard glance into the face of the short man against the farther wall. There was ice in his voice when he spoke.

"Cut him loose!" he commanded. "And if you make a move for a gat, next Christmas Santa Claus will page you in hell!"

There was no mistaking the danger, and the short man snapped into obedience. Wade Stone was soon standing on his feet.

"Take their gats, Wade," Lenoir ordered tersely.

Stone, a grin of relief and triumph on his leathery visage, promptly disarmed both men, thrust each into a chair, then turned to Lenoir.

"Chief," he said huskily, "I'm right glad to see you!"

"And that's mutual!" Lenoir declared fervently. "Boy, you had me in a sweat! Where did these two skunks come from, and are there any more here?"

"Two is all, an' them's enough!" Wade declared. "They trapped me slick as a whistle th' minute I got in. Here waitin' for me, chief. Then they made me decoy you over here. Thank God you decoyed them chief!"

Jim holstered his guns, took out his cigarette case, extracted a smoke and passed the case to Stone.

"Take a look around, Wade," he suggested, noting that there was a small kitchenette and a bathroom to the suite.

"We're going to have a nice little session here, and don't want to be interrupted."

CHAPTER THREE

Prosecuting Attorney

LENOIR took a seat near the door while Stone searched. There was nobody else in the small apartment. Lenoir tossed the end of his cigarette into an ash tray, then turned hard eyes upon the man whom he had surprised at the door.

"Speak up, hombre," he invited. "Anything you want to say?"

"Just what would you expect me to say?" came the query in a voice of culture—plus rage. "That it's a nice day, or something like that?"

"I expect you to talk turkey and talk it quick!" Lenoir snapped, "For instance, where is Mora Surrat?"

"That, my dear cop," came sneeringly, "is something I could not tell you if I would. Try another."

"You want to go down to the station?" Lenoir asked evenly. "They have a way of asking questions down there that beats mine all hollow. They ask things with a piece of rubber hose. Better play with me."

The short man spoke up.

"Th' gal," he said calmly, "is on her way—whar at you'll have one helluva time findin' Do that answer satisfy you?"

"It does for a fact," Lenoir told him. "She's on her way to the Black River region. I knew that before you spoke. What I wish to know now is this. Do either of you birds want to spill the works, or do you prefer to stick here and take what you'll get in the end? There's a chance for the man who will give me the lowdown to get off light. Who will be first?"

For all of Jim Lenoir's nonchalant manner, there was beneath it something a wise man would have feared. He was keyed up as he had never been before, and in his gray eyes danger signals were flaring.

"Go to hell!" the more polished man snapped at him. "We are not telling you anything. And that goes from here on out!"

"Search 'em, Wade," Lenoir ordered.

The search revealed nothing of consequence.

"These birds were waiting here when you came?" Jim then asked his operative.

"Well, they was here," Stone replied ruefully. "They'd come up th' servant's stairway. I asked downstairs if there was anybody in Miss Surrat's apartment, and they told me no. But there was, just the same."

"And they were not here as a reception committee," Lenoir said, glancing at a section of baseboard which had been torn loose. "They were here as wreckers. Wanted to find something—eh, boys?"

His answer came in scowls.

"Well, well!" he exclaimed. "Still hunting it, and still far from the goal! What a pity! Now, boys, maybe if you'll ask real pretty I'll tell you where it is. No? Well, I'll tell you anyhow."

Lenoir suddenly hardened. He stood up, eyes like blue glass. He took a step forward, brought the muzzle of his six-gun against the vest of the short man.

"It's in the muzzle of this gun! Talk—and do it quick!"

Was Lenoir bluffing? Was this merely a form of third degree? Perhaps. At any rate, it had a measure of success. The short man quailed away from the gun and the menace of those eyes.

"I'll tell!" he screeched, holding his hands in quivering horror before his face. "We want to get—"

With an oath that fairly sizzled, the second crook leaped from his chair, seized it by the back, and, before anybody could interfere, swung it down upon the short man's head. There was a crashing, sickening sound—and the would-be informer died with his squeal in his throat.

Lenoir leaped, his sixgun swung high for a blow. The killer, fury blazing in his eyes, swung for him with what remained of the chair. Lenoir side-stepped, and the infuriated man went down.

"Grab him, Wade!" Lenoir shouted to his aide.

Stone threw himself upon him. There was no resistance. Stone got up, face pale, hands blood-smeared.

"Chief," he said, his voice queer, "something's happened! He—he musta hurt himself!"

Lenoir turned the man over, then stood erect.

"We lose," he said quietly. "A jagged end of that chair is in his heart."

WADE STONE swore savagely. "That bozo was fixin' to spill it all!" he wailed. "Killed before he could let out the squawk!"

Lenoir stood grim-lipped in silence, his brow knitted.

"Wade" he said, after a bit, "these birds are only the hirelings. The place to find the prime mover in this affair is in the Black River country. The trouble is, right now, that I can't get a line on Mora Surrat. Where is she? What was the motive in her abduction? Those are the questions we have to answer. To hell with all this! The safety of our client is the first responsibility."

"Maybe she is safe, chief," Stone suggested. "The bozoes that got her won't hurt her until, at least—"

"That's it!" Lenoir snapped in. "Un-til at least. There is something Miss Surrat has, or they think she has, that they will demand of her."

At that instant the phone rang. Lenoir seized it.

"Mr. Lenoir?" The voice was that of Clara.

"Yes. What now?" Lenoir demanded.

"Steve Kelley on long distance."

"Can you switch the call?"

A moment. Then, very clear, came the drawly voice of the operative:

"Chief, I come up with th' party yuh named," said Steve. "We had a short argymint—an' I won. Th' gal is here with me—"

"Where?" Lenoir broke in.

"At th' hotel at Marion," came the prompt reply. "I'll wait fur yuh here."

"Anybody hurt?" Lenoir asked, fearful of the answer.

"Naw. Jist one feller killed is all. Th' feller that drove th' car got away," Steve drawled.

"What about the third man?" Lenoir asked.

"Wa'n't none, as I seen," Steve told him. "Jist th' two fellers an' th' gal. I got her safe. She been give a hypo, Jim, but she's come outa it now. Yuh comin' right down?"

"As soon as I can get a car to take me there," Lenoir told him. "Watch out for further trouble, Steve," he warned. "We're up against a pretty stiff gang."

"Don't worry yuhself none about that, Jim," Steve interrupted. "I don't aim to take anybody's foolishment. I aim to shoot fust, then ask questions of the coroner. Yuh git down here as soon as yuh kin because th' gal shore wants to see yuh."

"Right!" Lenoir hung up—with a warm glow around his heart.

She wanted to see him! Well, thank

God she was safe—and wanted to see him! Lenoir turned toward the door.

"Come on, Wade," he said, "we're done here. Steve has something corralled down at Marion."

THERE came a heavy rapping on the door, and Lenoir stopped his intended exit suddenly. He glanced at Wade, and that individual made ready for action. Lenoir himself made sure his gun was easy in its holster. Then he cautiously opened the door.

"I wish to see Miss Surrat," announced the man who had knocked, and his voice had what might be called a legal tender.

"Come in," Lenoir invited, swinging the door wide. "I am sorry Miss Surrat is not at home, but I assure you that she will be glad to see you when it is possible to do so."

The man who came in was slender, wiry, about five feet and ten inches tall. His age would be around thirty-five. Eyes black and unreadable, skin swarthy and thick. There was a quality about him that suggested strength and authority.

"I am Arthur Reed, of Black Rock," he announced, 'and a friend of Miss Surrat's uncle. At the present time I am the prosecuting attorney of Lawrence county—"

He stopped abruptly, eyes, having become accustomed to the dark interior, discovering the two dead men on the floor. He started back toward the door but Lenoir grasped him and dragged him inside.

"All right Mr. Reed!" he rasped, kicking the door shut behind him. "You have called at the right place even though it may be not at the right time. Sit— and hold your hands high!"

"Er—my hands what?" asked the legal gentleman, sitting down and looking about him in bewilderment.

"High!" Stone snapped, with a gun against the back of his neck.

"I—I don't understand this business!" Mr. Reed declared, the red of anger beginning to show in his cheeks. "What's it about?"

"High hands when ordered," Stone grunted. "What now, chief?"

Lenoir was studying the newcomer thoughtfully.

"Rather a nasty mess we have here, sir," Lenoir said at last. "But I assure you it is as unpleasant to us as you. And maybe you can help us to arrive at the reason for it. You have said you are a friend of the uncle of Miss Surrat. Where is he?"

Reed, still horror-stricken at sight of the dead men on the floor, answered slowly.

"He is dead. Thomas Surrat, the uncle of my client, Mora Surrat, is dead."

Lenoir sat down in front of the attorney, eying him narrowly.

"How long dead?" he asked.

"It is not possible to say," Reed replied.

"Why not?" Lenoir demanded.

"Because we have not arrived at that perfection in science when it is possible to tell—"

"Get down to cases!" Lenoir snapped in interruption. "Tom Surrat is dead. All right. When did that fact become apparent? Under what conditions? Give us the gist of it all, and do it quick!"

"May I smoke?" Reed asked, fishing for a cigar case with hands that were trembling.

"If you like," Lenoir told him.

The lawyer withdrew a cigar and, without offering his case to the others, replaced it. He lit a smoke with care and thought.

"Tom Surrat was found dead in his pearling shack on Black River," he informed them quietly, "on the day before yesterday morning. He had been stabbed in the heart. Our coroner could not determine the time of death, except to say that the body was dead at least twelve hours before he was called to view it."

"And there is no suspicion against anybody?" Lenoir asked.

"Well, that is as may be," Reed returned thoughtfully. "Our sheriff, John Copeland, had what he thought to be a hot trail—but he was shot and nearly killed in the hills above Surrat's old shack. Some people believe he was too close on the heels of the man who killed Surrat. John refuses to divulge any information until a certain private detective from this city arrives at his residence. He is in bed, guarded by a trusted deputy. Now, gentlemen, will you tell me what has occurred here?"

Lenoir wheeled upon Stone.

"Tell them to send my car here!" he ordered crisply. "Gas it and prepare it for a grind. Mr. Reed," he went on as Stone snatched the phone from the desk, "I think you have given me a clue that will explain all this business better than I can myself. At any rate, I hope you will not insist upon an answer here. The answer is in the Black River country—and that is where we are going!"

CHAPTER FOUR

Black River

A LONG blue sedan drew up at the front porch of the Traveler's Hotel in Black Rock, and a worn traveler got out. No word was said to the fat proprietor, who stood with bulging eyes to receive his guest, because all arrangements had been made in advance.

"Right this way, Mr. Reed!" he called. "All th' rooms air fixed an' ready. Breakfus' is all ready to sen' up, too. My place is honnered to have th' nex' governor of th' state as a——"

"Never mind!" snapped Lawyer Reed, who got out of the car with considerable difficulty. He was cramped from the trip from Memphis. "Just send a boy for the grips!"

Wade Stone, who sat beside the driver, grinned widely. The driver grinned too. It had been a hard trip from Marion down to Black Rock, but neither showed signs of fatigue. They were old in the service, and expected long grinds.

"There is another car coming," Reed told the landlord, as he stretched his long legs on the sidewalk. "Mr. James Lenoir, Miss Surrat, who is my client, and the gentleman who is driving. They all will have breakfast when they wish, and I particularly desire that you give them the best service of which you are capable."

Mr. Reed went up the stairs to his room, followed by a black boy with his grip. Wade Stone asked the way to the nearest garage, and the long sedan was soon parked there.

"Come on, Bulger," Wade invited the chauffeur, "le's us get a drink before the boss gits here."

They repaired to a bar of the small Ozark village and ordered. Prohibition evidently made no difference down there. The potion that arrived presently was strong enough—in spite of the sign which announced the place to be a soft drink stand.

While they were refreshing themselves, another car arrived at the Traveler's Hotel. It also was a sedan. In the front seat were two men, and in the back sat a man and a woman.

"Mighty glad to make you welcome to our city, Mr. Lenoir," the fat landlord exclaimed when the tall man got out of the rear seat. "Prosecutor Reed has got everything fixed for your party. And the young lady—my wife is waiting to take care of her. Come right in!"

Jim Lenoir assisted Mora out of the car and turned her over to the fat wife of the fat landlord. The girl looked pale, but far from unhappy. In fact, Lenoir himself had an expression that would have defied an analyst at his best. They had ridden together from Marion, sixty miles away, and day had just dawned.

On the front seat was Steve Kelley. He was neither pleased nor sad; tired nor full of pep. Steve was Steve. That was all. He had that night sent one man to his reward, and put another in a hospital. But it did not seem to trouble him. It was all in the day's work.

"Park th' car sommers," he said to the driver, Bill Mooney. "I'm goin' to git me some breakfust—an' a big drink. Yuh can eat an' drink on th' chief. He won't want nuthin', onless that leetle gal sends him a hoppin'."

Kelley, who had pursued the black sedan from Memphis after the killing of Tom Burdick, and who had overtaken that same sedan and sent one of the occupants to other spheres forever, did not show the least sign of recent conflict. His natty appearance had not been altered, and his nerves were as steady as the ground upon which he trod. But, for all that, Steve Kelley was as alive to the situation as was Jim Lenoir himself. His boredom was merely assumed. His black eyes took in everything, analyzed what they saw, and the result was stored away. Steve Kelley, fast with a gun, was also fast with his brain. He had his drink, his breakfast, then returned to the hotel porch and took up a good position in a chair. He appeared thereafter to sleep.

Upstairs there was a conference between Lawyer Reed, Miss Surrat, and Jim Lenoir.

"The fact is, Miss Surrat," Reed told the girl, "I am at the same time your appointed legal advisor and the executor of your uncle's will. He left you all his worldly possessions, and made me his executor. There is not much that we can find, but what there is will be duly turned over to you."

"Thank you, Mr. Reed," Mora said. "You are very kind."

"And was that why you came to Memphis, Reed?" Lenoir asked. "To find Miss Surrat and advise her that her uncle had died, left her all his possessions—and that they amounted to nothing?"

Reed's eyes developed steel. He shot a glance at Lenoir, then let his lids fall.

"Exactly, my dear Lenoir," he answered quietly. "I did my duty as I saw it. There was a poke of pearls found on the premises where Surrat was killed, and they, when sold, will perhaps net a couple of thousand. That amount will pay my fee, and certainly defray any other expenses attendant upon the burial of the deceased."

"And do you suppose," Lenoir suggested sarcastically, "that that burial fee is what those gorillas were after in Memphis? Why they shot down one of my men, abducted Miss Surrat—"

"My dear Lenoir!" Reed snapped irritably. "How do you suppose I can answer your absurd questions? I am forty years old, have practised law since I was twenty-one—and never before have I seen such an unreasonable a client as you, as Miss Surrat's advisor, make her to be! You will not listen to reason——"

"Yes we will," Lenoir interrupted. "We know that there is something back of all this. We know that Tom Surrat left an estate that is of great value. I suspect that you are aware of all this, and I intend to see that you come through. Also, there is a little matter of murder in the first degree attached hereto. My friend and employee, Tom Burdick, was killed——and I mean to know why. Have you anything really pertinent to say?"

Reed's tall form snapped erect, his dark eyes blazed.

"You are not in Tennessee, Lenoir," he said quietly. "You are in Arkansas. Down here, we hold a man to account for such talk as that!"

"By the gun——or the law?" Lenoir asked ironically. "Either way, I'm standing by my client."

"Please," Mora pleaded, "don't let us quarrel——"

"Your man Lenoir is the quarrelsome sort!" Reed snapped.

Lenoir laughed.

"How about the wounding of the sheriff?" he asked, switching the subject. "He sent me a telegram to come and aid him. Did you, as prosecuting attorney, know about that?"

"I did not," Reed asserted positively. "Copeland was wounded by a hunter I think, while he was searching for a trail above the shack where Surrat was killed. Nobody purposely shot him."

"But he said in his message that banditry was on the rampage," Lenoir broke in, purposely irritating the lawyer. "What did that mean?"

"It meant," Reed declared venomously, "that Copeland was trying to discredit my administration of the office of prosecutor! He wanted to make it appear that everything is on the loose

down here! That is what it meant!"

Lenoir narrowed his eyes for a moment, then laughed.

"Let's have breakfast sent up," he suggested. "I am afraid we have too long neglected the inner man. Certainly Miss Surrat deserves consideration, and we have given her very little. What say, Reed? Shall we all eat here, as a sort of family, so to speak?"

Prosecutor Reed smiled suddenly, bowed to Mora, and pressed a thumb against a button.

"I hope before we have finished breakfast," he said, "to convince Miss Surrat that she is perfectly safe under my care, and that the services of a detective are not necessary."

Mora looked at Lenoir, then shook her head negatively.

"I am afraid, Mr. Reed," she said—and there may have been a double meaning——"that they are."

Lenoir looked at Mora sharply, could make nothing of the veiled eyes, and nodded very regretfully.

"I must deny myself the pleasure you suggest, Mr. Reed. You see, I am under agreement with Sheriff Copeland. Immediately after breakfast I shall have a talk with him. While I'm gone, I hope you will take good care of Miss Surrat——you and Wade Stone."

A FEW hours later Jim Lenoir, very much in the dark, yet convinced that in some way Mora Surrat was both in danger of her life and in danger of being defrauded, sat beside the bed of Sheriff John Copeland, at Powhattan, the county-seat.

"It air this way, Jim," Copeland was saying. "This feller Surrat war camped in that shack down clost to Jackpot. He made a cleanin', an' that much air knowed. Then he war found dead in th' shack, with a knife stickin' in his

heart. Th' shack had done been searched frum top to bottom. Mebbe th'
killers foun' th' cache. Mebbe they
didn't. Anyhow, I war down thar
huntin' fur 'em, an' got this here bullet
in my laig.

"I was expectin' bullets. Th' Black
River country is plumb rid to death with
bandits. Thar has been a eperdermic of
'em here of late. Don't seem like nuthin'
will stop 'em. An', Jim, I'm plumb
sartin that Tom Surrat perished by
thar hands. So I sent fur you to come
down here an' help me out."

"Your deputy, Bill Sneed," Lenoir
told him, "seems like a pretty good man.
What about him? Shall I work with
him or not?"

"Bill Sneed?" Copeland queried.
"Why, Bill is all right, so fur as guts
is concerned," he asserted. "But fur
brains—well, Bill ain't thar. You got
to use some of yore own, Jim. That's
a fact."

Lenoir wondered. There was the
big, awkward Bill Sneed. His name
had two "e's" and a "d". Lawyer Reed.
His name had the same ending. But,
for that matter, so had others in the
community. Sneed certainly had not
been in Memphis the day before, so he
had an alibi in so far as the torn bit
of envelope was concerned. Lawyer
Reed did not seem a likely subject for
Lenoir's net. There were no fish, in
fine. Lenoir was no further on his way
than he had been in Memphis.

"You haven't a thing to tell me that
may help me to trap these birds?" he
queried.

"Not a dang thing!" Copeland declared. "Jist that I knows they air
raisin' hell on th' river—that their
leader is a damn smart devil—an' I
want 'em ketched! You air employed
by th' county, Jim, with my riccomin-
dation. Jist go to it!"

"How about Reed?" Lenoir asked.
"What will he have to say?"

"He'll have to prosecute whoever you
fetch in," Copeland replied. "No matter whut he thinks erbout it, he'll have
to go by th' evidence!"

"Regarding evidence," Lenoir said.
"I'd like to examine the personal effects
left by Tom Surrat. Are they available?"

"Bill Sneed wil fetch whut leetle
thar was," the sheriff answered. "Nuthin' much left in th' shack whar at Tom
war killed. Jist his pocket stuff, pipe,
knife, an' sich. He had a notebook, too.
A powerful feller fur writin' down
things to do tomorrer. That dang book
air full of such stuff."

"Who has had access to that book
since Tom was killed?" Lenoir asked
suddenly. He sat erect, eyes beginning
to glint.

"Jist me an' Reed," Copeland replied.

"Are you sure?"

"Course I am."

"Then let Sneed bring the book,"
Lenoir requested, after a moment of
thought. "The book will be all I shall
require tonight."

"Git th' notebook outter th' safe,
Bill," Copeland ordered the deputy.
"An' make it snappy!"

Bill Sneed departed at once, to return
within a short while with a small, cheap
book in his hand.

"Here she be, Mr. Lenoir," he said,
passing the book to the detective. "I
don't reckin you'll be able to make no
more outter it than Lawyer Reed did,
an' he couldn't make nuthin'."

Lenoir said nothing in reply. He took
Tom Surrat's little book in hand, began leafing it through.

> Get shells for shotgun.
> Buy sack of meal
> Get tobacco.

Make oar for boat.

Mend socks.

The entries would seem foolish to anybody but a man who had suffered from absent-mindedness himself. To such a one the record would have appealed. Lenoir kept reading the notations—and suddenly became absorbed in one. It read:

Make plan for self. Make duplicate for Mora.

He got up suddenly, his eyes shining. "John," he queried the sheriff, "did you find anything in this book that interested you?"

"Not a dang thing," groaned the suffering officer. "Jist th' record of a absent-minded feller—"

"Did Reed say anything about the notations?" Lenoir broke in.

"Naw. Art never said nuthin' to me erbout th' book."

Lenoir slipped the memorandum into a pocket of his coat. He arose.

"These bandits you spoke of," he said as he approached the door on departure, "are due to get some new business pronto, John. Just you keep your ear to the ground!"

CHAPTER FIVE

Bandit Bait

HE WAS a stranger in the village but that was not what distinguished him from the herd. Jackpot, on the west bank of Black River, swarmed with strangers; they had, in fact, built the place. Pearl-hunters had found it, named it, and maintained control over its destinies. A gathering place for rough and careless men who sought entertainment in exchange for cash, the village bore a hard name, and one well-deserved.

So the stranger in question was not remarkable for the fact that he was such. It was his appearance and manner that set him apart from the crowd. drawing attention and begetting comment. His spare frame would measure a full six feet, which was not unusual; there were many six-footers on the river. But there was not one other who chose to clothe himself as did this particular stranger. His immaculate gray trousers, highly polished boots, long black frock-coat, starched shirt, and black string tie, not to mention his wide-brimmed, black Stetson, formed an ensemble to which the river country was wholly unaccustomed. Nor was that all.

The stranger's swarthy, lined face, deep-set gray eyes, and thin-lipped mouth adorned with a slight gray mustache and even slighter goatee, would have distinguished him in any company. There was an air of good breeding about him, and his quiet voice and courteous manner marked him as one of those whom the world calls a gentleman.

On his first night in Jackpot, to which place he had come so unobstrusively as to enter unnoticed, the stranger found himself taking a drink in "Long Jack" Brome's crowded barroom. The liquor was good, but the atmosphere of the place was distinctly bad. Unwashed men smoked vile pipes and equally vile cigars, creating a blend of odors which, further blended with the smell of stale beer and uncorked whiskey, would have turned the stomach of a wet dog on a hot night.

At one end of the bar was gathered a crowd of rowdy pearlers, drinking, singing, and spouting friendly but lurid profanity. They were a distinct disturbance to the card players in the room, and to the peace of the quieter tipplers. Also to the bartender.

"Why don't you put that damned gang out, Jack?" queried a man at the stranger's elbow.

The bartender cast an apprehensive glance toward the bunch at the far end of the counter, then spoke in low tones.

"Don't let 'em hear ye spakin' abaht 'em, Mark!" Long Jack cautioned. "Them lads is bad ones, I'm tellin' ye. 'Whiskey Mike' Bradley an' his gang of pearlers. They're best let alone."

But Whiskey Mike wouldn't permit himself to be let alone. He craved attention. Pushing and shoving, he and his three cronies crowded toward the front end of the bar. They brushed aside any and all who had not the celerity to get out of their way. The man who had queried the bartender concerning them slipped out of the front door.

The dark-faced, quiet-voiced stranger, however, did not even turn his head. He sipped a glass of brandy.

Mike, brawny and bull-voiced, reached the stranger's side, seized him by an arm and faced him about. Then he released him, stepped back and eyed him quizzically.

"By Gawd!" he cried, after a moment during which he had been compelled to shift his reddish eyes from the level grip of the others blue, cold ones. "Look whut th' cat done drug in, fellers! Whut air it? Name it an' take it!"

"By gollies!" exclaimed Pete Higgs. "From th' gineral appearance of him, them clothes an' all the rest, I'd say he's a jedge!"

"Hear that, feller?" Mike demanded. "Pete says you-all air a jedge. Air you?"

The stranger answered, his voice quiet and showing not the least tremor.

"A judge of some things," he said slowly. "Of cattle, in particular."

"Hey!" cried Mike, on whom the insult was wasted. "Pete done guessed right th' fust pop! So you-all air a judge? Well, you shorely done brung ernother name with you. Whut air it? Jedge whut?"

With a movement so swift nobody was ever able to say just how it was done, the stranger's long, slender fingers sprouted a pair of blued-steel 45's, and his thumbs were seen to curve over the hammers. He spoke again, and this time his voice was slightly higher, and clear as a bell.

"Speed!" he snapped. "Does that satisfy you—or do you want me to demonstrate?"

The room became silent on the instant. Mike, utterly astonished at the turn his play had taken, hardly able to believe that anybody would cross him in such a way, drew back from those steady muzzles, and most especially from the dangerously glinting eyes above them.

"I—I—why, hell, jedge!" he exclaimed, careful not to move a hand toward the gun which swung from his own belt. "I war jist foolin'! Can't you-all take a little joke?"

"I am a good judge of jokes, too— and your kind of jokers," was the cold answer. "Now, get out, all of you. Take your jokes elsewhere."

Whiskey Mike Bradley hesitated briefly, while a scowl of rage clouded his face. His three cronies edged closer to him. Then the man who had called himself Judge Speed, spoke again.

"Get!"

Just the one word, but it cracked like the report of a gun. Just the one word —but it got results.

Whiskey Mike Bradley and his gang, cowed for once in their noisy and vicious careers, obeyed the order to a man. In the silence produced by the unexpected and submissive exit of Bradley, the river's bad man, the soft voice of the stranger cut through.

"The house drinks on me," he said quietly, tossing a bill upon the bar. "And if there is a little game going somewhere, where a gentleman can sit in—well, lead me to it."

They drank. But they did not respond to the invitation to the little game. For some reason the crowd seemed shy of the strange man.

JIM LENOIR walked out of the bar, hiding a grin under his false mustache. Down the uneven board walk he sauntered, reached the end toward the dark river, then stepped aside into deep shadows.

"Steve!" he called, his voice raised slightly.

"Here," came the answer, and Kelley appeared abruptly at his side.

"It's working," Lenoir told him. "Just as I said it would. I've made myself conspicuous, as I told Reed I would, and the game is on."

"Yeah. But you want to watch your step, Jim," Kelley cautioned. "This chief of th' Black River bandits ain't no fool. Yuh can make a piece of bait outter yoreself if yuh wants to, but yuh shore better keep your hand on yore gun."

"I will," Lenoir agreed. "Anything to report?"

Lenoir had left Black Rock in the early evening, leaving Mora Surrat under the care of Lawyer Reed. He felt that she was safe, yet yearned strangely to hear word of her.

"Nuthin'," the slim gunman replied. "All quiet—"

He broke off, ear cocked toward the river. A motorboat was disturbing the night with sound. It was running with full speed, and rapidly approaching.

"Lissen at that boat!" he exclaimed.

"Somebody's in one hulluva hurry. Whut yuh think about things so fur, Jim?" he asked, dismissing the boat from his mind.

"Tom Surrat made a big find. He cached the pearls somewhere, drew a plan of the place for himself, and intended to draw one for Mora. He made a note in his little book to remind him of doing it. Whether he actually did or not we don't know. But it is a cinch somebody—the keen mind that searched the pages of the little book—thought he did. That explains the attacks upon Mora. They were trying to get the duplicate."

"Whut yuh reckin become of th' plan Tom made fur hisself?" Steve asked thoughtfully.

"That's beside the point," Lenoir said.

"It's certain it hasn't fallen into their hands, though."

"Yeah," Steve agreed. "Who do yuh think is at th' bottom of it all?"

"Listen, Steve, nobody but you and Art Reed knew that I was coming down here in my present character—as bandit bait. Now, I get a bite before I'm here half an hour. Does that spell anything to you?"

"Yuh figger, Jim, that Reed warned his bunch? That he aimed fur them to pick a quarrel with you—"

"Exactly that!" Lenoir broke in to declare. "And when Whiskey Mike made his play I found out all I need to know about who is the leader of this gang of gorillas down here. The thing that stumps me now is how to pin it on him."

The motorboat had swung into a landing. The night was quiet. Steve stood stroking his chin in thought, his black eyes lidded. Suddenly he started erect, eyes wide. A whistle had sounded shrilly from the wharf. A signal that both Lenoir and Steve Kelley knew. Both were on the run at once. They neared the shore and saw a man running toward them—running raggedly as though the effort cost him much.

"Wade!"

The exclamation burst from Lenoir, as he recognized Stone.

"Jim!" Wade gasped. "They got Lawyer Reed—an' th' gal! Got 'em —both! Two hours ago! Kidnaped on th'—river—between here—an' Powhattan! Bill Mooney was—killed! Kidnaped—th' lawyer—an' th' gal—"

He collapsed in Steve Kelley's arms.

He was out for only a few minutes. A bullet had seared a channel across his ribs and he had lost blood. While Lenoir and Kelley were examining him they were joined by a short little man with a husky voice. He had appeared from nowhere.

"You gentlemen need a doctor," was the first warning of his arrival. "When I'm sober I can find my way around. Was in the saloon, judge, when you made that play, and I sure admired it. Sober now. Let me have this man."

Lenoir and Kelley, astonished, drew back. The ragged little chap, his hands working swiftly and expertly, exposed the wound on Wade Stone's side in a jiffy. He ran his fingers along the channel, then turned to Kelley.

"Get my bag from the hotel!" he snapped authoritively. "Tell them that Doctor Creed sent for it! Hurry!"

Kelley was off at once. By the time he returned, Stone was conscious, laughing deprecatingly at himself.

"I ain't got no excuse to offer, Steve!" he declared. "Just went out like a school gal! Oughta be ashamed of myself—"

"You lost blood," Dr. Creed broke in. "Rest for you, and a drink for me. Anybody got one?"

KELLEY produced a flask and passed it to the little derelict man of medicine. Stone, now bandaged, got to his feet. Lenoir looked at him with querying eyes.

"Jim," said Stone, "we got your message to come down to Jackpot."

Jim's eyes narrowed. "What message?" he asked.

"Yuh wanted Miss Surrat an' Lawyer Reed at once. Some evidence yuh had uncovered. So Reed an' us, with Bill Mooney to drive th' motorboat, started out. We hadn't hardly got started—just passed Powhattan in fact —when we was overtook by another motorboat. A fast baby it was. Th' feller hailed us, ordered us to run to shore—an' then I went into action. Reed grabbed my arm. Begged me to stop. Ordered me to, I reckin is whut he done. I slapped him off like he was a fly, an' then I got this slug in my side. Bill tried to handle th' boat with his left, while he swung his gun with his right, but he didn't have no chance. Th' damned snake that bit him was too clost—"

"What do you mean, Wade?" Lenoir demanded. "Who shot Bill Mooney?"

"Reed!" Stone's voice crackled. "Reed's th' bozo we want, Jim, an' he's th' worst devil in th' Black River country!"

The ragged little doctor, now half drunk at least, exclaimed approval.

"That is right! Art Reed, damn him, is the curse of this whole country! He's a fraud!"

"Then that there capture on th' river was a fake?" Steve Kelley drawled, his black eyes going harder. "An' th' message to come down here was Reed's play? Yuh figger that, Jim?"

"Exactly," Lenoir snapped. "Do you feel like action, Wade?"

Stone laughed. "Give me a chance, Jim!" he pleaded.

"What about it, doctor?" Lenoir asked the derelict.

"He'll be all right by morning," was the answer. "And maybe you'll take me along? You may need me. Besides, I owe Art Reed something. I'll make a hand, gentlemen, believe me!"

"Where to, Jim?" Kelley drawled, his black eyes now half-lidded. "Le's git goin'. I feel somethin' comin' on. Got some idea where to hit?"

"Yes!" Lenoir snapped. "The point on the River where that motor boat swung out—if you think you can find it! It's time for us to play our hand. And," he ended, thinking of Mora Surrat, "we'll play it!"

Steve Kelley knew nothing about motorboats. He was a gunman, pure and simple. He sat in the bow on the way up the river. Doctor Creed, his flask in his pocket, sat beside him. Lenoir steered.

"Here we are!" Wade Stone cried suddenly. "Right here is where we was overtook by th' other boat."

At that point the Black was joined by a creek. Sand Creek it was called. Too shallow to admit a motorboat for more than a mile up stream.

"What about this creek, doc?" Lenoir asked the medical man. "How far up do you know this section?"

The little man shook his head, tossed an empty flask overboard, and answered.

"A mile up stream is where Art Reed has got his summer cottage. Damn him!"

"And where does Mike Bradley live?" Lenoir went on.

"At the head-waters of the creek," Doc answered. "That's four miles further up."

Lenoir considered. Then he made his decision.

"Either at Reed's cottage or at Mike Bradley's place," he said to Kelley, "is where we're going to have trouble. Watch your step, Steve."

The thin gunman nodded.

"Trouble, right now, is what I'm cravin', Jim," he said quietly. "Just yuh go ahead an' figger th' deal—an' leave th' trouble to me."

They headed into Sand Creek.

"What I want to know," Wade Stone said uneasily, "is where this here cache of Tom Surrat's is. That's whut done caused all th' trouble, an' it's goin' to keep on causin' it until we git our hands on them pearls. You ain't got no idea where at th' cache is, have yuh Jim?"

"I think," Lenoir said quietly, "I have a——"

Wham! Wham!

Jim Lenoir shuddered, tried to get to his feet—then fell back, clutched at the gunwale and went overside!

Devil's Jackpot

CHAPTER SIX

LENOIR heard sounds that beat against his ear-drums without meaning. His hands grasped weeds and grass. He drew himself up on the shore, laid resting there for a moment, then sat up. He had blood on his face, in his eyes, on his hands. Darkness surrounded him.

Wham! Wham! Wham!

Up the shore there was firing. He struggled to rise, then sank back. Toward him a dark shadow was running. He aroused himself and drew his gun.

"Stop!" he called unsteadily, muzzle trained upon the oncoming man.

"Lenoir!"

It was the voice of the little derelict doctor, Creed.

"Here!" Lenoir answered.

"I have been hunting you!" panted the little doctor. "We were attacked from shore! Your man Kelley has already accounted for two! Whiskey Mike Bradley is dead! That Kelley man is a demon with a gun—"

"To hell with that!" Lenoir snapped, staggering to his feet. "They waylaid us, huh? Attacked from shore! Steve Kelley and Wade Stone are still alive and in action! That's all I need! Get away, doc, I don't want your services!"

"Listen to me!" the little doctor broke in. "I know what I'm about! I know where the entrance to Art Reed's cave is—and I'm the only one who does! Listen to me, Lenoir—for God's sake!"

Lenoir grasped the little man by a shoulder.

"Why didn't you tell us so in the first place?" he demanded, his brain beginning to clear.

"I meant to, if there was cause," Creed replied. "Now, let's get going!"

Lenoir followed fast upon the heels of the doctor. He arrived at the door of an out-house back of a large cabin which he knew was the summer residence of the county prosecutor, Arthur Reed. There he stopped. Steve Kelley stood in the entrance.

"What's on, Steve?" he queried. "You got any dope on this thing?"

"Yes!' Kelley snapped. "The woman you love, Jim, is down there with th' mangiest devil I ever seed! Lawyer Reed!"

Lenoir reached for the guns on his hips. They were there and in good condition. He made sure of that by drawing them and wiping them dry with Steve's handkerchief.

"How do we get down?" he asked with cold quietness.

"Set of steps down a shaft—"

"Wait!" doc broke in. "There's an exit on the bank of the creek! That's got to be guarded!"

"Can you guard it, doc?" Lenoir asked.

"Give me a gun and see!"

"Here!"

Jim Lenoir whipped one of his guns from a holster and handed it to the little doctor. Steve Kelley grasped his wrist.

"Careful, Jim!" he growled.

"I know a man when I see one!" Lenoir snapped. "And I'm playing the doc for a friend! Now, Steve, let's get going!"

"It's cost us enough already!" Steve choked. "Wade Stone—"

He said no more. The ladder was exposed under the trap he raised as he said the words. Lenoir, face blood-covered and grim, set his foot on the first round. Doctor Creed looked straight into his eyes.

"I'm with you, Lenoir!" he snapped, his frail form erect. "They won't get out past me!"

"Jim!"

The hail came from the creek, and Lenoir turned to see Wade Stone and another coming. Wade Stone, whom he had thought killed on the creek bank, staggering along the path, herding a man before him.

"Whiskey Mike," Stone said, wiping the blood-stained water out of his eyes, "has got somethin' to say. Speak your piece, Mike!"

STONE'S revolver wavered uncertainly in the general direction of the wet and sullen native. Lenoir recognized him at once. Whiskey Mike

Bradley, thoroughly cowed, stood before him.

"I got a crease across my head," Stone was explaining. 'Steve thought he'd got Mike. But Mike wasn't hit. His pal, Lafe Simmons, took Steve's lead. Another minnit, an' I was in th' water, swimmin' to th' shore. Must of passed out for a little while. Then I found this hombre standin' over me. He thought I was one of his men, but he damned soon learned different. He's willin' to talk now, Jim—so put on th' pump."

Lenoir turned to the now subdued bandit.

"All right, Bradley," he said quietly. "What have you got to say? Reed is the chief, and you are his lieutenant. I know that already. Reed's regime is about over, and you'd better talk."

The big bandit, now wilted as a rag, spoke.

"That there cave of Reed's," he bleated, "air dangersome! Don't go down! It air mined with dannamite—an' Reed aims to blow it up!"

"With himself in it?" Lenoir demanded, a chill assailing him.

"In it—hell!" Bradley excalimed. "He ain't in it! He's on th' river, runnin' up stream fur my place. Thar's two exits from th' cave, an' Reed has done gone!"

"He expected to trap us down there, eh?" Lenoir demanded.

Before Bradley could answer there came a thunderous explosion, and the ground caved in about them!

Out of the chasm created by the explosion the five men crawled. Reed had missed, granting his idea had been to trap Lenoir. Where the out-house had stood was now just a heap of debris.

"Jim!"

It was Steve Kelley calling.

"Here!" Lenoir answered.

"We gotta git to that place up river!" Steve shouted. "This feller Reed means business!"

In the motorboat Lenoir's brain cleared. Reed had been forced to show his hand, and he was now out in the open. His band had been disrupted, and he knew that his mask had been torn off. But he had still one trump card. He had the girl!

"How many men has Reed got with him?" Lenoir demanded of Whiskey Mike.

"Not none," Mike answered. "Yuh kilt off my men. Reed will be at my place, where at he keeps a car. If he gits thar an' in th' car, then he'll make it away—"

"He won't make it away!" Lenoir snapped. "We'll get him."

There came a sudden shout from above, on the left side of the creek. Stone, who was steering, slowed down. A man stood on the bank, hand waving.

"What's wanted?" Lenoir called, squinting through the dawn.

"Are you willing to make a deal?"

The voice was that of Arthur Reed, prosecutor of Lawrence county—and he held the slim form of Mora Surrat between himself and the men below!

Lenoir stood up, at the same time motioning Wade Stone to run the boat to shore.

"What sort of deal?" he called.

"Give me twenty-four hours," came the answer, "and I'll give you the girl!"

"His motorboat air wrecked!" Wade Stone cried, pointing to where the white outlines of a long boat showed against the shore. "Don't make no deal with him, Jim. We got him, th' danged coyote!"

"But Mora—"

"Jim!" came clearly from the shore.

"For you, Mora," Lenoir cried. "I'll do anything."

"Then don't compromise!" she broke in. "Anything but that!"

Steve Kelley, very calm, drew a revolver.

"Yuh want him fur evidence, Jim," he said quietly. "So here goes!"

The gun in Steve's hand cracked. Lawyer Reed trembled as though an ague had gripped him. Then he went down on his face.

"Jist creased him," Steve said, holstering his gun. "An' that ain't bad shootin', considerin' th' light I had. Jist th' top of his head showin' above th' gal's —but I got it. Mebbe when he comes to we kin persuade him to tell us where them pearls are."

"He doesn't know," Mora broke in. "Uncle made a big find—got hold of a fortune in pearls—but Mr. Reed doesn't know where they're hid. He thinks I know."

Jim Lenoir smiled. "And so you will in a minute," he said softly. "They're quite safe."

"What!" Stone exclaimed. "Yuh know where that cache is? How did yuh have time to find that out?"

"It wasn't so hard," Jim answered. "Why, Wade, would a man buy boxes of shotgun shells—when he didn't own a gun?"

Stone looked at Lenoir dazedly, then he gasped.

"In th' shells?"

Lenoir nodded.

"I found that there was no shotgun in the shack when Tom Surrat's possessions were taken out," he said quietly. "But in his notebook were several entries calling for the purchase of shells. Four boxes of those shells are in the office of the sheriff—and there is where Tom Surrat's cache lies."

"He took th' shot an' powder out, then filled th' shells with pearls?" Stone's voice was full of awe. "That it, Jim?"

"It's what I figured—and I'll bet I'm right," Lenoir told him quietly.

He was right. A little more than an hour later he, Mora, Steve Kelly, the doctor and Wade Stone sat in the sheriff's office at Powhattan, examining some boxes of shotgun shells which held pearls in place of powder. State Prosecuting Attorney Reed, his head bandaged, was securely lodged in an iron-barred cell and Whiskey Mike occupied a similar domicile nearby.

Bradley's confession had made everything clear. Reed had been the leader of the bandits on Black River, and his power was now broken.

"I reckin we done a right good job down here," Steve Kelley remarked to Wade Stone as they traveled back to Memphis. "We got another boss hooked onto us, Wade. An', if yuh ask me, she ain't no pearl in th' rough!"

HOW ABOUT IT?

NOW, if you've got your breath back—if the goose flesh has stopped crawling and the shivers ceased racing up the old spine—

How do you like it?

We hate to begin patting ourselves on the back at this stage of the game—it's only the first issue of DIME DETECTIVE MAGAZINE after all — but we rather think we've done ourselves proud taking everything into consideration.

How about it?

Honestly now—no hedging—have you ever run into a finer line-up of action-mystery-adventure stories than we've gathered together for you in this first number of DIME DETECTIVE MAGAZINE?

And it's going to be this way from now on.

On the 15th of every month it's going to be waiting for you on the newsstands, thrill-packed from cover to cover, with the fastest-moving yarns that the modern masters of detective fiction can concoct. And all for the astonishingly low price indicated in the title.

For only ten cents you will be able to get stories by such writers as Erle Stanley Gardner, J. Allan Dunn, T. T. Flynn, Edward Parrish Ware, Earl and Marion Scott, Frederick Nebel and a score of other favorites whose work continually appears in magazines that sell for twice the price of DIME DETECTIVE MAGAZINE.

We are confident that never before in magazine history has there been planned such a month-after-month fare of headliners as we are going to give you in DIME DETECTIVE MAGA-ZINE. And we want to know what you think of the idea.

You won't find any reader's contests, space-filling "departments" or prize puzzle pages in the issues which are coming. DIME DETECTIVE MAGAZINE is going to be without any bolstering props, firmly planted on a solid foundation of the best stories money can buy by the best authors we can find to write them.

You won't find any coupon on the next page but if you feel like writing in and telling us what you think of DIME DETECTIVE MAGAZINE, pro—yes, and con, too, it will help to guide us in making the magazine the sort of magazine you want it to be. What authors would you like to see on the contents page? We'll get them for you. What type of stories do you like? We'll go after them if you'll give us the word. Do you prefer novelettes to short stories? We want your help in making that decision.

In order to give the readers the high type of fiction we want to give them at the amazingly low price of only ten cents per copy of the magazine it is going to be necessary for the circulation to be large and steady. We are confident that this first issue of DIME DETECTIVE MAGAZINE is going to make for just that state of affairs and that you readers are going to be watching avidly for the 15th of next month when another striking new cover will let you know that the second issue of DIME DETECTIVE MAGAZINE is ready to thrill you.

AND speaking of covers, a story is back of this month's masterpiece. We wanted something extra special in which to dress the new baby and everyone around the office was frantically cudgelling his or her brain for a swell idea. But even editors and art directors draw blanks, it seems, and no one could hit on anything that would fill the bill.

Finally, one rainy afternoon, after much prolonged and footless argument over innumerable bowls of chop suey, sent up from down-stairs, it began to look like the new magazine was going to have to go coverless. Each idea put forth seemed to have less merit than the last and time was getting short if the publication date planned on was to be met.

At last Mr. Reusswig, the artist, wandered in. Noticing the baffled, careworn faces of the staff his pity was aroused.

"If you'll trust me until tomorrow," he said, "I'll have a cover idea for you in the morning."

We told him we wouldn't trust him around the corner with a plugged dime —he was helping himself to someone else's chop suey at the moment—but he seemed to be a last resort so we told him to go ahead and do his worst.

The chef d'oeuvre in blue on the cover was the result. He walked in the next day with the "Shadow of the Vulture" tucked casually under his arm and walked out five minutes later with the enthusiastic cheers of the whole organization ringing in his ears.

But that isn't all! J. Allan Dunn who happened to be in the office when the cover arrived was so taken with it that he promptly went home and wrote the lead story that opens this issue. The "Shadow of the Vulture" is unique in that it was inspired by the artist's illustration instead of, as is usually the case, the illustration being drawn to fit the story. The combination turned out so successfully that we're thinking of putting our carts before our horses as a regular procedure! How about it?

Curious chances often combine to create a story and this was just such an occasion. Sometimes it may be an apt title that may start the leaven to working in an author's mind. Other times it may be an item from the daily newspaper or an incident from the personal experience or knowledge of the yarn spinner that gives the initial impetus to his pen.

Mr. Dunn, the author of "The Shadow of the Vulture," is himself in many ways as interesting a character as the fictional figures he draws to move through his ingenious and thrilling yarns. South Sea trader, world explorer, traveler and holder of navigation certificates he has led an action-crammed life.

It takes more than the merely unusual to excite him, but when he first saw Mr. Reusswig's cover the reaction was immediate.

"Great!" he said. "I've been kneading a story in my subconscious for a long time. It's tied up with the subterranean water conduits and channels of New York."

"Got a title?" he was asked.

"A dozen," said Dunn. "Take your choice!"

"The Shadow of the Vulture" was finally decided on. We thought it was a pip of a choice. Dunn thought so. Reusswig thought so. We hope you'll think so. Let us know now that you've read it. How about it?

Next month at the end of the magazine we'll have some more interesting material on the men who are making DIME DETECTIVE MAGAZINE a success. How they write their stories, who they are and what they do when they're not pounding out thrillers for your hungry eyes. You'll like it.

Five Sure-Fire Magazines That Never Miss A Punch

---o---

UNDERWORLD ROMANCES

Mystery, romance and crime in—

THE SILVER RING

by Earl and Marion Scott

Shrouded in mystery, covered with ancient dust—the old pawnshop was a spot of sinister crime. Yet Patsy worked and even dreamed there, dared to let a perilous romance enter its creaking doors.

---o---

WESTERN RANGERS

Danger and six-gun action in—

THE MASKED DEATH

by Ralph Cummins

A yelling mob, roaring sixguns, frightened cattle in mad stampede—And face down in the dirt lay a nervy sheriff, his gold star soaked with blood. Masked mystery! Yet one slim clue sent "Brick" down that blood trail, sent him riding rough-shod over danger and death!

---o---

BATTLE ACES

Conflict above the clouds—

BAT WINGS

by Steuart M. Emery

One by one pilots had disappeared from patrol—and now their bodies were being returned, drained of blood, accompanied by a living bat. Who were the fiends responsible for this horror? In what secret place was their staffel? Silently, sternly, two Yank flyers took forth into the night, determined to pierce the mystery—or meet the fate of their lost comrades.

---o---

DETECTIVE ACTION

Hair-raising thrill after thrill in—

THE FACE OF DANGER

by J. Allan Dunn

"$50,000 in 2 days—or Norman Foster will be dead!" This note and three postmarks were the only clues to the prominent millionaire's disappearance. Yet in one of them, or all, lay the key to the strangest mystery Henry Smith had ever tried to solve —a key that he meant to find within 48 hours.

---o---

GANG WORLD

Flaming smoke-rod action in—

MURDER C.O.D.

by Carl Bernard Ogilvie

Gangsters crammed in a sinking yacht on the storm-tossed waters of Lake Michigan—the crack of thunder and of flaming gats. And "Cub" Buckley knew that he was pitted against death, caught in the meshes of Chicago's most powerful mob.

Why waste time on *old fashioned methods*

—when you can learn to play at home without a teacher

DON'T let the thought of long years of tiresome practice scare you away from learning to play! Don't let the thought of an expensive private teacher keep you from letting your dreams come true! For you—*anyone*—can easily *teach yourself* to play—right in your own home, in your spare time, and at only a fraction of what old, slow methods cost!

It's *so* easy! Just look at that sketch at the right. The note in the first space is *always* f. The note in the second space is *always* a. The way to know the notes that come in these four spaces is simply to remember that they spell *face*.

Now, isn't that simple? You don't have to know one note from another in order to begin. For the U. S. School way explains everything as *you go along*—both in print and picture—so that, almost before you know it, you are playing *real tunes and melodies* right from the notes.

You simply *can't go wrong*. First you are *told* what to do, then the picture *shows* you how to do it—then you do it yourself and *hear* it. No private teacher could make it any clearer.

Easy as A~B~C

If you can read the alphabet you can learn to play your favorite instrument *in just a few months.*

Easy as A-B-C

No wonder over 600,000 men and women have learned to play this easy way! For this famous course is based on sound, fundamental musical principles, highly simplified. It's not a "trick" or "stunt" method. You learn to play from notes, just as the best musicians do. You learn to pick up any piece of music, read it, and understand it.

No time is wasted on theories. *You get all the musical* facts. You get the real meaning of musical notation, time, automatic finger control, harmony.

You'll find yourself studying the U. S. School way with a smile. Your own home is your studio. The lessons come to you by mail. They consist of complete printed instructions, diagrams, all the music you need. There are no dry-as-dust exercises to struggle through. Instead, it's just like playing a game—you learn so fast!

No Talent Needed

Forget the old-fashioned idea that you need "talent." Just read the list of instruments in the panel, decide which one you want to play, and the U. S. School of Music will do the rest. And remember—no matter which instrument you choose, the cost in each case will average just the same—only a few cents a day.

You'll never regret having learned to play. For those who can entertain with music at parties—who can snap up things with peppy numbers—are always sought after, always sure of a good time! Start *now* and surprise your friends!

Free Book and Demonstration Lesson

"Music Lessons in Your Own Home" is an interesting little book that is yours for the asking. With this free book we will send you a typical demonstration lesson that proves better than words, how quickly and easily you can learn to play your favorite instrument by note—in less than half the time and at a fraction of the cost of old, slow methods —the U. S. School way. The booklet will also tell you all about the amazing new *Automatic Finger Control.*

If you really want to play—if new friends, good times, social popularity, and increased income appeal to you—clip and mail the coupon NOW. Instruments supplied when needed, cash or credit. U. S. SCHOOL OF MUSIC, 3611 Brunswick Bldg., New York City.

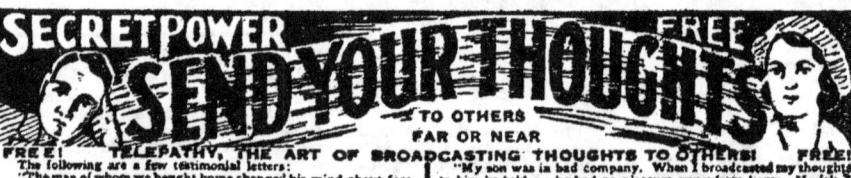

DRAWING
turns INK *to* GOLD

THE small crude sketch (1) was drawn by Herschel Logan before he had Federal School training. The large drawing of Lincoln (2) shows his recent work. Note the improvement. Today his drawings are seen in National Exhibits. Recently he made $100.00 over his regular monthly salary. He says, "Any average fellow with the same instruction should be able to accomplish similar if not greater results."

Many Earn $500 Monthly

Opportunities for artists have never been better. Publishers pay millions for illustrations every year. The Federal Home Study Course has been prepared by over fifty of the Nation's leading artists. If you like to draw, cash in on your talent. It's easy to learn the "Federal Way." You may have talent lying dormant in you, just as Logan had. Our Vocational Art Test will find that out. Send your name, address, age and occupation and we will send you the chart free. Act today.

Federal School of Illustrating

11441 Federal School Bldg., Minneapolis, Minn.

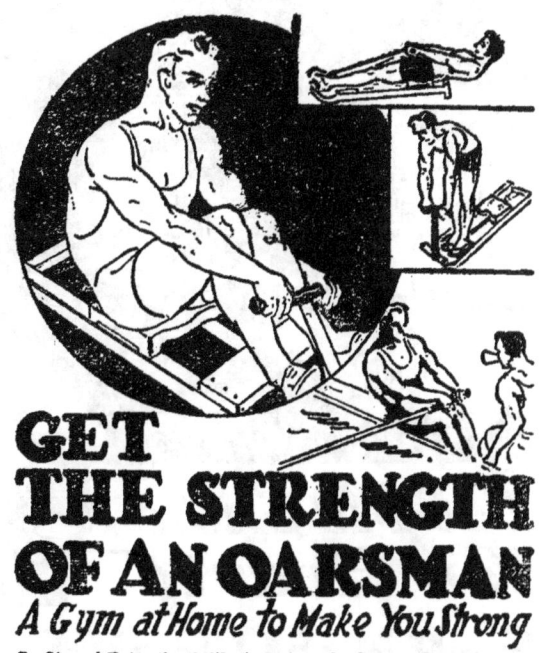

GET THE STRENGTH OF AN OARSMAN
A Gym at Home to Make You Strong

Be Strong! Enjoy the thrill giant strength gives to the varsity oarsman. He must be "there" to stand the strain and endure the greatest and most terrific strength test put to any athlete. If you want massive shoulders—a mighty chest—arms like iron—a powerful back—legs like pillars of steel, and an all around perfect athlete's body—stop dreaming—wake up! The invention of the VIG-ROW is the answer to your dream. The VIG-ROW was created and built by a man who built his own body from a weakling to that of a champion. The VIG-ROW offers body-building principles never revealed to the public before—the perfect device for keeping fit and getting strong. Be sure to investigate the VIG-ROW. You will agree that it is the greatest and most perfect rowing machine ever marketed, regardless of price. Its many features and beauty will amaze you. Send no money—write now for additional free information.

Examine the VIG-ROW First

Space doesn't permit the entire story about the VIG-ROW. There are too many reasons why you should select the VIG-ROW. We don't ask you to purchase from this advertisement—we do ask that you write for our large photographic circular and realize the difference yourself. Write for free facts now. Don't buy now from us or anyone else — compare — examine — test — don't buy a cat in the bag — write us now and get the wonderful complete VIG-ROW story.

EXCLUSIVE VIG-ROW FEATURES

Inclined Frame

Sliding, Form-Fitting Aluminum Seat

Progressive Exercise Springs — Instantly Adjustable

Arch-Supporting Foot-Rest —Aluminum Front

Noiseless Rubber Wheels — Oilless Bearings

Free Instructions

We don't think it enough just to sell you the finest rowing machine in the world and trust to luck that you will use it and get strong. We furnish a course of instruction, without extra cost, that is complete in every detail, showing how to develop every part of the body with the VIG-ROW—prepared and written by a master of physical culture. And it's yours free —if you write at once.

$11⁸⁵ $11.85

Rush Coupon!

Don't send a cent! Fill in coupon and mail. Full details free by return mail.

www.ingramcontent.com/pod-product-compliance
Lightning Source LLC
Chambersburg PA
CBHW080911020726
47502CB00008B/2424